A FEARFUL THING

Christopher Nicole

Severn House Large Print
London & New York

This first large print edition published in Great Britain 2006 by
SEVERN HOUSE LARGE PRINT BOOKS LTD of
9-15 High Street, Sutton, Surrey, SM1 1DF.
First world regular print edition published 2005 by
Severn House Publishers, London and New York.
This first large print edition published in the USA 2006 by
SEVERN HOUSE PUBLISHERS INC., of
595 Madison Avenue, New York, NY 10022.

British Library Cataloguing in Publication Data

Nicole, Christopher
   A fearful thing. - Large print ed.
   1. Jones, Jessica (Fictitious character) - Fiction
   2. Policewomen - England - Fiction 3. Suspense fiction
   4. Large type books
   I. Title
   823.9'14[F]

ISBN-13: 9780727875600
ISBN-10: 0727875604

Printed and bound in Great Britain by
MPG Books Ltd, Bodmin, Cornwall.

Please return / renew by date shown.
You can renew at: **norlink.norfolk.gov.uk**
or by telephone: **0344 800 8006**
Please have your library card & PIN ready.

10/4

NORFOLK LIBRARY
AND INFORMATION SERVICE

A FEARFUL THING

Alas! The love of women! It is known
To be a lovely and a fearful thing!

George Gordon, Lord Byron

Prologue

The pebble arced out of the darkness and landed lightly on the windowpane. Jeremy Lenghurst held his breath. He loved adventure, and with his strikingly handsome looks, his athletic build, and his mother's money he had been able to find enough of it in his brief life, but this was the ultimate. Now he inhaled mimosa and night-blooming jasmine, listened to the distant roar of an automobile on the highway, then held his breath again. If she had changed her mind...

A light glowed in the bedroom. Now the window opened. The girl stood there for a moment, silhouetted. Her face was invisible, but her long dark hair fluttered in the dawn breeze. Jeremy flicked his cigarette lighter to allow her a single gleam. She raised her hand and left the window, to return a moment later with a suitcase. Jeremy had already moved forward to stand against the wall; he caught the case without difficulty, even though it was surprisingly heavy.

He set it on the ground and looked up, just in time to catch the girl herself, as she lost her grip on the drainpipe down which she had been climbing. He held her in his arms as she slid down his body.

'Oh, my God!' she gasped. 'Oh, my God!'

'It's OK,' he said. 'We're nearly there.'

'Where's the car?' Her southern drawl contained only a slight foreign intonation.

'On the road. You all right?' His English accent was in the strongest possible contrast to hers.

He could feel her trembling against him, but now she stepped away from him and straightened her clothes; she wore jeans and a loose blouse that did not reach her waist, exposing several inches of pale-brown flesh, and sandals on her bare feet; but in the warm Florida night this was not a problem. Only standing as high as Jeremy's shoulder, she had delightfully piquant features and lively black eyes to go with her slender body; her most striking feature was the wealth of silky black hair.

'I'm all right,' she said.

'Then let's get out of here.' He picked up the suitcase, held her hand, and led her across the lawn to the fence.

'Hey,' a voice said.

They stopped. 'Oh, my God!' Theresa whispered. 'Oh, my God!'

'Who is that?' Jeremy asked.

'Rodrigo.'

'You said he was going away for the weekend.'

'He did go away. He must have come back early. What are we to do?'

Jeremy watched the large figure coming

8

towards them, indistinct in the moonlight. 'We could make a run for it. Once we reach the car...'

'He would have the highway patrol after us in a moment. Anyway, he carries a gun.'

'Shit! Well, then...' Jeremy laid the suitcase on the ground, but continued to hold Theresa's hand with his own left.

The big Hispanic came up to them. 'What you doing?' he demanded. He peered into the uncertain light. 'Señorita Theresa?' His gaze shifted to Jeremy. 'And you! I have seen you.'

'Well, why don't you go back to bed, and you won't see me again?' Jeremy suggested.

'You are running off with the señorita!'

'Actually, old boy, we are eloping. So we'd be very grateful if you'd not interfere. As I say, if you were to go back to bed, and do nothing until tomorrow morning, we should be ever so grateful.'

'The patron will wish to see you.'

'And I look forward to meeting him, in due course. But as he is in Colombia, and I am in Florida, it will have to wait until after the señorita and I have married and had our honeymoon. So I must ask you to bugger off.'

Theresa's fingers were so tight on his he could feel her nails eating into his flesh.

'You come with me, señorita,' Rodrigo said. 'You will go back to bed. I will deal with this creature.'

Theresa drew a deep breath. 'I love him, Rodrigo. Please do not interfere. I am asking as an old friend.'

9

'And I must do my duty,' Rodrigo pointed out. 'Release her and step aside.'

'Or what?' Jeremy asked, pleasantly.

'Do not make me use force, señor.'

'Jerry,' Theresa whispered, urgently.

Jeremy squeezed her hand. 'Such as?' he inquired, still speaking quietly.

Rodrigo reached for his pocket, and Jeremy did release Theresa, giving her a push which sent her sprawling on the ground. In the same movement he drew the knife, which Rodrigo had not previously noticed, from the sheath at his waist, stepped against the big Colombian and drove the blade into his chest with tremendous force. Rodrigo did not even have the time to scream before he died, his body slumping to the ground, while Jeremy leapt away from him to prevent blood from staining his clothes.

Theresa pushed herself up. 'What ... oh, my God!' Her voice rose an octave. 'Oh—' The incipient scream was cut off as Jeremy stooped and slapped her across the face.

'He was reaching for his gun,' he said.

She licked her cut lip and got to her knees. 'Is he...?'

'I would say so.' Jeremy knelt beside the dead man, choosing his right side to avoid the blood which had flooded the shirt and jacket. Rodrigo's right hand was still in his pocket, and Jeremy felt the inert fingers and then the pocket itself; there was no weapon, only a small notebook. He kept his back turned to the girl. 'He's dead, all right.'

10

'Oh, my God!'

'For Christ's sake stop saying that.'

Theresa drew a deep breath, noisily. 'What are we going to do? The police...'

'We have to get out of here before the police get involved. Are you with me?'

'Well...'

'Look, do you love me?'

'You know I do.'

'Then stick by me. Does anyone know about us?'

'If Rodrigo says he saw you, then Greta may have done so too.'

'Who is Greta?'

'His wife. She is my aunt's housekeeper.'

'OK, she may have seen me with you, some time. But she can hardly have any idea who I am.'

'Well...'

'For God's sake, Terry, pull yourself together. Does anyone *know* about us?'

She bit her lip.

'Who? Who did you tell?'

'I didn't tell anyone. But your photo ... the one you gave me...'

'Didn't you bring it with you?'

'I meant to. But I forgot it. I think.'

'You *think*?'

'I was so excited. Let's look in my case. It could be there.'

'We have no time for that. Come on.' He wiped his knife clean on Rodrigo's trousers, sheathed it, held her hand to pull her to her feet, picked up the suitcase and dragged her

11

towards the fence.

'But the photo...'

'So you have a photo of a guy in your bedroom. No one knows who it is, any more than Rodrigo's wife can know who I am, and by the time they find out we'll be long gone.'

'Gone where? They'll track us down. They always do.'

'We'll be out of the country. You *did* bring your passport?'

'Oh, yes.'

They reached the fence, and he helped her over it. The hired car waited in the darkness. He threw her suitcase in the back, sat beside her.

'When you say out of the country, you mean Mexico? We'll never get there. It's right across the States. Anyway, Papa will find us there. He has friends in Mexico.'

Jeremy gunned the engine and roared towards the highway. 'We aren't going to Mexico.'

Theresa realized they were driving north. 'The airport? But it's the middle of the night. There won't be any planes.'

'Not at Miami, but there'll be planes flying by the time we reach Atlanta.'

'Atlanta?' she cried. 'But that's hours away.'

'That's the idea.'

'But ... by then the police...'

'Will still be poking around your auntie's house. So you'll have disappeared, and your minder has gotten himself killed. Clearly you've been kidnapped.'

12

'The photo...'

'Is of some good-looking guy you have a crush on. Oh, they'll look for him, and I guess the guys at the Dive Centre will recognize me, but by the time they do that, we'll be long gone.' He squeezed her hand. 'Quit worrying. We're going to Mumsy. She'll look after us. She always does.'

The New Girl

The bells pealed as the couple left the church. A small crowd had gathered outside, idly curious, but becoming more interested as they saw the bridal pair – the woman tall and slender, her somewhat aquiline face strongly attractive rather than pretty, and surrounded by a wealth of straight auburn hair disappearing behind her white satin headdress; the man even taller, with handsome features and glowing ebony skin. He wore a blue dress uniform with red facings, and now that they were out of the church he placed his blue peaked cap on his head.

But by now the spectators' interest was being taken by the couple next in line. The best man was also a black police officer, immaculately dressed if by no means as striking as the groom. The woman beside him, wearing a pale-blue long gown, was no more than half his size, with exquisitely carved features and smooth yellow hair which escaped her floral headdress to lie on her shoulders. She looked around herself with a peculiarly alert air, her gaze utterly confident and all-embracing.

As her companion noticed. 'You ain't on

duty, Sergeant,' he remarked, glancing at her décolletage, decorated by the pearl pendant nestling between breasts that indicated a very mature figure.

'It' a way of life.' She spoke quietly, and accompanied him down the steps to the waiting Rolls; the bride and groom had already departed in the first car. The onlookers had now pressed closer, and as she got into the car, someone pointed and muttered to her companion. Then the best man sat beside her, the door was closed, and they were driving away.

'The price of fame,' he remarked.

'I'm sure they think I'm someone else.'

'Aren't you the most famous copper in England?'

'Let's say I get into trouble more than anyone else.'

'Shooting people.'

'When it has to be done, sir.'

He mused for a few moments while they proceeded slowly through the busy streets. Then he asked, 'Andie is your best friend, right?'

'We've worked together a lot.'

'So you must be sorry to see her go.'

'I am. But I want her to be happy. I'm sure she will be.'

'Amen.'

Detective-Sergeant Jessica Jones preferred not to add to the comment. She did wish Andrea Hutchins, or Andrea Kahu, as she now was, all the happiness in the world, but

16

she was aware that racism was very much a fact of life, both in and out of the police force, and that not everyone approved of Andrea's marrying her Nigerian beau and going off to the wilds of West Africa – and that went for the Nigerian police as well. But she did feel like shedding a tear when she remembered the stupendous adventures they had had together, from the jungles of South America to the deserts of North Africa, all in the service of the Special Branch Protection Unit. Of all her original squad Andie was the last: Louise was dead, murdered in the line of duty; Cleo was retired, crippled in the line of duty ... Andie was at least going to happiness, she hoped and prayed. So where did that leave her?

'How come a gorgeous chick like you never got married?' Inspector Boroku asked. They had only met at the church.

'I've been married.'

'And it didn't work out? The guy must've been nuts.'

'Faults on both sides.'

'Because you shoot people, eh?' White teeth gleamed at her.

'As you say, sir.' Jessica began to feel irritated by his constant reference to her reputation, no matter how deserved it might be.

'So that big guy you came with...?'

'My partner. Sergeant Lawson.'

'Ah.' The inspector digested this for a few moments, then turned his head, sharply. 'What's that?'

'My mobile. Would you believe it?' She opened her handbag, took out the phone. 'Jones.'

'Where are you?' Mrs Norton had a somewhat abrasive voice, which became more abrasive when she was speaking with Jessica: the two women did not like each other.

'I am on my way from a wedding to a wedding reception,' Jessica said. 'I am not on duty today.'

'You are now. The commander wishes to see you.'

'I am about to attend the lunch. I happen to be matron of honour.'

'You can have your lunch,' Mrs Norton said. 'But don't linger. Three o'clock.'

Jessica restored the phone to her bag.

'You don't look a happy bunny,' Boroku remarked.

'Oh ... bugger off. Sir!'

'He is an old shit,' Andrea said, holding Jessica close. 'I was going to toss you my bouquet.'

'I'd probably have dropped it. Why don't you throw it at Tom?'

'He'd probably catch it.' Andrea kissed her. 'I am going to *miss* you.'

'Not as much as I am going to miss you. Listen. Be happy. And you, sir,' she told Douglas Kahu, who had hurried over to say goodbye.

'We're going to see you again,' he protested.

'Well ... next time I'm in Nigeria.'

18

A last hug and then she joined Tom Lawson, large and rugged, awkward in his hired morning suit. 'You don't have to come,' she pointed out.

'You look too good to be loose on the streets by yourself.' He had already summoned a taxi, and she sat beside him with a rustle of taffeta. 'You're not even armed.'

She blew a raspberry. 'I happen to be attending a wedding, not a stake-out.'

'Any idea what it's about?' he asked.

'No. But it had better be good. What are you going to do with your afternoon?'

'I'm going back to the reception. Having paid a small fortune for this clobber, I don't mean to take it off till tonight. Will you be home?'

'Will you be sober if I am?'

Heads turned and there were some whistles as Jessica strode through the lower office, her long blue dress floating behind her, as did her hair – she had abandoned her floral coronet in the taxi. Jessica ignored them and got to the lift, entered Mrs Norton's office on the stroke of three.

'How pretty you look,' the secretary remarked. Small and dark, with heavily permed black hair, she looked as intense as she actually was. 'Was it a nice reception?'

'I never had the chance to find out. It's three o'clock.'

Mrs Norton's expression became one of sucking a lemon, as she pressed the switch on

19

her intercom. 'Sergeant Jones is here, Commander.'

'Send her in, Mrs Norton.'

Mrs Norton jerked her head towards the inner door, and Jessica opened it and went in.

'JJ?' Commander Adams peered at his most famous employee; only rarely had he ever seen her out of uniform, and never in a long gown. He was a big man whose head seemed even bigger and was inclined to droop between his shoulders, giving him the appearance of a somewhat unhappy bloodhound – at the moment, a bewildered bloodhound. 'Good heavens! Have you been to a ball? In the middle of the afternoon?'

'I was attending Detective-Constable Hutchins' wedding, sir.'

'Good heavens! Of course. To that, ah...'

'To that Nigerian police officer, sir, whom we met when on assignment in Kano.'

'Ah, yes. I remember. Big chap. And you came straight from the, ah, party?'

'Mrs Norton said I was to be here at three, sir, and I did not have the time to change.'

'Well, I'm sorry to have interrupted the festivities, what? Although I must say that you look most becoming. Most becoming. This is Mrs Lenghurst.'

Jessica hadn't realized there was another woman in the room, seated on the far side, but now standing. She frowned. There was something familiar about the name, but she had never seen the woman before, as far as she could remember. Mrs Lenghurst was a

20

few inches taller than herself, slim, with crisply attractive features and short, straight dark hair; Jessica put her down as early forties, and thus only a few years older than herself. Her clothes were expensive, and the rings on her fingers were worth at least a year's pay. 'Mrs Lenghurst.'

'You are not the least as I expected,' Mrs Lenghurst remarked. Her voice was as upper-crust as her clothes and jewellery.

Jessica did not take offence; she was used to this sort of treatment from her various 'clients', a group she had no doubt this woman was about to join. Besides, the commander hurried to her rescue. 'Sergeant Jones does not wear evening dress when on duty.'

'Except where the duty requires it, sir,' Jessica pointed out.

'Oh, quite.'

'You're so ... well ... little,' Mrs Lenghurst observed.

Jessica looked at the commander.

'You know what they say about small packages,' he suggested.

'They say you are the best,' Mrs Lenghurst commented. 'Is that true?'

'As I don't know who "they" are, ma'am, I couldn't possibly offer an opinion.'

'She is the best,' Adams said. 'Shall we sit down?'

Mrs Lenghurst resumed her seat, and Jessica sat before the desk.

'Mrs Lenghurst especially requested your services, JJ,' the commander said.

'May I ask in what capacity, sir?'

'I wish you to protect my son,' Mrs Lenghurst said.

Again Jessica looked at the commander.

'Jeremy Lenghurst has received a death threat,' Adams explained. 'Well, I suppose it could be called a death threat.'

'Of course it's a death threat,' Mrs Lenghurst snapped, and Jessica felt that she refrained with difficulty from adding, 'You cretin.'

'Ah ... I think Sergeant Jones should be shown the letter,' Adams said mildly.

'It's an e-mail,' Mrs Lenghurst said, and gave Jessica the printout.

Jessica read:

I WANT MY DAUGHTER BACK, AND YOUR SON'S BALLS. I INTEND TO HAVE THEM, AND TO MAKE HIM PAY FOR RODRIGO. YOU CANNOT HIDE FROM ME.

'Disgusting, isn't it?' Mrs Lenghurst said.

'He seems pretty upset. But, as the commander said, it isn't exactly a death threat.'

'Oh, really!'

'May I ask where your son is now?'

'He is here in London, at the moment.'

'And the young lady?'

'She is here as well.'

'And the irate father?'

'God knows. Colombia, I suppose.'

Jessica looked at the commander.

'Mr Abriga deals in, ah, drugs.'

'Tell me about it,' Jessica muttered.

'Sergeant Jones has encountered Colombian drug smugglers before,' Adams explained.

'And she's still here?'

'She killed an estimated dozen of them.'

'What did you say? This little girl killed twelve of those thugs?'

'It's not quite as it sounds,' Jessica said, defensively. 'I and my unit were being attacked from the air. We returned fire, and I happened to hit the fuel tank of the helicopter. It was crowded at the time.'

'Well!' Mrs Lenghurst said, her tone suddenly warm. 'I've heard a lot about you, Sergeant Jones, but never that one.'

'It was not publicized, for obvious reasons,' the commander said.

'It still sounds good to me. You going to come in on this, Jessica? You don't mind if I call you Jessica?'

'She prefers to be called JJ,' Adams said.

'Right. JJ it is. Welcome aboard, JJ. And you must call me Rowena.'

'Ah ... right. Could you fill me in, Rowena? Your son has...?'

'Eloped with Theresa Abriga.'

'From Colombia?'

'No, no. She was at school in Florida, and Jerry was in Florida, doing a diving course, and they met, and ... well, one thing led to another.'

'Did you say she was at school?'

23

'She was actually living with her aunt. But she was attending school in Miami.'

'May I ask how old she is?'

'Well...' Rowena looked sulky. 'She'll be sixteen in three months' time.'

Yet again Jessica found herself looking at the commander, who waggled his eyebrows; he clearly intended to leave the ball in her court. She turned back to Rowena. 'Are they married?'

'Well, not yet. It appears she cannot marry without the consent of her parents, and this we have not yet obtained.'

Jessica looked at the printout, which was lying on the commander's desk. 'Do you suppose you are going to?'

'It may be difficult. But I have lawyers working on it. Anyway,' she added brightly, 'it won't matter, once she's eighteen.'

'Which you say happens to be more than two years off. I hate to be indelicate, but have the happy couple consummated their relationship?'

'Well, you know what young people are like.'

'So your son is guilty of statutory rape. They take this even more seriously in the States than we do here. He could go to gaol for life. And you want us to protect him?'

'He's my son.'

'I should say,' Adams intervened, 'that the initial ... ah, crime, took place in Florida, not on British soil.'

'But it is continuing on British soil, sir.'

'Only for another three months,' Rowena said. 'Then it will be legal.'

'Do you think Mr Abriga will think it is legal?'

'That is what we are trying to ascertain. But until we have reached a settlement with Abriga, my son's life is clearly in danger.'

Jessica switched tacks. 'May I ask why the Florida police have not asked for an extradition order?'

'Because they don't know anything about it.'

'Abriga doesn't deal with the police,' Adams said. 'He is virtually a king in his part of Colombia, and he takes care of those who commit crimes against him personally. Or he has his henchmen do it. Apparently, this aunt, on discovering Theresa was missing, e-mailed her brother and left it up to him.'

'Right. So they eloped together from a house in...?'

'Coral Gables.'

'Intending to go to Miami Airport?'

'No, no. Jerry is a smart boy. Obviously they eloped at night, and he knew he couldn't get a flight until the afternoon. But he also knew that Miami Airport would be the first place they would look for him. So he drove up to Atlanta.'

'As you say, a smart boy. And I assume he had sufficient money...'

'He has his own credit cards.'

'Of course. Silly of me. And presumably the girl had a passport ... what about the car he was driving?'

'It was hired; why?'

'I'm just trying to establish whether or not your son committed any other crimes while carrying out this romantic adventure.'

'Of course he did not. Jerry is not a criminal.'

'Except when it comes to sex.'

Rowena glared at her, and then at Adams.

'JJ believes in getting to the nub of the business,' the commander explained. 'We regard it as one of her strengths.'

Rowena snorted.

Jessica smiled at her. 'So, the Miami police, or the FBI, are not involved. Only this understandably irate drugs baron. So who is this chap Rodrigo?'

'Some man Abriga intended as a husband for Theresa. But she hates him. She told me so.'

'I see. May I ask, what is Mr Lenghurst's take on all this?'

'My husband keeps a very low profile.'

Jessica waited a moment, hoping for an explanation of the cryptic remark, but as there obviously was not going to be one, she turned back to Adams. 'What exactly is my brief, sir?'

'Normal, round-the-clock protection.'

'In what conditions?'

'You'll move into my London flat,' Rowena said. 'Prevent people getting in unless I say so, accompany us when we go out – that sort of thing.'

'For how long?'

'As I said, we are working on sorting this out diplomatically, but it may take a little while.'

'How long, sir?'

'Well, it could be for a month or two. Obviously you will be relieved. Shall we say, a fortnight to begin with?'

'Round the clock. I'll need a team.'

'We'll discuss that in a moment. Was there anything else, Mrs Lenghurst?'

'You understand that I do a lot of travelling.'

'That will not be a problem.'

'Then that seems settled. When will Jessica take up her position?'

'Tonight, if you wish.'

Jessica stared at him with her mouth open.

'That will be very satisfactory.' Rowena stood up. 'Shall we say, six o'clock? The commander has my card; it's the Aspern Building, the penthouse. I look forward to entertaining you. And do wear that dress tonight. It's so attractive.'

The door closed and Jessica faced the desk. 'Have we got Home Office clearance for this, sir?'

'She came to us via the Home Office – in fact, via the Home Secretary. Apparently that e-mail arrived last night, and she has been twisting arms ever since.'

'And she can twist arms?'

'Very easily. Her father is Lord Blandin.'

'The billionaire?'

27

'Correct. He also happens to be a principal donor to the government. So he carries clout. He is also prepared to pay for the whole operation, no matter what it costs. I don't think he is so worried about his errant grandson as that his daughter may get in the way if any Colombian hit man turns up. Mind you, I think that is highly unlikely, when they realize who they are tangling with. Still, we must keep the lady, and her daddy, happy. So, you see, you are actually protecting Mrs Lenghurst as much as her son.'

'Then I will need an even larger team than usual, as they are hardly likely to spend all their time in the same room. As for this Abriga character, my experience of South American drug barons is that they do not make threats idly.'

'Well, then, it's up to you to keep the lad intact.'

'I will do my best. However, six o'clock tonight ... that's impossibly short notice. The place has to be inspected, I have to round up my team ... it's not as if I could just telephone Andie. I'm starting from scratch. And this business about travelling ... where?'

'Mrs Lenghurst owns an island in the Bahamas.'

'You're kidding.'

'However, it is her custom to spend the summers in England, and only the winters out there. I believe that she does not normally return there until the end of October – that is, after the hurricane season. As that is three months off, this business will surely have been brought to an acceptable conclusion by then. Now, your team...'

Jessica tried to concentrate. 'I'll need at least three people, to begin with.'

'Ah ... that won't be possible.'

'Say again, sir?'

'The department is both short-handed and cash-strapped, due to this latest government drive for economic efficiency. And as Mrs Lenghurst requires round-the-clock surveillance, that means you and your back-up will be totally lost to the department for the length of your assignment.'

'But if her father is paying...'

'Lord Blandin is paying for the protection of his daughter and grandson. He is not paying for anything else, as, for instance, a desirable expansion of the department. We simply do not have the staff to deploy four or more of our officers to a single assignment for what may be a considerable period. So we are offering our very best. You may have one back-up.'

Jessica was not mollified by the compliment. 'Would you give me a moment to catch up? I am required to move in with this woman, lock, stock and barrel for a fortnight, with just one back-up – who will be a partner with whom I have never worked before and of whom I know nothing.'

'Oh, come now, JJ. I'm sure we can find you someone with whom you've worked before. What about Lawson?'

Jessica needed only the briefest consideration. 'I don't think that would be a good idea, sir.'

The commander raised his eyebrows. 'Don't you live together?'

'We do, sir. And thus we know each other very well. Tom is a great guy. But we could never work together. There can be only one leader in the field.'

'And he'd want to be it. I take your point. Well, go and see Inspector Morton – find out who's available. It has to be now. And get a move on. You only have a couple of hours.' He gave her Rowena's card. 'There's the address.'

'My word,' Inspector Morton remarked. 'Is that the new uniform? I like it. At least on you, Sergeant Jones.' A heavy-set man, he hunched over his desk as if about to eat it.

'I have just come from a wedding.'

'Of course. Hutchins. What a damned shame.'

'Sir?'

'Well, you know...'

'Hutchins has married the finest man she has ever met. Or I have ever met. Sir.'

'Ah. Well ... what do you want of me?'

'I need a partner, female, for a two-week spell of duty which will take up all of her time for that period.'

'And of course Hutchins is no longer available. You say, a partner. Just the one?'

'It appears that's all I'm allowed.'

'Well, it shouldn't be difficult. I'll make up

a list and you can mull over it, see which ones you would like to interview. Is there a time schedule?'

'There is. We are on duty at six o'clock this afternoon.' She looked at her watch. 'That's just over two hours.'

Morton leant back in his chair. 'I, sadly, was not invited to this wedding, and therefore have not been indulging in champagne. So I would like you to be serious.'

'Maybe you should give the commander a call. Sir.'

Morton glared at her.

'I am on duty at six,' Jessica went on. 'My partner does not have to be there then, but she has to be available tonight.'

'That is quite impossible.'

'If I can do it, so can she.'

'You are saying that your partner has to be a woman.'

'I would prefer that, sir. We are likely to be spending a lot of time in very close proximity. There must be someone available.'

'There may be. But are you also saying that you will take someone virtually sight unseen, someone you have not been able to evaluate, on a two-week tour?'

'I would prefer it to be someone I know, yes. But I will have to leave it to your judgement. I am going home now to get ready. The venue is here in town, so I will leave the flat at five thirty. If by then you have found someone, and she is able to give me a call – or, better yet, drop in for a moment – I would be

31

grateful; but in any event, she must report at the venue by nine o'clock tonight.' She laid Rowena's card on the desk. 'That is the address.'

Morton wrote it down as if signing a death warrant, returned the card. 'This is most highly irregular.'

'Tell me about it, sir. Or better yet, tell the commander.'

Jessica took a taxi home; it was not practical to catch a bus or a tube wearing a long gown. Predictably, the little flat was empty; Tom was undoubtedly still enjoying the reception, nor was there the least chance he would be home by five thirty. On the other hand, once this business was set up, she should be able to get back for an hour, both to complete her packing and put him in the picture.

She stripped off her gown, had a shower, but did not bother to dress; the flat was comfortably warm and she enjoyed being naked, in private. She placed her small suitcase on the bed and packed a change of underwear and shirt, then opened her top drawer to take out her Skorpion blow-back machine pistol, her favourite weapon. Unloaded it weighed just over a kilo, but it carried a twenty-shot magazine, and would stop a man at seventy-five metres. Years of practice on the police range had made her an expert markswoman, but the little gun had the additional value of an extendable butt which allowed it to be aimed like a small rifle. It also fitted neatly into the shoulder bag she always carried on duty. Beside it she packed the other essentials of her job: a spare magazine, her first-aid kit, a flashlight, two pairs of handcuffs and her mobile. These made the bag quite heavy, but her shoulder was used to that.

She had completed her packing by four thirty, made herself a cup of tea and sat down to think. Not for the first time in her now quite long career – sixteen of her thirty-eight years had been spent in the Force, and eight in the Protection Unit – she did not care for the job she had been given. But she loved her work and, as she was in the habit of being honest with herself, she also knew that she loved her reputation – 'the deadliest woman in England', as a tabloid had recently described her.

She had not sought such a reputation. It had arisen entirely by circumstance, combined with her exceptional skill with firearms and her unusual powers of making instant decisions. Thus she had increasingly been given high-profile jobs, on one occasion even being seconded to, and having to train with, the SAS, in order to track down the terrorist Korman.

The media had lapped it up. Her colleagues, and even more her superiors, were not sure what to make of her. Even Tom, who, when she had been at a loose end emotionally, following her divorce, had persuaded her to join him in the Protection Unit, was, she felt, vaguely afraid of her, for all that he was six foot two to her five foot four. For the last couple of years her only true and unequivocal friend had been Andie Hutchins, but that had caused eyebrows to be raised even higher, as Andie had been well known to be at least bisexual. In fact, they had never exchanged more than a squeeze of the hand in moments of extreme danger, even though Jessica knew the temptation had from time to time been very present.

Now Andie was gone, having finally made the choice, and she was on her own. She thoroughly enjoyed Tom, who had been her sexual partner now for several years. He was good in bed, most of the time, and they shared common interests, not only in their work, but in music and cinema, food and drink. There had been a time, early in their relationship, when she would have married him, if he had asked her; but she had rapidly realized that it would have been a mistake. She had wanted children; he had not. And the essential difference in their temperaments, which made it impossible for them to work together, would have made marriage a disaster. The present arrangement, whereby they shared a flat and their bodies (when they were both available, which owing to their profession was not on a very regular basis), but kept their finances and their opinions on most matters strictly separated, was as good as it could get. Of course, she had from time to time considered moving out and in with someone more likely to give her what she really wanted, but she never had. Partly this had been because, after her first husband, it had been a case of 'better the devil you know', but more importantly it was because she knew she was looking for the impossible: someone who would let her continue in her high-profile and often high-risk and basically unfeminine job, and yet be an attentive and ever-loving male companion.

Dreams! So now she was stuck with protecting a rich bitch who had a criminal son, however much Rowena might protest his innocence of criminal intent. All because her father supported the government! Policemen were not allowed to hold political views, at least when on duty, but this set-up stank like a garbage pail that had not been emptied for a week.

She picked up the phone, called the Yard. 'Sergeant Jones. Put me through to Records, will you?'

There were some clicks. 'Curtis.'

'Jimmy. JJ. I'd like anything you have on the name Lenghurst.'

'How soon?'

'A.S.A.P. But if it's after five thirty, or tomorrow, call me on my mobile.'

'Will do.'

She replaced the phone, contemplated her empty teacup, got up to make herself another, and the doorbell rang. 'Shit,' she muttered. She went into the bedroom, pulled on a dressing gown, hesitated, then took the Skorpion from the shoulder bag and held it against her own shoulder as she went to the door. She did not consider herself to be paranoid, but she knew she had made many enemies over the years, and she could never forget that her worst experience, the occasion when she had been famously kidnapped by someone her evidence had once convicted of murder, had happened simply because she had been in a glow of contentment after a game of tennis with Andie, and had not given a thought to the rather pleasant man who had engaged her in conversation as she had walked home, until it was too late.

The bell jangled again. Jessica picked up the phone. 'Who is it?'

'Sergeant Jones?' The voice was softly feminine, but also tense. 'Detective-Constable Hewitt. Inspector Morton sent me.'

'Oh. Right. Come up.' Jessica released the catch for the street door, unlocked the flat door, stepped back, and gazed at an extraordinarily young woman – at least in her opinion. Detective-Constable Hewitt was only a couple of inches taller than herself, and slender, for all the fact that she wore uniform. Her dark hair was in a ponytail but was clearly quite long, and her features were gamine rather than pretty, or even regular, but Jessica estimated they could have been quite attractive had she not been so terribly nervous. Her condition worsened at the sight of the pistol. 'Just habit,' Jessica explained. 'Enter.' She locked the door behind her.

'If I hadn't been me, would you have shot me?'

'There's a conundrum. Tea? I'm just making a cuppa.'

'Oh, thank you. I'm Felicity.'

'Welcome.' Jessica went into the kitchenette, switched on the kettle; as it was still hot, it boiled almost immediately. 'I'm Jessica.'

'JJ,' Felicity Hewitt said, in an awed tone.

'That's right.' Jessica poured. 'How did you know that?'

'Everyone knows of JJ.'

'Hm.' Jessica gave her the cup. 'Sit down. Be comfortable.' She did so herself, leaning back in the armchair, one naked knee draped across the other.

Felicity removed her hat and sat opposite, on the settee, black-stockinged knees pressed together. 'My friends call me Filly,' she ventured.

'Then Filly it shall be. So Inspector Morton sent you. How old are you, Filly?'

'Twenty-six.'

'Good heavens. That's young to be in the Branch. How long have you been a member?'

'Two weeks.'

Jessica hastily put down the teacup before she dropped it.

'They think I'm quite good,' Felicity said, ingenuously. 'I'm "A" in marksmanship, and I have a black belt ... but I suppose you do too.'

'Yes,' Jessica said absently, wondering if Morton was playing a joke on her, or if this girl was truly all he could come up with at such short notice. 'So, have you ever been on assignment before?'

'Oh, no. This will be my first. But to be with you ... I'm so excited.'

'Don't be. If we're lucky, it won't be an exciting job. But as it may well be ... you know the rules?'

'Yes, ma'am. We defend the client – with our lives, if need be – and we only shoot if their life is in danger.'

'Don't be melodramatic. We are also allowed to defend our own lives. And if we ever have to shoot, we shoot to kill.'

Felicity swallowed. 'Yes, ma'am.'

'Which is something I assume you have never done before.'

'No, ma'am.'

'Unfortunately, it is quite likely in this case that we may have to defend our clients. I want you to know that this is a potentially dangerous assignment, and if you wish to opt out you should do so, now.'

'I want to work with you, ma'am.'

'In that case, do stick to JJ. Right. I'll just put you in the picture.'

Felicity listened with her mouth open. 'A drugs baron! Oh, Lord!'

'I shouldn't think we'll be dealing with him personally. What I want you to do now is go home and pack an overnight bag and join me at the Lenghurst flat this evening. We'll sort out a rota later. You will not, of course, wear uniform; you need to be tastefully and quietly dressed.'

'Do I wear jewellery?'

'Studs, if you wish.'

'Necklaces? Bangles?'

'They get in the way.'

'Yes, ma'am.'

'And do remember to call me JJ. There is one more thing: what do you carry?'

'Ma'am?'

'What weapon do you use?'

'Oh. I haven't been issued with one yet.'

'Then go back to the Yard now, get a requisition from Inspector Morton or whoever is on duty, and equip yourself. I'd prefer you to have a pistol than a revolver, but it should be as small and light as is compatible with stopping an aggressor. Make sure it is loaded and that you have a spare magazine.'

Felicity gulped. 'For tonight? Here in London?'

'London is at least as dangerous as any other place in the world, particularly when it comes to the drugs industry. And you will be on duty tonight.'

'Yes, ma'am. I mean, JJ.'

'OK. I'll see you later on. Oh, by the way: eat before you join me.'

'Right.'

Jessica closed the door behind her. Could enthusiasm make up for experience and proven reliability? Definitely not, but it at least promised to be fun to work with. She looked at her watch: quarter past five. Time to make a move.

She went into the bedroom, and the telephone buzzed. 'Yes?'

'JJ? Jim Curtis.'

'Jimmy! That was quick.'

'It wasn't difficult. The name rang a bell when you mentioned it.'

'You mean they're in Records?'

'Lucian Lenghurst is. A very high-profile case, fifteen years ago. He was convicted of being the head of a paedophile ring, right here in London.'

The First Attack

Jessica sat down. 'Would you repeat that?

'You must remember the case. It was only fifteen years ago.'

'Only fifteen years ago, Jimmy, I was walking a beat and thinking about my forthcoming marriage. Anyway, it can't possibly be the man I'm thinking of; mine is married to Lord Blandin's daughter.'

'That's the one.'

'What?'

'That's what made it so high profile.'

'Give me the details.'

'This was before the days of the Internet gangs. Lenghurst lured these kids to his flat, where his pals would come, and they'd photograph them, and well...'

'How long did he get?'

'Six years.'

'*Six?*'

'The kids weren't harmed in any way, except perhaps psychologically. They weren't raped. They were fondled a bit, and they had to do a bit of gross indecency...'

'And he got six years. Nowadays he'd be sent down for life. And his pals.'

'His defence was that he had paid the kids

good money – hired them, in fact – and that they had been perfectly willing.'

'Big deal. Don't tell me: he had good lawyers.'

'The very best. Paid for by his wife's family.'

'You mean she stood by him?'

'Indeed she did.'

Like son, like father, Jessica reflected. 'So presumably he came out after four.'

'That's right.'

'And what happened then?'

'He left the country. There was no sex offenders register then.'

'So where is he now?'

'Haven't a clue. Being kept out of sight by his wife, I suppose. Talk about standing by your man...'

'Yes,' Jessica said, grimly. 'Thanks a million, Jimmy.'

'You got something on him?'

'Not yet.'

Jessica called the office.

'I'm sorry,' Mrs Norton said, 'the commander has just left. And I wouldn't call him at home, Jones. He was in a hurry. He and Mrs Adams are going to a cocktail party at Downing Street.'

'Shit,' Jessica said.

'What did you say?'

'I said, shit. Shit, shit, shit. Have a nice evening.'

She dressed in her usual working outfit of a blue trouser suit with a white shirt, and, as she was now running late, took a taxi to the

Lenghurst address. As she had anticipated, it was an extremely up-market neighbourhood, and an even more up-market apartment building; but by the same token she recognized at a glance that it would be an impossible place to make secure. The buildings across the street were all several storeys high, with masses of windows that would undoubtedly overlook every window in the Lenghurst apartment; there was a constant flow of traffic and pedestrians to and fro on the street outside, and the downstairs double doors were open to allow the warm July evening air to flood the lobby.

'Shouldn't these doors be locked?' she asked the uniformed black concierge.

'There ain't no air-con down here,' he pointed out, rising to look over his desk and take in her overnight bag. 'You have business?'

'Mrs Lenghurst is expecting me.'

He checked his list. 'You got a name?'

'Jones.'

He grinned. 'That's what they all say. Says here there'd be two of you.'

'My friend is coming later.'

'She named Jones too?'

'Her name is Hewitt.'

He wrote it down.

'Are you on duty all night?' Jessica asked.

'I go off at eight. If that Cully turns up.'

'And when do these doors get locked?'

'That's up to him.'

'I see. Thank you. The penthouse, is it?'

43

'That's right. I'll ring and let them know you're coming up.'

'That is probably a good idea.' Jessica got into the lift and rode up. Her mood had not improved. She crossed the penthouse lobby and pressed the bell.

At least the door was opened immediately, by a man wearing a morning suit and a severe expression. 'Miss Jones?'

'Right first time. And you are?'

He raised his eyebrows.

'Don't tell me you're ashamed of your name?'

'My name is Jerningham.'

'I'd prefer what comes first.'

'It is James, madam.'

'Isn't that great? We have the same initials. You going to let me in?'

He stepped aside, reluctantly. 'I understand Mrs Lenghurst is expecting you.' His tone indicated that he didn't see how that could be possible. 'But she said there'd be two of you.'

'Hang about and all things may be possible.' She passed him, into a lobby with sufficient chairs, tables and potted plants to have been in an hotel. From the lobby a wide corridor led further into the flat.

Jerningham regained the lead, and she followed him, but only as far as the second door on her left. This he opened. 'This will be your, ah, quarters, Miss Jones. And that of your friend, whenever she gets here.'

He switched on the light and Jessica gazed at a perfectly comfortable double bedroom,

44

with twin beds, as well as a washstand. She placed her suitcase on the nearest bed, but, as always, retained her shoulder bag.

'The, ah, bathroom is just across the hall,' Jerningham explained.

'Sounds great. Where do you sleep?'

'I am not resident, madam.'

'So when do you go off duty?'

'Is that any business of yours?'

'Didn't Mrs Lenghurst give you any idea why I'm here?'

'She merely said that two young ladies would be coming to spend a few nights.'

'Then I'll have to ask her. Where do I find her?'

'Don't you wish to, ah...' He looked at the door across the hall.

'I can manage for the time being, thank you. So...'

Jerningham gave a strangled exclamation as he was unceremoniously pushed to one side and Jessica found herself facing quite the most handsome man she had ever seen – tall, dark haired, strongly built and with classical features. Jeremy Lenghurst took after his mother, but Jessica had to suppose that his father had been even better-looking. 'Good God!' he remarked.

'I know,' Jessica conceded. 'I often affect people that way.'

'You're not the famous JJ?'

'I'm JJ. As to whether I'm famous, I suppose the jury is still out.'

Jeremy looked her up and down, slowly.

'You ... are going to protect ... me?'

'If I have to.'

'I beg your pardon, Mr Jeremy,' Jerningham said. 'Did you say "protect"?'

'Oh, get out, there's a good fellow,' Jeremy said.

The butler hesitated, then left the room.

'Now you've got him all confused,' Jessica commented.

'I could pick you up with one hand,' Jeremy said.

'Which hand do you value more? Because that's the one I would keep.' She smiled at him. 'I think it's time I paid my respects to your mother. Where should I go?'

'She's in the drawing room. At the end of the hall.'

'Thank you.' She stepped past him, and he caught her round the waist. 'Please,' she said. 'We don't know each other well enough – yet.'

'I am going to have *fun* with you.' He lifted her from the floor, effortlessly.

'Jeremy,' she said, as reasonably as she could, 'if you don't put me down, I am going to have to hurt you.'

For reply he hugged her against him and began to nuzzle her neck.

Jessica sighed. Her arms were free, and she was tempted to thrust two of her fingers into his eyes. But that would blind him, perhaps permanently. Instead she reached down and closed her hand on his crotch. Years of train-ing had made her fingers as strong as steel, and his initial grunt of anticipated pleasure changed to a piercing shriek, which, as his mouth was against her ear, all but deafened her. Then he let her go. She landed on her feet, and stepped away from him, while he dropped to his knees, clutching at himself and moaning.

'Sorry about that,' she said. 'But you would not listen.'

'Bitch,' he snarled, tears running down his cheeks. 'When I get up...'

'I may have to really hurt you. So be a good boy.'

The hall had filled with people. Jerningham had returned, accompanied by a maidservant complete in black shirt and white apron and cap. 'Oh, Mr Jeremy,' she squawked. 'What happened?'

Jessica looked past her at a brown-skinned, very young woman, with attractive Latin American features, and then to Rowena, wearing evening dress and looking like an avenging angel. 'I'm sorry I was late,' she said. 'I was delayed, by one thing and another.'

Rowena echoed the maid. 'What happened? Do get up, Jeremy.'

Jeremy staggered to his feet. 'That bitch...'

'Your son attempted to molest me,' Jessica said. 'I tried to reason with him, but...'

Rowena looked at her, then at Jeremy, then at the other faces. 'For God's sake,' she said. 'Pull yourself together, Jerry.'

'That bitch...'

'If your son calls me a bitch again, I really will hurt him,' Jessica said.

'Oh ... look after him, Terry,' Rowena decreed. 'JJ, let's see if we can start again. Jerningham, drinks.' She led Jessica along the hall and into a sumptuously furnished lounge, with a huge plate-glass window overlooking London but also overlooked by the building opposite. 'I'm sorry about that. Jerry, well...'

'He just can't keep his hands off women,' Jessica suggested.

'Well, they have to be good-looking.'

'Thank you. And the girl – Theresa – goes along with that?'

'She's very much in love with him. Well, who wouldn't be?'

'I won't comment.'

'Do sit down. Don't you think he's handsome?'

'Errol Flynn was handsome, but I suspect I would have had to hurt him as well.' Jessica sat on the settee.

Jerningham bustled in with a tray containing a bottle in an ice bucket and two glasses of champagne.

'Thank you, Jerningham,' Rowena said.

'May I have a word, madam?' He glanced at Jessica. 'In private?'

'I'm sure it can keep until after dinner.'

Jerningham hesitated, then gave a brief bow. 'Very good, madam.' He placed the tray on the sideboard and left the room.

'Servants,' Rowena remarked. 'If one could

do without them, one would.'

'Does that go for me, too?' Jessica inquired.

'Oh, my dear ... of course I wish it wasn't necessary to, well...'

'Employ me.'

'Need your assistance,' Rowena said firmly. 'But as I do, I wish to regard you as a friend. I will speak with Jerry. He will not trouble you again.'

'You'd better mention my partner as well. She'll be coming in later tonight.'

'Ah. Is she as pretty as you?'

'You'll have to make your own judgement on that. But she's certainly attractive. And she's more Jerry's age.'

'Oh, well...' Rowena raised her glass. 'Welcome.'

'Thank you. There are a couple of things we need to discuss.'

'I said I'd speak to Jerry.'

'I'm not the least bit concerned about Jerry, except that I'm here to protect him. So, do you have another residence in this country?'

'Why do I need another residence in this country?'

'Simply because this building would not keep out a ten-year-old boy armed with a water pistol.' She gestured at the window. 'Just as that is the dream of any assassin armed with a high-powered rifle.'

'But...'

'Yes. If we take your threatening e-mail seriously, that Abriga's aim is to regain his daughter, and, shall we say, punish your son...'

49

'The thought makes my blood curdle.'

'Quite. But as I say, as it wasn't actually a death threat, I think we may discount that high-powered rifle, at least for the time being. But if Abriga really means to counter-kidnap, there is damn all to stop him.'

'You are going to stop him. With your partner.'

'I will do that, certainly. But our main aim in life is to prevent trouble, rather than encourage it. You need to remember that if it comes to a shooting match, while I have no doubt that my partner and I would win it, I can't say who might get hurt in the process. That includes you.'

Rowena got up to fetch the bottle and replenish their glasses. 'So what is the point in employing you? I mean, police protection.'

'Physical protection is the last resort. Our principal duty is to prevent anyone getting at you in the first place and, as I have said, to make this place secure would require a team of at least a dozen, which I do not have. For instance, are you aware that the street doors downstairs are wide open?'

'The concierges complain of the heat down there, in summer.'

'That's a problem between them and the management. I'm concerned that anyone can walk in there and reach the desk without anything to stop him.'

'What am I supposed to do about it?'

'You can move.'

Rowena looked left and right. 'This is my

English home. I've lived here for twelve years.'

'But you have never been in this position before. Can't you move to your father's house? Or one of his houses?'

'That would not be a good idea. Daddy doesn't like Jerry.'

'That's not too difficult to understand. But in the circumstances...'

'Daddy mustn't ever know of the circumstances. He'd cut Jerry out of his will.'

'Tricky. Well, then, may I suggest you go home to the Bahamas?'

'Now? In July? That's not possible. It's far too hot. Besides, it's the hurricane season.'

'When last was Nassau hit by a hurricane?'

'We don't live in Nassau. We have our own island.'

'Of course. I *am* a silly girl. May I ask where it is?'

'On the north-eastern fringe. That is very exposed to hurricanes.'

'How big is it?'

'About a mile long, and half a mile wide.'

'And you actually own it?'

'Of course we do.'

'What sort of population has it got?'

'Just the staff and the families. About thirty people.'

'And your husband?'

Rowena stared at her. 'What makes you say that?'

'Well, as he isn't here...'

'What do you know about my husband?'

51

'Is there something to know? Something you'd like to tell me?'

Rowena continued to stare at her for several moments. Then she said, 'I think we should have dinner. Did you bring your long dress?'

'No. These are my working clothes. Would you like me to eat with the servants?'

'Of course not, my dear.' She rested her hand on Jessica's. 'It's just that I have never seen your legs.'

Jessica decided not to attempt to analyse that remark, not even to comment that Rowena wouldn't have seen her legs anyway, if she had been wearing the gown. As was so often the case in these circumstances where she found herself thrust into the centre of a family or group of whom she had never even heard twenty-four hours before, it was necessary to take one step at a time, and concentrate on the main issue. Fortunately, Rowena was also concentrating on this.

She sat at the head of the table, with Jeremy at the foot. Jessica and Theresa were opposite each other in the middle, while Jerningham served. Like her prospective mother-in-law, Theresa wore a long dress with a deep décolletage, although she did not have much to fill it with; she struck Jessica as being extremely nervous, which, in her circumstances was perfectly understandable.

'Detective-Sergeant Jones is willing to forget what happened this evening,' Rowena announced over the soup. 'Providing it does not happen again. You may apologise, Jerry.'

'Forgive me, Sergeant.'

'Accepted.'

'As I attempted to explain earlier,' Rowena went on, 'Sergeant Jones and her partner...?' She looked at Jessica.

'Detective-Constable Hewitt.'

'Are joining us for a few days until we can ascertain whether your father's threat is to be taken seriously, Terry.'

'Papa is always serious.'

'Well, then...'

'I still can't get hold of the concept that this little lady, if you'll forgive me, Miss Jones,' Jeremy said, 'is capable of protecting us from the sort of heavy old Abriga is likely to send after us.'

'How many men have you killed, JJ?'

'I don't make notches on my gun.'

'You have a gun?' Jeremy asked. 'Where?'

'In here.' Jessica touched the shoulder bag she had draped over the back of her chair.

'Convince me.'

Jessica looked at Rowena, who shrugged. 'It would be nice to see it.'

Jessica finished her soup, opened the bag, and drew the Skorpion.

Jerningham all but dropped the plates he was gathering.

'Wowee,' Jeremy said again. 'I apologize again. What sort of cartridge does it fire?'

'Seven-point-nine millimetre.'

'And you have actually fired it at someone?'

'JJ once killed a dozen men with a single shot,' Rowena said proudly.

53

'Holy shit!' Jeremy commented.

Theresa spilt her wine.

Jerningham staggered about the room trying not to drop the steaks he was carrying.

'It wasn't quite like that.' Jessica restored the pistol to her bag. 'I'm not very proud of it.'

'Nevertheless,' Rowena said, 'you'll see that she is not to be trifled with, and that we must do what she says, while she is in ... while she is assisting us. For heaven's sake, Jerningham, put the goddamned plates down.'

Jerningham obeyed, and hurried from the room.

'And he's spilled the gravy,' Rowena said. 'Where does one get good staff, nowadays? What was I saying. Oh, yes – we must listen to JJ. Sergeant Jones. She's not happy with our situation.'

'What, up here?'

'This building is totally insecure,' Jessica said. 'It's overlooked from every possible direction, and anyone can enter or leave at will.'

'Surely it's the concierge's job to stop them doing that?'

'I wouldn't bet on it – certainly if the person who wishes to gain access carries a weapon.' Jessica looked at Theresa.

'Yes,' Theresa said. 'The man Papa will send will carry a gun. Just like...' She stopped, and gave her lover an anxious glance.

'I get you,' Jeremy said. 'Just like in that movie we saw in Miami.'

Jessica reflected that they must go to very few movies if one with a man carrying a gun in it stood out in their minds. But she had more important things on *her* mind. 'So I'd like to introduce a few house rules. Well, only three, as a matter of fact. Number one: stay away from the windows. I don't mean you can't walk past them. Just don't stand in front of them for any length of time. I know that Mr Abriga did not specifically threaten your life at this time, Jeremy, but there is always the possibility that he might change his mind. Number two: do not answer the front door, even if the concierge rings up to say someone you know is on the way up. Leave the answering of the door to either me or DC Hewitt. And number three: no one is to leave the building, for any reason, unless accompanied by either me or DC Hewitt. That shouldn't be too difficult to remember.'

'And just how long does this go on?' Jeremy demanded.

Jessica looked at Rowena.

'JJ feels that we should leave this place.'

'And go where?'

'Back to Tiger Cay.'

'In July?'

'It would be safer,' Jessica said. 'As I understand it, this cay ... Is there a reason for it being called Tiger Cay?'

'Not really,' Rowena confessed. 'When we bought it we thought it should have a romantic name.'

'But it is an island. How far is it from its

nearest neighbour?'

'Oh, about a mile, I suppose.'

'This neighbour being?'

'Cat Island.'

'Is that a big place?'

'Oh, very, by Bahamian standards.'

'Is it populated?'

'Well, of course it is. There's a town: Arthur's Town. That's the nearest what-you-might-call centre of civilization.'

'But you say the only inhabitants of your cay are your own servants.'

'And their families.'

'So presumably you know them all by sight.'

'Well, yes.'

'So any stranger on the island would be instantly recognized as such.'

'Well ... people do come across from the mainland, from time to time.'

'And there's no way we can stop someone turning up in the middle of the night,' Jeremy said. 'The whole island, save for the southern ridge, is one big beach.'

'But he'd have to come by boat, right? And I don't think the most dedicated hit man is going to paddle a mile to do his stuff, so at the very least he'd use an outboard. An efficient system of nightwatchmen would surely make it secure. Anyway, don't you have dogs?'

'Well, yes.'

'What breed?'

'Two goldies.'

'Hm. Not very fierce. But they do bark. I

think you could make the island pretty tight. Do you have weapons?'

'Well, Lucian – that's my husband – has a revolver.'

'And there's the shotgun,' Jeremy put in.

'Well, then,' Jessica said, 'I have to say that in my professional opinion you'll be a lot safer there than here.'

'You mean we'd be safer on a virtually uninhabited island than here in Central London?'

'Being surrounded by people is often far more dangerous that being well away from anyone.'

'But the island – it's deadly there. Nothing to do. And then, there's—'

'We'll discuss it later,' Rowena positively snapped.

Conversation flagged while Jerningham served the dessert. Then Jessica ventured, 'I don't suppose, Miss Abriga, that you have considered going home? I mean, just to patch things up. If you could sort it out with your papa, all of this wouldn't be necessary.'

'Oh, I...' Theresa bit her lip, and looked at Jeremy.

'That's not an option,' he said. 'You don't know her dad, Sergeant. He's still living in the eighteenth century when it comes to his womenfolk. Terry would be beaten insensible and then locked up for the rest of her life.'

'You said you were negotiating a settlement,' Jessica said to Rowena.

'Well, we're trying. But we haven't had any

response so far. On the other hand...'

'You reckon the problem will be solved when she's eighteen. But from what you say her daddy isn't likely to accept that. Are you looking for police protection for the rest of your life? Or, indeed, Jeremy's life?'

'I'm sure something will turn up before too long.'

Ah, Jessica thought, *you are hoping that, before too long, Abriga will not be here, either by murder or by reason of the DEA.* Well, she supposed, that was a possibility.

The doorbell rang. Rowena, Theresa and Jeremy all sat bolt upright, and Jerningham spilled the coffee he was pouring.

'It's almost certainly Hewitt,' Jessica said. 'You stay here, Mr Jerningham. I'll get it.' But she took her bag, just in case, went along the hall, and encountered the maid, hurrying into the lobby. 'Leave it,' Jessica said. 'From now on you don't open the door.'

'I'll have to check with Mr Jerningham.'

'Do that.' Jessica had no doubt that it *was* Felicity, but she was still not prepared to take any risks. So, as was her practice, she stood to one side of the door, and drew her pistol.

'Oh, my God!' the maid cried, and ran back along the corridor.

'Who is it?' Jessica asked. There was not even a peephole.

'Filly. Sorry I'm late.'

Jessica unlocked the door. 'How did you get in?'

Felicity was also wearing a blue trouser suit,

58

and also carrying both a suitcase and a shoulder bag. 'Through the front door. It wasn't locked. In fact, it was wide open.'

'That's what I thought you'd say. At half-past nine at night. What about the concierge?'

'He was reading a book.'

'He didn't try to stop you?'

'He waved his hand at me. Is anything wrong?'

'You should ask is anything right. Come in.'

Felicity stepped into the hall, and faced Jeremy and Theresa, standing in front of the drawing-room door. Jessica locked the hall door. 'These are Jeremy Lenghurst and Theresa Abriga. They're the people we're protecting.'

'Hi,' Felicity said.

'Well, hello.' Jeremy advanced.

'She's bigger than me,' Jessica pointed out. 'And stronger.'

Felicity raised her eyebrows, but politely held out her hand.

Jeremy squeezed it. 'I'm sure we're going to be friends. I must say, I never knew the police employed so many attractive women. Do you two chicks ever wear uniform? I love women in uniform.'

'Never on duty,' Jessica told him. 'Now if you'll excuse us.'

'Mum will want to meet ... ah?'

'Miss Hewitt. We'll be along in five minutes.' She opened the bedroom door, showed Felicity in, closed it. 'He gropes,' she explained.

59

'He's awfully good-looking.'

'And knows it. But there's something fishy about him, and his girlfriend. Still, that's only our business if it affects our job. If you're interested, the bathroom is across the hall.'

'I'll manage for now.'

'So sit down and I'll bring you up to date.'

Felicity sat on the bed and listened. 'You seriously think someone is going to try to bust in here?' she asked.

'I don't know what to think. But I'm pretty damned sure there is something – or maybe several things – going on which we do not know about.'

'You mean something to do with the father?'

'There certainly, although I'm hoping to get some clarification on our attitude to that when I contact Adams tomorrow morning. As for the rest – well, we just play it by the book.'

'You mean, watch and watch?'

'I don't think that will be necessary. We're right next to the front door, which is the only reasonable point of access, unless Abriga employs Spiderman.'

'What about a helicopter drop on the roof?'

'It's possible, but we'd surely hear the chopper in time to do something about it. When the flat has settled for the night, we'll sleep with this door open, so we'll hear the slightest sound at the front door or up top.'

'Um. Suppose our groping friend attempts to join us during the night?'

'I think I have already put him off that idea. Now...' she turned sharply as the door opened without a knock. 'Oh, Rowena, this is Detective-Constable Felicity Hewitt. I was just going to bring her to meet you.'

Rowena ignored the introduction. 'Jerningham has quit.'

'You mean he's given notice?'

'No. He's walking out.'

'What about his pay?'

'He's foregoing any severance pay. He says he is not working in a place where people carry guns and boast about killing people.'

'Oh, I'm sorry.'

'It's not your fault. It's Jerry's, for being so boorish.'

'Can't you make this man...?' Felicity asked.

'Jerningham,' Jessica said. 'The butler.'

'Well, isn't he legally obliged to give notice?'

'Of course he is,' Rowena snapped.

'Well, then...?'

'He says if I take him to court he will sell his story to a tabloid newspaper.'

'He's probably going to do that anyway,' Jessica said.

'It's such a *nuisance*. As if I didn't have enough to worry about. Yes, what is it?'

Jerningham stood in the hall. 'I am leaving now, madam. Good night.' He looked past his erstwhile mistress at Jessica, but made no comment.

'Oh, get out!'

'Goodnight, ma'am,' the maid said.

'Are you coming in tomorrow?'

'Well, ma'am...'

'Oh, get out,' Rowena snapped again.

The maid followed Jerningham out of the front door, and Jessica went behind them to lock it.

'What a balls-up,' Rowena growled. 'Well, I'm going to bed. What did you say your name was, girl?'

'Felicity, ma'am.'

'Felicity. I'll speak with you in the morning. Maybe things will look brighter then. Goodnight.'

The door closed. 'I don't exactly feel welcome,' Felicity remarked.

'Her trouble is that she can't make up her mind whether to treat us as servants, friends, or necessary evils. Have you eaten?'

'You said I should.'

'Good girl. And drunk?'

'Not alcohol.'

'I can see you are going to be a treasure. So, did you equip yourself?'

'Oh, yes. I had to take advice; I don't know too much about guns.' She opened her bag, took out the little Ingram Mac 10. 'Inspector Hadow said this is all the rage.'

'It is, amongst gangsters.'

Felicity's face fell. 'Oh.'

'It's used by various police forces as well. Why did Hadow recommend it for you?'

'Well, I told him you'd said it should be something light.'

'That's true enough.'

'He also reckoned that, as I didn't know the

gun and wouldn't have time to practise with it, this was the best.'

'Because it's virtually a sub-machine gun. It empties its entire magazine in the blink of an eye, so being able to shoot accurately is meaningless. It's a killing machine.'

Felicity looked more crestfallen yet. 'Should I get something else?'

'If we're dealing with Colombian assassins, it is probably a very good weapon to have. But for God's sake keep it on single shot and don't ever fire except to back me up. I'll tell you when to go into machine mode.'

'Yes, ma'am.'

Jessica squeezed her hand. 'I'm JJ, remember? We're a team.'

They used the bathroom, returned to the bedroom to undress, Felicity's eyes becoming saucers as she realized that Jessica was not going to put anything on.

'It's habit,' Jessica explained.

'You said we'd leave the door open.'

'That's right.' Jessica opened the door. The hallway was in darkness.

Felicity hastily held up a white nightdress with a Grecian design in red. 'Would you mind?'

'Wear whatever you like.' Jessica slid beneath the sheet.

Felicity dropped the nightie over her head, smoothed it, also got into bed. 'I was just wondering...'

'Because I sleep naked, or because Andrea was my friend?'

'I don't believe in gossip, myself.'

'Then you're unique.' Jessica switched off the light. 'Just remember that we're on duty.'

She was asleep in seconds, as she always was – to be awakened by a rumbling crash. She was out of bed before she was actually certain where she was, instinctively reaching for the shoulder bag, which was, as ever, on the floor beside her.

'What the shit—!' Felicity sat up and switched on the light. 'Did the earth move? Gosh, what a dream!'

Jessica was at the door, pistol in hand.

'You've nothing *on*!' Felicity hissed, and gasped as there was another explosion, much louder than the first; the entire building seemed to shake. 'Jesus!'

The corridor was in darkness, but now they were surrounded by sound – calls from inside the apartment, shouts from outside it, and some screams.

Jessica closed the door, laid down her gun, and dressed. Felicity followed her example. 'What was it?'

'That's what we have to find out.'

'JJ! JJ! What's happening?'

Jessica tucked her shirt into her trousers, ignored her jacket, and went outside, to encounter Rowena, in a nightgown with her hair in pigtails. 'There's been an explosion.'

'I know that. Was someone trying to get at us?'

'Of course that was someone trying to get at

64

us,' Jeremy said from along the hall. He wore pyjamas and had his arm round an obviously terrified Theresa, who was in a dressing gown.

'It came from downstairs,' Jessica said, 'which can hardly have been meant for us. Anyway...' She decided against reiterating her theory that Abriga would not wish to harm his own daughter. 'We'll check it out. You go back to bed.' She sat on the bed to put on her shoes. Behind her Felicity was finishing her own dressing.

Rowena stood in the doorway. 'You're not going to leave us here alone.'

'One of us will be here,' Jessica promised. 'Please go back to bed, Rowena; you're in no danger.'

'Well, report to me the moment you find out what has happened.' She stepped back into the corridor, and the lights went out. 'Aaagh!' she screamed.

'It's just a power failure.' Jessica delved into her bag, found her torch, and switched it on. 'Filly!'

Felicity produced her own torch.

'It must be a fuse,' Rowena said.

'Where is your box?'

'How should I know? Somewhere in the kitchen.'

'And I assume you have candles?'

'I have no idea. Jerningham looks after things like that.'

'But he isn't here.'

'The bastard!'

65

Jeremy had joined them. 'I think I can find them. And the box.'

'There's a good lad. Here, take my torch until you get something going.' She handed over the light, watched them retreat along the corridor. 'You'll have to hold the fort here,' she told Felicity.

Felicity had moved to the window, was looking down. 'There's something going on.' Jessica joined her. 'All those people. And listen: that's a fire engine.'

'Coming this way. That figures. That explosion must have set off any number of alarms. Now listen: I'm going down to see what's up. You stay by the front door, and let no one but me in.'

'Got it.'

Predictably the lobby was in darkness. Jessica tried the switch, guided by Felicity's light from the doorway, but there was no response. 'Hm.' Then she realized there was no light on the lift panel either. 'I think this whole building may be blacked out. Give me the light.'

'What do I do?'

'Sit tight in that doorway. I won't be long.'

Felicity extended the torch, and Jessica squeezed her fingers. 'Just don't shoot anybody. Especially me.'

She followed the beam to the stairs, started down, and was suddenly joined by several other people, emerging from the ninth-floor flat. They had two torches, but fortunately Jessica had restored her pistol to her shoulder bag.

'Anybody else up there?' a man asked.

'Yes. Why?'

'They should get out. This building is on fire.'

'The building?'

They had descended another floor, and were joined by yet more people, waving torches and chattering excitedly; but then they were suddenly impeded by other people, coming back up.

'Can't get down,' someone shouted. 'The stairs are on fire.' And now they could smell smoke.

A woman screamed.

'How far up?' Jessica snapped.

'Second floor. But it's coming up.'

'OK. Get down to the sixth floor, break the windows, and summon help. The ladders will reach you there.'

'Who the hell are you,' someone demanded, 'giving us orders?'

'I'm a police officer,' Jessica told him. 'And if you don't do as I say, you're all going to die. That smoke is going to travel fast.'

That brought a fresh chorus of screams, but already curling wisps of smoke were making the air difficult to breathe. Jessica could do no more for them; she had her own situation to worry about. She left them and ran back up the stairs, panting now.

'Stop right there!' Felicity snapped.

'Good girl. But it's me. We have a problem.'

'I can smell smoke.'

'That's the problem. Stand by.'

She ran along the hall and into the lounge, where Rowena, Jeremy and Theresa were gathered. Jeremy had found some candles and the room was quite bright. 'There doesn't seem to be anything wrong with the fuse,' he said. 'Must be a general outage. I tried calling, but the phone is dead.'

Rowena was standing at the window, looking down. 'There's a hell of a crowd down there,' she remarked. 'And four fire engines. But I don't see any fire.'

'It's right beneath you,' Jessica told her.

'What?'

'I smell smoke,' Theresa said.

'That's it. We have to get down a couple of levels before it gets up here. Hurry now.'

'But all my things!' Rowena said. 'I can't just abandon my things.'

'Are they more valuable than your life?'

Felicity arrived. 'I do think we should hurry.'

'Let's go,' Jessica said.

She held Rowena's arm to escort her down the hall, followed by Felicity. Jeremy came behind, his arm round Theresa's shoulders. There was certainly smoke drifting up the stairs, and Jessica almost felt she could hear the flames: the heat was intense, but so was the noise that surrounded them.

They passed the ninth and eighth floors, reached the seventh, and the smoke was swirling, making them cough and choke. Jessica wondered how the people on the sixth floor were getting on; she could only hope they had managed to get out.

'We're trapped,' Jeremy said. 'My God, we're *trapped.*'

'Back to the eighth,' Jessica said.

'Will they get a ladder up that high?' Felicity asked. She was obviously scared, but to Jessica's great relief was keeping her nerve.

'That we'll have to find out.' Jessica led them to the eighth-floor lobby, tried the door: 'Locked.'

'We're trapped,' Jeremy said again.

Jessica looked at Rowena, who appeared to have entered a catatonic state, although she was still on her feet. 'Take her,' she told Felicity. 'Stand her against that wall. Level the torch. You too, Jeremy.'

They retreated against the wall, and Jeremy and Felicity both sent their torch beams against the door. Jessica drew her pistol. 'Arms over faces,' she said, and emptied her magazine into the lock. Sparks and splinters flew in every direction, but the door opened to her kick.

'Holy shit!' Jeremy commented.

Rowena moaned, but she did not appear to have been hurt.

'Inside,' Jessica commanded. They rushed past her, and she closed the door, then turned and surveyed the flat by the beam of Felicity's torch. There was the usual lobby, and then an open door to another large lounge – with another picture window. 'Sit Mrs Lenghurst down,' she said. 'Then, Felicity, you and

69

Theresa find the bathrooms, gather all the towels you can, soak them if there's still water, and press them against this door, along the floor. Jeremy, smash that window.'

Jeremy gulped. 'Is that legal?'

'The only illegal thing we can do now is to die.'

'But what do I use? That's plate glass.'

'I'll give it a start.' She replaced her magazine. 'Stand clear.' She fired three times into the glass. It didn't shatter, and the bullets ricocheted around the room, bringing a scream from Rowena. But the glass was cracked in several places. 'There you go. A heavy chair should get through that. Try not to cut yourself.'

She retreated against the far wall, used her mobile: 'Scotland Yard ... This is Detective-Sergeant Jessica Jones, Special Branch. Take down my number.' She gave it. 'Now, I and four other people are trapped on the eighth floor of the Aspern Building, which is presently on fire. We need a ladder brought up to take us down. Please get on to the Fire Service and arrange this. Tell them we have at most fifteen minutes to live. They can call me on this number. Got that?'

'Yes, Sergeant Jones. But—'

'No buts. We now have fourteen and a half minutes. Get with it.'

She switched off, watched Jeremy take a second swing at the window with a heavy chair. The cracks spread. 'The next one will do it,' she said encouragingly and went into the lobby, where Felicity and Theresa were obediently packing towels at the foot of the door.

'I think we're winning,' Felicity panted. Certainly the air was quite clean.

'It's not something we can win,' Jessica said. 'We're fighting a holding action. Come through.'

They followed her into the lounge. As they got there the window splintered with a huge crash.

'Got the bugger,' Jeremy shouted.

Clean air drifted into the flat, and with it a huge burst of sound: shouts, screams, sirens, loudspeakers.

'Can they reach us?' Felicity asked.

'I'm waiting to find out. Now get back to work. This door must be blocked as well.'

'We've used all the towels we can find,' Theresa protested.

'So use bed sheets, pillows, cushions, clothes, if necessary.'

'Won't that stuff burn like a firelighter?'

'It will. But if the fire gets up here before the ladder, we'd be dead anyway. It's the smoke that will kill us first.'

They hurried off, and Jessica's mobile buzzed.

'Jones.'

'Was that your window that just fell out?'

'Affirmative. We helped it.'

'You're a hell of a long way up. Can you get down another floor?'

'Not without breathing apparatus.'

71

'OK, then you'll have to go back up. We can't reach you where you are.'

'So what do we do if we go back up?'

'Can you access the roof? We've sent for a chopper.'

Jessica looked at Jeremy, who was standing beside her.

'No problem,' he said. 'There's a small roof garden. But it's not big enough to put a helicopter on.'

'So he'll have to hover,' the fire officer said. 'Are all your people fit and able to cope with heights and ropes?'

Jessica looked at Rowena, who had curled herself into a ball. 'I would say not.'

'OK. We'll be with you as soon as we can.'

'Where are the flames now?'

'Fourth floor. The floor has just fallen in.'

'Did those people get out?'

'Thanks to you.'

'So how long do we have before the whole shebang collapses?'

'Where you are, ten minutes. On the roof, could be double that. Move it, sergeant.'

Jessica stowed the phone. 'You heard the man. Jeremy, you're in charge of your mother. Let's shift this gear.' She began removing the padding.

'All that work,' Theresa panted.

'It's not wasted. Wrap the towels round your heads and over your faces.' She attended to Rowena, who came to with a shriek. 'She's trying to smother me! Help!'

'It's OK, Mother. We're trying to help you,'

Jeremy said. 'Trust us.'

He lifted her from the settee, and she nestled against him. 'Oh, Jerry, you are such a good boy.'

'Bring her along,' Jessica said, and joined Theresa and Felicity. Smoke was seeping under the door. 'Now,' she said. 'Speed is the order of the day.' She drew a deep breath, threw the door open, involuntarily stepped back. Smoke and heat filled the lobby and surged at her like living enemies; she could hear the crackle of the flames. 'Go, go, go,' she shouted, inadvertently inhaling some smoke and coughing.

The two women dashed past her and up the stairs. Jeremy followed, his mother wailing again. Jessica stumbled behind them, holding the towel across her nose and mouth, eyes smarting, hardly able to see. But on the next floor the smoke was thinner, and there were only wisps on the penthouse floor: they had actually only been gone ten minutes.

Jessica closed the door behind her, and they staggered along the hall, all of them now gasping and coughing. 'Where?'

'Through the kitchen,' Jeremy said. 'But as we're here, can't we pick up some gear. Some clothing?'

'Not if you want to see sunrise. Move it.'

They went into the kitchen, from which a flight of stairs led up to a small door. 'Take your mother up first,' Jessica commanded. 'Then you, Theresa.'

The Columbian girl followed her lover.

There was a rumbling crash from below them. 'Oh, Jesus,' Felicity said.

'That's another floor gone. Probably where we just were. Up you go.'

Felicity went to the steps, hesitated. 'You *are* coming?'

'You bet.'

Felicity went up. Jessica cast a last look around; the floor beneath her was now hot, and the kitchen was starting to fill with smoke. She followed Felicity up the steps, emerged into the clear night air, and was immediately bathed in the searchlight of the helicopter hovering overhead.

The Island

'Are you sure you're all right?' the commander asked, peering at Jessica. She wore uniform, and from the neck down was as precise as always; but her eyes were red from smoke and lack of sleep, and her normally immaculate hair, though brushed, was untidy.

'There's nothing the matter with me that an hour with the hairdresser won't sort out,' Jessica said. 'I am going there as soon as I leave here. But I felt I should report first.'

'Absolutely. What a terrible thing. Have you seen the doctor?'

'Yes, sir. I am suffering from a bit of smoke inhalation, which is why I am hoarse. Apart from that I am perfectly all right.'

'And Hewitt?'

'She behaved magnificently, sir.'

'Oh, good. I think you two should stick together. I gather that the Lenghursts are in the Savoy. We have a guard mounted there for the time being. So there has been no catastrophe.'

'With respect, sir, the Lenghursts have lost all their clothes, and some personal belongings which I believe they value highly. As, no

75

doubt, have quite a few other people.'

'Well, they're wealthy enough to be able to replace them.'

'Detective-Constable Hewitt and I also lost some clothing.'

'Put in a claim and it will be replaced. But as I say: as regards us, all's well that ends well. Of course it was dashed bad luck that this happened on your first night on the job, as it were; however...'

'There was no luck involved, sir.'

Adams frowned. 'What do you mean?'

'The fire was not an accident, sir. It was caused by an explosion.'

Adams nodded. 'So I understand. The fire people are working on the probability of a leaking gas main.'

'It was not a gas main, sir. It was a bomb. In fact, two bombs.'

'Eh?'

'There were two explosions, sir. I would say the first was in the control room, knocking out the phones and causing a fire which very rapidly knocked out the electrics as well, and of course the lifts, so that the only way out of the building was by the emergency staircase. The other, greater explosion took place at the foot of that staircase, thus making sure that it couldn't be used.'

'My God! But ... you know this?'

'Let's say it's an educated guess.'

'And you think...'

'It was the Lenghursts the bomber was after.'

'That's a bit hard to swallow. A whole building, to kill one man? What is your theory?'

'The concierge has not been found. I believe he will be found, when the police can get into the building. He will be dead.'

'Well, of course he'll be dead, if he's still in the building.'

'Unless the body is too badly burned, a post-mortem will reveal that he was dead before the fire started.'

'Proof?'

'Circumstantial, sir. But I am certain that the police will find supportive evidence as to where those bombs were placed. If they also find the body...'

'Far-fetched, JJ. There were some thirty people in those flats.'

'So have them checked out, sir. I think you'll find that only the Lenghursts are in the firing line.'

'Hm. But...' he pointed. 'That can't be right. Abriga wants his daughter back. He's not going to burn her alive.'

'I agree, sir. It wasn't his work. But it was still aimed at the Lenghursts, no matter who else got hurt.'

'I'm afraid you've lost me, Sergeant.'

'There is a great deal about this business that we don't know, sir. I don't believe that Mrs Lenghurst knows the whole story either. I believe something happened when Jeremy and the girl Theresa eloped, and that there is more involved – and more people involved than the Abriga family. I believe that it has

77

to do with this mysterious Rodrigo, who Theresa says she was due to marry. I think it would be worthwhile investigating their true relationship and his background.'

'I see what you're driving at, but that is hardly our business, is it? And it would require involving the Miami police.'

'It is our business, sir,' Jessica insisted. 'In the context of our protection of Mrs Lenghurst and her son. Those bombs last night were meant to kill – everyone in the penthouse, and that includes Theresa. That people on the other floors might also have to die seems to have been irrelevant to the bomber. The point I am making is that the bomb cannot have been planted on Abriga's orders, unless the man is an absolute monster.'

'He is supposed to be a monster.' The commander seemed unaware that he was contradicting himself.

'As you said just now, sir, no man kills his own daughter unless he's deranged. And to attempt to do so the day after sending a note demanding her back is totally illogical. I believe there is another party in the field, who is not interested in regaining possession of Theresa Abriga, but who wishes her dead. And Jeremy, of course. And if anyone else gets in the way, too bad.'

'And you think it's this chap Rodrigo.'

'I hope it's Rodrigo. If it isn't, we don't have a clue what we're up against.'

'And you think the two young people know

what his problem is, and are not letting on. That the story of him merely being a jilted lover is a red herring.'

'I would say so – yes, sir.'

'It's an interesting theory. I'll put someone on to liaising with the FBI to find out if they have anything on this character, though as we don't have a last name it may be difficult. That's something you will have to obtain as soon as possible.'

'Me, sir?'

'They still want you looking after them. In fact, they want you more than ever now. They seem to feel you saved their lives. Well, very probably you did.'

'But surely, as long as they're in the Savoy...'

'They have no intention of staying there. Or even in England. Mrs Lenghurst is returning to the Bahamas tomorrow.'

'I thought she didn't like it there, in the summer and the hurricane season.'

'She dislikes being burned out of her flat even more. You'll take Hewitt with you, of course. If you really are pleased with her.'

'Would you give me a moment to catch up, sir? You are requiring me to accompany this woman to the Bahamas as her bodyguard? What will the Bahamian government think of this idea?'

'They won't think anything of it, because they won't know anything of it. You and Hewitt will go as friends of the family. Think of it, JJ: blue sea and sky, white beaches, endless sunshine...'

'Been there, done that.'

'Ah, but those circumstances were different. You were kidnapped, a helpless prisoner...'

'I was not a helpless prisoner, sir,' Jessica snapped. 'By the time we were shipwrecked on that island I was in control. We just couldn't get off for a while.'

'Well, you'll be in control again this time. And enjoying yourself.'

'Holding off at least one hit man. How do we get our hardware out?'

'The usual way. I'll arrange for you to by-pass security. After all, they're quite used to having people on board carrying guns nowadays. I mean legitimately.'

'And what happens if, while I'm in the Bahamas, I have to shoot someone?'

'We'll sort it out.'

'After I have spent a month in a Bahamian gaol.'

'You'll get a commendation. Anyway, hopefully it won't happen. This fellow Abriga, and this other fellow, if he exists, won't even know where you've gone.'

'I'm sure they'll be able to find out, before too long. But there is one other matter: Mr Lenghurst.'

'What about him?'

'I have a suspicion that he is living on this island of theirs.'

'That's certainly possible. But he does not appear to be under threat.'

'He is a convicted paedophile, sir.'

80

Adams raised his head. 'Now, how do you know that?'

'I believe in finding out the background of who I am dealing with, sir.'

'All right, so Lenghurst went down.'

'For something peculiarly nasty.'

'He paid the penalty. It could be said that he is still paying the penalty in being permanently self-exiled from this country. So you may have to shake his hand. I,' he said reminiscently, 'once had to shake the hand of Idi Amin. It goes with the job.'

'I still think I should have been informed, sir.'

'So now you've briefed yourself. I have never doubted your efficiency, Sergeant. Was there something else?'

'We are still to be relieved in a fortnight?'

'You have my word.'

'And you will keep me briefed about anything that is learned about the fire?'

'All right. I suppose this island is linked to the Internet.'

'With respect, sir, the Internet is very public. It would be better if you would use my mobile.'

'Do you realise what that will cost? Oh, very well, I will use your mobile. Now, as I was saying: Mrs Lenghurst and party are leaving on tomorrow morning's flight to Nassau, and your seats are booked. She and her son will be under general protection until their departure; after that she's in your hands. I'm sure you have some things to do before then.'

'Yes, sir,' Jessica said grimly.

'So, off you go. Report to me when you come back.'

'Lucky for some,' Mrs Norton remarked. 'You know, very blonde people should stay out of the sun as much as possible. They're more susceptible to things like skin cancer than ordinary people.'

'Like you, you mean,' Jessica suggested. 'You are an ordinary person, aren't you, Mrs Norton?'

She went down in the lift. 'Is Hewitt in?' she asked at the duty desk.

'She telephoned, Sergeant. Said she's suffering from smoke inhalation, and has been told by the doctor to spend twenty-four hours in bed.'

'Well, you get her on the phone and tell her to get herself out of bed and round to my flat A.S.A.P. I'll be waiting for her.'

Actually, she told herself, as she took the tube home, she had no reason to be grouchy. This assignment might be rather fun. With different people. But she didn't like Rowena Lenghurst; she actively disliked her son; she distrusted his doe-eyed girlfriend ... and the thought of having to live in the same house as a convicted paedophile, even for a fortnight, made her skin crawl. But it would be only a fortnight, and she felt she had some unfinished business with the bomber, supposing he was going to try again. Her emergence from obscurity had really begun, four years previously, with that bomb in Alicante, which had all but killed her – her back still had one or two little pits caused by flying glass – and had killed both the minister she had been protecting and her then partner. She did not like bombers.

Her hairdresser's was just round the corner from the flat, and she spent a pleasant hour being restored to her normal neatness before going home. She knew Tom would be there because he was not on duty today. He also had a king-sized hangover, which had not been improved when she had staggered in at dawn, looking a total wreck. To make matters worse, she had offered virtually no explanation, merely told him to watch the morning news, showered and exchanged her tattered clothes for uniform, and gone out again.

Now he was sitting morosely in front of the TV, naked and drinking beer. 'How the shit did you get mixed up in that?'

She peered at the screen, on which they were showing again her interview by eager reporters. 'God, what a sight.'

The picture flickered to a shot of the helicopter hovering above the burning building. 'Is that you on the end of that rope ladder?'

'No. I was still on the roof. That's Hewitt, my new partner.'

'Do I know her?'

'I doubt it. She's only been in the Branch a fortnight.'

He got up to hug her. 'You all right?'

'I need to sleep, which is what I intend to do, and then I have to pack. Oh, there's the door.'

'I'll get it.'

'Not like that you won't. This is an innocent young girl. Go and put something on.' She used the intercom. 'If it's you, Filly, come up. If it's anyone else, get lost.'

'It's me.' Felicity arrived a few minutes later. She was also wearing uniform, and looked surprisingly unruffled. 'You don't look too good,' she remarked, peering at Jessica. 'You should be in bed.'

'Which is where I am actually going, as soon as we have had a chat.'

'Didn't you see the doctor? He sent *me* to bed.'

'He made noises about it, but I told him to forget it: I had to report to the boss. Come in.' She closed the door. 'I don't suppose you've met Sergeant Lawson.'

'Well, hello.' Tom was in the bedroom door-way, wearing a dressing gown.

'I've heard a lot about you, Sergeant.'

'Well, now.' Tom came forward to shake hands. 'That is either an invitation or a challenge.'

'It's neither,' Jessica said. 'Sit down, Filly, and I'll make coffee.'

'Filly,' Tom remarked, sitting beside her on the settee. 'I like that.'

'He's always randy in the middle of the morning,' Jessica explained, handing out cups. 'Now, you just have time to drink that, listen very carefully, and then go home and pack. We're off tomorrow morning.'

'Off where?' Tom and Felicity spoke together.

'Not you,' Jessica said; 'Filly and me. We're off to the Bahamas for a fortnight.'

'The Bahamas?' Felicity cried. 'I've always wanted to go there.'

'Just remember you'll be working. But there's no reason why we shouldn't have some fun.'

'You mean we're going with that woman?'

'And her son and his popsy, yes. Now, as far as I know, we don't actually need shots or visas, but we do need passports. I assume you have one?'

'I got mine a couple of weeks ago. They said it went with the job.'

'Good girl. So off you go, pack, and be at Heathrow at nine o'clock tomorrow morning. And have a full night's sleep.'

'And don't forget a couple of bikinis,' Tom suggested.

Felicity cast Jessica an anxious glance, finished her coffee, and left.

'Cute kid.'

'Yes. And you need to remember that she is just a kid, relatively speaking.'

'I was just kidding with her.'

'Of course you were. Because you knew that, if I thought you weren't, I'd break both your arms.'

He gulped. Although he was more than twice her size, he knew better than anyone the extent of her skills, with or without weapons, the intensity of her mind when she

85

switched it to either attack or defence mode. Besides, she was the most compelling woman he had ever known, even if she could also be the most frustrating and irritating. But he had no desire to change her, for anyone. 'So you're really off to the Bahamas with this client?'

'That's what the boss says. Now, I am going to make a large brunch, and then I am going to bed.'

'That sounds great. I'm not on duty until four.'

'Will you be back tonight?'

'About ten.'

'I'll wait up for you. Right now, all I want to do is sleep.'

'Detective-Sergeant Jones,' remarked the Airport Police inspector, his tone redolent of disapproval. 'I have heard of you. And this is...?' He regarded Felicity with even more disapproval; both women wore their spare blue trouser suits and white shirts without ties.

'Detective-Constable Hewitt.'

The inspector picked up the Skorpion, gingerly, turned it over, and laid it down again. 'And is she also armed to the teeth?'

'Show the inspector your weapon, Hewitt.'

Felicity delved into her shoulder bag and laid the Ingram on the desk.

'And do you know how to use this, ah ... Hewitt?'

'DC Hewitt holds a marksman's certificate,

86

sir,' Jessica said, before Felicity could blow her top.

'And I assume she also knows when not to use it.'

'Our guns will not be used on this flight, sir, unless it becomes necessary to protect the lives of our clients.'

'Correction, Sergeant. Your clients are three people in a flight which will contain over two hundred. These people have no involvement with your people, nor will they wish such involvement. You have no authority to put them at risk. I see that you are travelling first class; therefore it should not be difficult for you to keep a low profile *vis-à-vis* the other passengers. Therefore your weapons will not be used, under any circumstances, within the aircraft. I wish you to be very clear about this.' He looked from one woman to the other.

'You are aware of the facts of the case, sir?' Jessica asked.

'Commander Adams has provided me with a résumé, yes.'

'Then you understand that the person, or persons, who destroyed the Aspern Building the night before last must have known that he was risking the lives of perhaps thirty other people to get at our clients. That indicates that he, or they, will hardly worry about endangering the lives of another two hundred-odd for a similar purpose.'

'I am aware that that is a theory which has not yet been substantiated. However, I consider it unlikely in the extreme that these people, if they exist, can know that it is your clients' intention to fly out this morning, and that if they do, they will have had time to put together a plan to destroy the aircraft. In view of the circumstances, however, I have allotted two marshals to this flight, and they will take care of any in-flight problems. You will not know who they are, but they know who and what you are. They're not going to trouble you, but they have orders that if you reveal either your identity or your weapons at any time they are to place you under arrest and hand you over to the Bahamian authorities on arrival in Nassau. Is this understood?'

'Yes, sir.' They spoke together.

'Very good. I intensely dislike this sort of thing, but as I am instructed by the Home Office, I have to go along with it. Take the corridor on the left and you will bypass Security and emerge into the Departure Hall.'

'Thank you, sir.' Jessica led the way from the office and into the indicated corridor.

'Officious bastard,' Felicity remarked.

'Only doing his job, as he sees it.'

'But he was so hostile.'

'A lot of this sort of fringe policemen are hostile to Special Branch.'

'He was hostile because we're women.'

'That too. Do you have a partner?'

'You're my partner.'

'I meant, a man about the place.'

'No way.'

'So who shares your flat?'

'I live alone.'

'On your salary?'

'Well, Mummy and Daddy pay the rent.'

'Lucky for some. Do they know what you do?'

Felicity giggled. 'They think I spend my time protecting the Queen.'

'So you're not into men.'

'I didn't say that. I love men, in small doses. I don't want to live with one.'

Jessica realized that was essentially her own point of view, but as she didn't have a wealthy mummy and daddy – or any mummy and daddy at all, now – she had to do the best she could.

She opened the door at the end of the corridor and they stepped into the crowded Departure Lounge. They made their way through this to the First-Class Lounge, and were greeted with a shriek from Rowena, rising from a deep armchair. 'JJ! I thought you weren't going to make it. I've been so scared.'

'We had various formalities to complete. Now you can relax.' Jessica looked at Theresa, who was sitting in a tense hunch, knees pressed together; like them, she was wearing trousers. 'Jeremy not with you?'

'He's at the bar.'

'That figures.'

Rowena lowered her voice to a whisper. 'Do you think they're here, with us?'

'No. They don't know where you are. By the

time they find out you'll be home.'

'And you'll set up that protection system you spoke of?'

'I'll see what I can do.' She sat beside her, while Felicity sat beside Theresa. 'Will you fill me in on a few things?'

'Anything.'

Jessica was tempted to begin exploring Jeremy's background and activities in Florida, but the immediate business came first. 'Would I be correct in assuming that Mr Lenghurst is in residence on the cay?'

'Is that important?'

'It could be. Are you going to bring him up to date on the situation?'

'Is that necessary?'

'You know him better than I do. Isn't he going to be a bit surprised when you turn up out of the blue?'

'I have sent him an e-mail telling him I am coming, and to have the helicopter waiting for us in Nassau.'

'Ah! You have the use of a helicopter?'

'It is my helicopter. Daddy gave it to me as a birthday present, ten years ago.'

'Of course. Who flies this machine?'

'Arnie Pleass.'

'Bahamian?'

'Welsh.'

'Right. And he works for you. Full-time?'

'He has to be there whenever I want him.'

'Which can't be every day. You mean he just lounges around the cay?'

'No, no. He doesn't live on the cay. He

owns a bar in Nassau.'

'I thought the Bahamian Government was a bit sticky about foreigners owning businesses in their territory?'

'They are. The bar is in the name of Arnie's wife. She's a Bahamian.'

'I'm getting there. So Arnie hangs round Nassau with his pals, and flies your chopper whenever you need to get on or off the cay, right?'

'What wrong with that?'

'You wouldn't consider him a security risk?'

'Arnie? He's been with me for ten years.'

'Since you had the chopper. So how often in those ten years have you, or Jeremy, been the object of a Colombian hit man?'

'Oh, my God!' She grasped Jessica's hands, tightly. 'I'm so *scared*. But ... why should Arnie turn against me? I pay him well...'

'I'm not saying that he would turn against you. But he's a weak link, simply because from time to time he holds your life in his hands, and because he is your link with the other islands.'

'Oh, we have a boat as well, a forty-foot cabin cruiser.'

'Of course you do. But you prefer to use the chopper.'

'Well, it's a long trip to and from Nassau by sea even at seventeen knots. And I get seasick. The boat is really for Lucian to amuse himself. And, of course, for bringing things up from Nassau or over from Arthur's Town. You know – fuel and bulk food. It's important

91

for that.'

'Lucian being your husband?'

'That's right.'

Jessica stood up. 'They're calling our flight.'

'What do you reckon?' Felicity asked. They were seated at the rear of the first-class cabin.

'I thought this thing stank from the moment I got involved, and it stinks more and more with every moment.'

'You seriously think this helicopter pilot may be a problem?'

'In himself, probably not. But suppose he gets hijacked? When the Lenghursts want to leave Tiger Cay, they call him up and he arrives the next day or whatever. But who's to know who he has on board until he lands?'

'You shot down a helicopter once, didn't you?'

'And I'd happily do so again, if I was sure it was full of Colombian hit men. But the same thing applies to this cabin cruiser. We won't know what or who it's carrying until it docks, or whatever it does.'

'You know a lot about boats too, don't you? Didn't you once spend several months on a small boat?'

'I spent several months on a sailing yacht, yes. But as the owner was running away from the law, we didn't dock anywhere.'

'This was the guy who kidnapped you, right?'

Jessica sighed. 'Right.'

'That must have been something. Couldn't

you take him out?'

'In the beginning no, because he kept me shot full of drugs and tied up.'

'Wow! Did he ... um...'

'Yes,' Jessica said. 'Let's watch the film.'

'But you got free eventually, and did him. And sailed the boat to safety.'

'I managed to get free and, as you say "do him", because we got caught up in a typhoon. And I didn't sail the yacht to safety. It sank.'

'What a life you've had. Will you tell me about it?'

'When you're older,' Jessica promised.

They landed at Windsor Field just after two, or just after seven English time. The flight had been totally uneventful.

'Wowee,' Felicity remarked as they emerged from the cabin. 'This is hot!'

'Hottest month of the year, July,' Jeremy said, immediately behind her.

'Do we stay the night in town?'

'No,' Jessica said.

She was braced for a possible crisis with Customs, but apparently Rowena was well known and none of their bags were opened. 'You going straight on, Mrs Lenghurst?' one of the officers asked.

'If my machine is ready.'

'Yeah. Arnie's waiting. These ladies with you?'

'They're my guests, yes.'

He scrawled on the various bags with a piece of chalk. 'You all have a nice visit, now.'

'What would have happened if he had opened our bags?' Felicity whispered, as they gained the security of the Arrivals Lounge. Rowena had gone off in search of her pilot.

'Mum would have sorted it out,' Jeremy assured her. 'Mum sorts everything out.'

'This is my first visit to the Bahamas,' Theresa confided to Jessica.

'I honeymooned here,' Jessica said. 'Not in Nassau. In a place called Eleuthera, an island to the north-east.'

'Honeymooned? Gee, that must have been great. I didn't know you were married.'

'I'm not, now. That was before you were born. You know, it puzzles me why you and Jerry didn't come straight here when you left Florida. It's much closer than England.'

'I guess it is. But Jerry felt Papa would have found us too easy to trace. There are only a couple of commercial flights to Nassau or Freeport every day, and they're all out of either Miami or Fort Lauderdale.'

'Did your father know about you and Jerry before you eloped?'

'Oh, no. But I foolishly left a photo of Jerry behind.'

'I see,' Jessica said, and took a stab in the dark. 'And you reckon Rodrigo found it?'

'Rodrigo?' Colour filled Theresa's cheeks, and then faded again to leave them more sallow than before. 'Oh, no. He couldn't ... I mean, my aunt would have found it, or one of the servants.'

'And she contacted Daddy. Or was it,

Rodrigo?'

Theresa had recovered her aplomb, at least partly. 'My aunt would have done that.'

'Because of course Rodrigo wasn't actually there, was he? He was in ... Colombia?'

'Rodrigo ... oh, I really don't know.' Theresa moved away to stand beside Jeremy, who was still deep in conversation with Felicity; he had clearly taken a shine to the pretty young policewoman, even if she was the elder. That was a looming hassle she could do without, Jessica decided, but before she could follow Theresa she was joined by Rowena, who was accompanied by a huge bear of a man, with yellow hair worn shoulder-length, just like herself, Jessica realized, surrounding curiously small and quite handsome features, the whole sitting on top of a massive frame; he was larger even than Tom Lawson.

'Arnold Pleass,' Rowena said. 'Detective-Sergeant Jessica Jones.'

Jessica glanced at her in dismay; she had not anticipated their identities being so casually revealed.

'Well, hello there.' Arnie's grasp was as gentle as his face. 'This sure is a pleasure. I never met a pretty policeman before.'

'And for me. I thought for a moment you were the other Arnie.'

'Yuh know, lotsa people make that mistake. But I ain't no good with a sword. Never owned one. That your partner?'

In for a penny, in for a pound. 'Detective-Constable Felicity Hewitt.'

'Well, I'll be ... And you two pretty little girls are gonna protect Mrs Lenghurst?'

Jessica sighed; she had begun to like this great oaf. 'Even from you, Mr Pleass.'

'Well, now, ma'am, that's a challenge I can't hardly resist. And the other little lady?'

'My son's fiancée. Come along,' Rowena said; 'let's get out of here.'

'Yes, ma'am.' Arnie stopped long enough to give a gentle squeeze to Felicity's hand, a quick bow to Theresa, then led the way out of the airport building by a side door which avoided the main concourse, still crowded with people seeking taxis and being greeted by friends and relations. A porter followed, wheeling a trolley on which were their bags.

'It's so close,' Rowena complained. 'I'm dripping sweat. What's the temperature?'

'Well, it was thirty-seven a couple of hours ago. Musta gone up by now.'

'Thirty-seven what?'

'Well, degrees, ma'am. Centigrade.'

'For God's sake give me that in English.'

'Well, ma'am, yuh double it, see. That's seventy-four. Then yuh takes away ten per cent. That brings yuh down to sixty-seven. Then yuh add on Fahrenheit's thirty-two. And yuh have ninety-nine. So that's what it is: ninety-nine degrees Fahrenheit.'

'Wowee,' Felicity said. 'That is hot.'

'You had any rain recently?' Jeremy asked.

'Some,' Arnie said.

'What about storms?'

'There's something knocking about out in

the Atlantic, name of Brigitte; but it's a long way south.'

'You mean that's a hurricane?' Felicity asked.

'Well, it's a tropical storm, right now. I guess it'll blow up a bit, but it ain't likely to come up here.'

'And as it's called Brigitte, it's only the second storm of the season,' Jessica suggested.

'That's right, ma'am. You could say they're running late: the season starts in June. And the weather sure has been hot. A bit of wind might cool things off. Here's the crate.'

The helicopter, attended by three mechanics, stood by itself on a short apron, shaded by a tall sapodilla tree.

'Up yuh get,' Arnie said. 'There's room for all.'

The mechanics began loading the suitcases.

'There's room up top as well,' Arnie remarked. 'You wanna ride co-pilot, Sergeant?'

Jessica looked at Rowena, who shrugged. 'Go ahead. I've done it a hundred times.'

Jessica climbed into the machine, made her way forward and up the short ladder to the flight deck, strapped herself in. She listened to various bumps and comments from behind her, and was then joined by Arnie.

'You ever flown in a chopper before?' he asked, as he fiddled with his instruments.

'Some. I crashed in one once.'

'Holy shit! Where was that?'

'In Africa. We ran out of gas over the desert.'

'Heck. So you're not keen on choppers.'

'I wouldn't say that.' But she couldn't resist adding, 'I shot one down, once, too.'

Arnie's head turned, sharply. 'Say again?'

'It was a bigger machine than this. Easier to hit.'

'You're putting me on.'

'Now, why would I want to do that?'

'Shit!' he muttered. 'Why did yuh do it?'

'Well, they were shooting at me, so I returned fire.'

'Holy Christ,' he muttered, and started the engine. The blades whirled; he chattered for some moment with the control tower, then gave the thumbs-up to the ground crew, and the helicopter rolled away from the trees before lifting. A few minutes later they were flying over the harbour and the bridge to Paradise Island, before changing course to just south of east to cross East End. Then they were over open water, mostly shallow, with several small cays emerging from time to time.

'Yuh know what Bahamas means?' he asked.

'Ah ... something like shallow sea.'

'Yuh got it. *Baha mar.* The Spaniards called it that when they were big around here. They tried to avoid it. Those sandbanks and reefs weren't good for their big ships. So the Flota – the treasure fleet out of Mexico – used the Florida Channel to get up the Gulf Stream and round the top of Grand Bahama and into the Atlantic before setting course for Europe.'

'But not all of them made it.'

'Yuh bet. They didn't understand the weather then. They didn't have things like barometers to warn them of trouble. So yuh know, yuh get a day like today – bit hot but with a nice sailing breeze – and everyone would be bowling along quite happily, totally unaware that just over the horizon there's a humdinger of a storm waiting to blow them to hell. Or into these sandbanks, as the case may be. This whole area is littered with wrecks, and those are only the ones documented. There's a lot of others that just disappeared. Because, yuh see, as the Spanish didn't want to know about this lot, it became a haven for the lawless. Guys with shallow-draft boats could nip out, especially after a storm when the Flota would have been scattered, pick off a straggler, loot it, kill the crew, scuttle it and nip back into the islands. Even if they were seen and chased by other ships, once they got into the shallows they were safe.'

'But weren't they subject to the weather as well?'

'Oh, sure. God alone knows how many pirate craft lie buried in these banks. Nobody ever bothered to document *them*. But those guys didn't reckon on collecting their old-age pensions in any event. If a hurricane didn't get them, or they weren't caught by the Dons and hanged, they died of drink or disease.'

'And eventually they became respectable.'

'Yuh gotta be joking. The pirates got cleaned out by the Royal Navy, when the British government decided they wanted the islands as a colony. So the Bahamians turned to wrecking. Then during the American Civil War they ran guns and munitions in to the Confederacy and ran cotton out. Then during Prohibition, they ran liquor. Then came drugs.'

'I thought the drug business was dead in the islands, since the DEA virtually closed Florida?'

'The drug business ain't never dead. It gets tight in some places, but they always find some other channel.'

He lapsed into silence, leaving Jessica to wonder if he was thankful he hadn't been around during any of those exciting episodes in Bahamian history, or if he might have enjoyed it. 'What's that big island over there?' She pointed to the north-east.

'Eleuthera.'

'Is it really? It doesn't look the way I remember it.'

'Yuh been there?'

'I honeymooned there.'

'You're kidding? You married?'

'Once upon a time, something like a hundred years ago.'

'So where did you stay?'

'Actually, on a little island off the main one: Harbour Island.'

'Oh, sure, I know it. But it's up the other end; that's why yuh don't recognize it.

Eleuthera is more than a hundred miles long, and is quite different up the north end. What you're looking at is Rock Sound. So what went wrong with your marriage?'

'It went wrong. That's another big island ahead.'

'Cat Island. Another long skinny one. But it's not as big as Eleuthera.'

'Mrs Lenghurst said that Tiger Cay is quite close to Cat Island.'

'It's just on the other side. When yuh get there, there ain't nothing between you and North Africa.'

'I thought San Salvador was the eastern-most of the islands. Isn't that where Columbus made his landfall?'

'Sure. That's bit further south. You'll see it when we reach the cay.'

The land steadily approached. 'How often do you make this trip?' Jessica asked.

'Whenever I'm called for. Not too often this time of year. Mrs L isn't out here as a rule.' He glanced at her. 'She tells me some guy has a contract out on her boy. Right?'

'If that's what she told you.'

'And yuh and that other cutie are here to make sure this guy doesn't collect. Right?'

'Supposing that were true, would you answer a few questions?'

'Ain't that what I've been doing since we left Nassau? But I'm happy to co-operate, ma'am.'

'Does Mr Lenghurst use you often?'

'No way. When he wants to go some place,

101

he uses the cruiser. He doesn't like planes of any sort, but especially choppers.'

'What does he use the cruiser for?'

'Mainly to go down to Nassau.'

'He goes to Nassau? Often?'

'Well ... this time of year. When Mrs L is in residence, he stays on the cay.'

'Does she know he strays down to Nassau when she isn't there?'

Arnie grinned. 'You'll have to ask her that. But I'd bet she doesn't.'

'So let me get this straight. During the months that Mrs Lenghurst isn't on the cay, Mr Lenghurst makes regular trips by boat to Nassau. Does he take anyone with him?'

'One of the boys usually goes along to act as crew.'

'And does he ever bring anyone back?'

Another grin. 'I guess he finds being alone on the cay, save for the servants, a bit tiresome.'

Shit, Jessica thought. 'Can you tell me anything about the people he takes up to the cay?'

'I reckon that's his business. Why don't yuh ask him? You'll be there in half an hour.'

'I didn't come here to investigate Mr Lenghurst's personal habits.' *Much as I would like to do so*, she thought. 'Nor did I come here to cause trouble between Mrs Lenghurst and her husband.' *Much as I would like to do that*, she thought. 'But I did come here to protect Mrs Lenghurst and her son from what may turn out to be an attempted murder. Now, obviously, the surest way to protect them from that is to make sure no stranger is allowed to land on the cay. But that is going to be difficult if Mr Lenghurst is in the habit of bringing up people from Nassau. So if you have any information on these people it would be very useful. The Lenghursts are your employers.'

'Part-time. I like flying this chopper. As for the old boy's guests...'

'You know who they are.'

'How do yuh reckon that?'

'Because I reckon you are used to fly them back down when the "old boy" is finished with them.'

'Maybe. But I'll tell yuh this, Sergeant: none of the old boy's guests could possibly have been a hit man.'

Jessica determined on another shot in the dark. 'You mean they were children?'

'I mean what I said. Now I need to concentrate.'

They were approaching the island, which, if once it clearly had been nothing more than a sandbank, was now a couple of hundred feet high in places, and under intensive cultivation. Some distance to their left Jessica could make out a sizeable collection of roofs. 'Arthur's Town,' Arnie said. 'And there's home.'

Jessica looked at the small island which lay offshore, and then back at the town. 'How far is it from the town?'

'Maybe five miles.'

'But it's much closer to this beach below us.'

'Sure. About a mile.'

'And I presume Arthur's Town is in regular communication with Nassau?'

'Sure. They have a ferry every couple of days, and they have an airstrip.'

Shit, she thought again. Tiger Cay had to be the most indefensible place she had ever been required to defend – certainly with just a single back-up who, despite the courage she had shown during the fire, had never fired a shot in anger.

Arnie was speaking into his mike. 'Going down. You guys should belt up.'

Jessica looked down at steadily shoaling sea, changing from blue to green to yellow. Then they were swooping over a thick grove of coconut trees. She saw the roofs of a small village and, beyond, a sudden large sheet of dirty white... 'Concrete?' she asked.

'Yeah. That's the catchment area. It's on a slight slope, see, and the rain runs down it into those two big concrete vats yuh can see. That's all the fresh water there is.'

Jessica realized that owning and operating a small island had problems that had never occurred to her. Now they were approaching the south end of the cay, where the land was distinctly higher, and to the left she saw a large, isolated house, in front of which there was a red concrete tennis court. The house backed the beach, while from the tennis court a path led through the trees to a small dock, alongside which there was a large cabin cruiser. To the right of the path was the helicopter pad, where some people were waiting. Arnie put the machine down expertly, the blades ceased to rotate, and the doors were opened.

'Darling,' Lucian Lenghurst said, embracing his wife as she stepped down. 'What a pleasant surprise. And Jerry? Good heavens!'

Somewhat predictably, in Jessica's opinion, he was a big man with a bald head and a goatee beard – considerably older than his wife, she estimated, or merely had not worn as well. He wore shorts and a loose shirt and sandals, and had a paunch but good legs. But her ingrained feeling of hostility towards him was not allayed when he said, 'And two such beautiful young ladies! Are they for me? Or are they yours?'

'Theresa, I would like you to meet my husband,' Rowena said. 'Theresa is Jerry's fiancée.'

'Jerry? Engaged? Nobody told me.'

'We are telling you now,' Rowena pointed out.

'You young devil.' Lucian shook his son's hand, and then reached for the Colombian girl. 'Come and give your father-in-law a kiss.'

Theresa submitted to a bear hug with considerable embarrassment.

'And you're Theresa's friend?' Lucian asked, optimistically, turning to Felicity.

'Let me introduce Detective-Constable Felicity Hewitt, of the Metropolitan Police,

Special Branch,' Rowena said, with, Jessica felt, a good deal of malicious pleasure.

Certainly Lucian's face turned quite pale. 'A policewoman? But...'

'She is here with her boss,' Rowena went on: 'Detective-Sergeant Jessica Jones.'

Lucian looked up at Jessica, framed in the helicopter doorway. 'Jesus!' he muttered.

'Detective-Sergeant Jones is quite famous,' Rowena said. 'She kills people.'

Lucian swallowed.

'And how,' Arnie said from behind Jessica, who stepped down and held out her hand.

'Only in the line of duty, Mr Lenghurst.'

Lucian stared at her, then at Felicity, then at his wife. 'Will someone tell me what the hell is going on?'

'Later. JJ, I'd like you to meet Truman, my butler.'

'Welcome to Tiger Cay, ma'am,' said the short, thickset black man.

Jessica shook his hand, apparently to his surprise.

'And this is Millie, my housekeeper.'

'Pleased to meet you, ma'am.' Millie was considerably taller than Truman, and larger, too.

'I'm glad to be here,' Jessica said, and for the first time felt that might be the truth.

'Have the boys bring the luggage up to the house,' Rowena commanded. 'Come along, girls, let's get out of this sun.' Which was drooping to the west, but remained hot.

Jessica smiled at the collection of men and

women, of all ages, including children, and became aware of two large retrievers frolicking around her feet.

'Hero and Leander,' Rowena explained. 'They like you.'

'They like everybody,' Jeremy pointed out.

Jessica patted the dog, who promptly took her hand into his large jaws, not making any attempt to bite, but just holding her.

'Leander, stop that!' Rowena commanded, and the jaws reluctantly opened. 'It's his way of saying hello.'

Jessica retrieved her hand. 'What's his way of saying goodbye?'

'What's that noise?' Felicity asked, as they proceeded along the path, Rowena leading, Lucian bringing up the rear, just in front of the servants with the bags.

'What noise?' Rowena asked.

'That continuous rumbling. As if you had machinery working somewhere.'

'We do have machinery working,' Rowena said. 'That's the generator – our electricity supply. I'm afraid it's on twenty-four hours a day. We actually have two, so that we can shut one down for servicing every so often.'

'You'll get used to it,' Jeremy promised.

'Where does the oil come from?' Jessica asked.

'Nassau.'

'That must be quite an operation.'

'It is, and damned expensive,' Lucian said, having regained some of his confidence as he realized they had not actually come to arrest him. 'We have a two-thousand-gallon tank, and burn about twenty gallons a day; they're slow-running machines. So every three months we have to have a tanker up from Nassau. The oil isn't all that expensive, but chartering the tanker costs an arm and a leg. Still, that's what you have to pay for complete privacy, nowadays. There aren't many places left where you can have that.'

They reached the tennis court. 'Any of you girls play?' Jeremy asked.

'Oh, yes,' Felicity said.

'We both do,' Jessica said. 'But we haven't brought any gear.'

'I'm sure we'll be able to fit you out. Mind the mess.'

On the far side of the court they arrived at a short flight of steps leading up to a verandah. The seats on the verandah were covered in multi-coloured dust cloths – with good reason, for the steps, the floor and the cloths were littered with fresh bird droppings.

'Peacocks,' Jeremy explained.

'I washes this floor every morning,' Millie said. 'And look at it.'

'They are a nuisance,' Rowena agreed. 'But they're such attractive creatures.'

'Except first thing in the morning,' Jeremy said. 'You won't believe the racket they make.'

'Where are they now?' Felicity asked.

'Probably sleeping in that mango tree.' The huge growth was situated on the north side of the house, actually leaning against it. 'They have more sense than to rush around in the heat of the day.'

'And the dogs don't trouble them?' The two retrievers were padding behind them.

'They're all friends.'

Jessica glanced at Lucian, and found him staring at her. He was clearly still haunted by the chance that his past might catch up with him, but unable to believe that his wife would actually bring two policewomen to their home. She felt that he deserved his discomfort, but, as she had told Arnie, she had not come here to interfere in the domestic lives of these people, except insofar as it might be necessary to do so to keep them alive.

They entered a not very large and completely conventional lounge-diner; the furniture was all unpolished white wood, including the television set and the little bar in the corner. The best thing about it was the suddenly cool air which surrounded them from the humming air-conditioning plant. Beyond, a door led into a much larger, if narrower, open area, where the only furniture, apart from some chests along the outer wall, was a table-tennis table. This room had its own small air-conditioning unit.

'The games' room,' Rowena explained.

At the far end of this hall, a screen door opened on to another verandah, beyond which could be seen the sand and the sea, some fifty feet below them. 'Our private beach,' Jeremy said. 'No one is allowed there unless they are resident in the house.' He grinned. 'That way we can swim in the nud. Say, there's a conundrum: where do you girls keep your guns when you're swimming naked?'

Jessica looked at Felicity, who rolled her eyes.

There were two other doors, on the inner wall. 'The kitchen...' Rowena gestured at the first. This was a surprisingly large room, mainly because of the huge chest freezer along one wall. 'We have to buy in bulk,' she explained. 'And this leads to the bedrooms.' She opened the other door to reveal a small lobby, in which there was a flight of stairs. 'That goes up to the master bedroom and the office. The others are out here.' She went through the lobby into a corridor, the outer wall of which was entirely screened window, let into which was another air-conditioning unit. On her right were four doors. 'The end one is Jerry's. I suppose...' She looked at Theresa, quizzically.

Who looked at Jeremy.

'She stays with me,' Jeremy said. 'Unless...' He could not stop a glance at Felicity.

'I'd like that,' Theresa said.

'How about you two?' Rowena asked. 'All these are en suite doubles.'

'Then we'll share one,' Felicity said before Jessica could offer an opinion.

'That's fine. Arnie, you can have this end one for the night.'

'Anything yuh say, Mrs L,' Arnie agreed.

'So, settle in. As soon as I've done that, I'm

110

going for a swim, before the sandflies get active.'

She returned to the lobby and the stairs leading up. Lucian had been standing in the doorway; he let her by and then followed her, obviously anxious for an explanation of what was happening. Jeremy and Theresa had already disappeared. Now Arnie opened the end door. 'See yuh girls on the beach.'

The servants arrived with the bags, and took them into the nearest of the remaining rooms. Jessica and Felicity followed, to find themselves in a very comfortable bedroom, with twin beds, the covers in pastel shades; an inner door led to an equally comfortable bathroom. The two men placed the suitcases on the floor beside the beds, bobbed their heads, and left.

'Should we have tipped them?' Felicity asked.

'I don't think so. This isn't an hotel.'

'I just have to go.' She returned a few moments later, 'There's a notice in there, saying please do not waste water.'

Jessica was testing the beds; both mattresses seemed firm enough. 'That makes sense. Arnie was telling me their only source of water is rain. I mean, literally.'

'What I mean is, do I flush?'

'I think you can do that. We'll check with Rowena later.'

Felicity returned. 'Isn't this air conditioning something? My tits are like ice picks.'

'Down, girl. Although...' Jessica touched her

111

shirt front. 'So are mine. I suppose we'll get used to it. Now...'

There was a buzz from her shoulder bag.

'Not already.' She took out the phone. 'Jones?'

'Where are you, Jones?'

'I am on a remote island in the Bahamas, about to go for a swim in a glorious blue ocean. Don't tell me you're still at the office, Mrs Norton? It must be about nine o'clock where you are. Tell me, is it raining?'

'It is not raining, and no I am not at the office. I am at home preparing my dinner and have just been called by the commander.'

'You *do* live an exciting life.'

'The commander was himself disturbed at his home, by a call from the Yard. He rather unwisely, in my opinion, left a message that he was to be informed the moment anything was turned up in a search through the wreckage of that burned-out building you were involved with.' Her tone indicated that she had no doubt that the apartment block had only burned down because Jessica had been involved.

Which, Jessica reflected, was at least partly true. 'And they've turned something up?'

'Apparently. The commander told me to deal with it, as he wishes to get a good night's sleep.'

'Mrs Norton, you are a loyal and devoted servant of the department. So what have they found?'

'The body of the night porter. It was

112

burned beyond recognition, but they have identified it through his dental records.'

'Is that all?'

'No, that is not all. There appears to be no doubt that he was murdered. The remains of a knife were found sticking out of his chest.'

Exploration

Jessica sat on the bed. 'Go on.'

'They even have a suspect. Well, maybe. There's a woman shown on the CCTV situated across the street entering the building just before midnight, and leaving again fifteen minutes later. The first explosion took place at midnight thirty. Apparently the street door wasn't locked.'

'Tell me about it. And what did she do while she was inside?'

'The camera in the lobby was destroyed in the fire.'

'That figures. I assume there is a description.'

'Well, you know what those CCTV cameras are like. It seems that she was tall, slim, and had long yellow hair.'

'Yellow hair? They're sure about that?'

'That's what they said.'

'But no facial description?'

'Apparently not.'

'They do realize that what they do have would cover about a million women in England. Are the Yard going for this?'

'It seems they were sceptical, but there is a vital additional piece of evidence.'

'Tell me.'

'The woman was wearing a knee-length cloth coat when she went in, but no coat at all when she came out. And they have actually found a trace of scorched material which could have come from a cloth coat, close to where the porter's body was lying. So they are looking for her, but they're not too hopeful. They're checking into the porter's background to see if anyone fitting the description may have been part of it.'

'Well, thanks a million, Mrs Norton. You go back to your beans on toast or whatever.'

'You don't sound very interested.'

'Oh, I am. Definitely. Call me back if the Yard turns up anything else.' She switched off.

Felicity was sitting on the bed beside her. 'Are we interested?'

'Yes, we are,' Jessica said. 'Very interested.'

'Oh. Right. Are we going to join them for a swim?'

'I am going to have a shower and go to bed for a couple of hours. That way I won't be falling asleep over my dinner. I also need to think.'

'Oh. Right. Ah...'

'You go ahead.'

'I was wondering ... well ... when in Rome, you know.'

'I think it would be a good idea to find out how Roman these Romans are,' Jessica suggested. 'Wear a swimsuit. You can always take it off.'

'I see what you mean. The thing is...'

'You did bring a swimsuit?'

'Well, yes. I brought this.' She delved into her bag and held up too small pieces of cloth.

'What is that?' Jessica asked.

'It's a bikini.'

Jessica took them. 'If I have my facts straight, the name bikini was taken from the island where the atomic bomb was tested after World War II, and was meant to indicate what might be left after such an explosion.'

'That's right.'

'But this is clearly the remnants of a hydrogen bomb. What exactly does it cover?'

'Well ... everything. Well, almost.'

'Do you mean almost everything, or almost bits of each thing? Show me.'

Felicity undressed and inserted herself into the bikini. The bra covered her nipples, but nothing else, and the pants were a pair of thongs.

'Do you mean that you have actually worn that in public, and not been raped? Or arrested for indecent exposure?' Jessica asked.

'Well, I have only worn it in the swimming pool at home. But I thought that, coming to the Bahamas, where anything goes...'

'Now there you are wrong. The average Bahamian is a good deal more strait-laced than anyone you are likely to meet on Brighton Beach.'

'Oh. You mean I shouldn't wear it?'

'By all means wear it. I wouldn't describe our hosts as average Bahamians. And you'll

116

have less to take off if you decided to follow fashion.'

Felicity hesitated, went to the door, and checked. 'Should I take my pistol?'

'As the man asked, where would you put it? Anyway, I think we're all right for at least twenty-four hours. None of the opposition can possibly have located us yet.'

'Well ... wish me luck.' Felicity closed the door behind her.

She was an absolute treasure; Jessica hoped she came through this without being hurt, either physically or emotionally; but she was a grown woman, in every way, and could only be protected so far. JJ had a shower, got into bed – beneath the sheet, as the air conditioning had her feeling quite cold, especially after the heat outside – and lay on her back to think. There were a great many questions waiting to be answered, the first priority being a serious talk with Theresa, supposing she could ever get the girl alone. She stretched, and sighed ... and awoke as the door opened.

Her initial reaction was one of extreme irritation: she was sure she hadn't been asleep more than five minutes. But that changed to real annoyance as she identified the intruder. Wrong room, she said, not sitting up but allowing her arm to droop beside the bed to find her shoulder bag. She was not the least afraid of a physical confrontation with anyone, but she had no real desire to wrestle with him in the nude, certainly when he was clearly also in the nude: he wore a towel round his waist.

Lucian closed the door. 'I need to talk with you. In private.'

'And I have no desire to talk with you, Mr Lenghurst, in private.'

He sat on the other bed, allowing his towel to fall open. He retrieved it, but not before qualifying as a well-endowed flasher, though Jessica reflected that his record indicated that he preferred his women about a quarter of her age. 'I am employing you,' he remarked.

'Correction. I'm employed by the British government.'

'But you are here, on my island.'

'I was under the impression that it is your wife's island. By the way, does she know you're here?'

His hands opened and shut. She was used to this syndrome; she knew that her ability to preserve a perfectly uninvolved demeanour, no matter what was happening about her, irritated most men who could not help regarding her as a cute little blonde liable to burst into tears if bruised. 'Why are *you* here?' he asked.

'Hasn't Rowena told you?'

'She said something about Jerry being in trouble with some Colombian drug baron, but that has to be rubbish. Jerry doesn't do drugs.'

'I'm glad to hear that. But he is certainly into under-age women, as you may have noticed.'

His head jerked. 'Just what do you mean by that?'

'What I said.'

'Look, I know I fucked up once. So I went to gaol. Do you know what it's like to be a sex offender in gaol?'

'I would say, lonely.'

'Not lonely enough. They get at you, mentally, even if they can't get at you physically. You can feel the hostility all around you.'

'How very sad. Tell me about the children you abused.'

'I never harmed any of them.'

'That's a matter of opinion. Look, Mr Lenghurst, I'm a police officer, and I don't really go for criminals, and sex offenders rank at the top of criminals I most dislike. But I have not come here after you. I'm here to do a job of work. While here, I am perfectly willing to be civil to you, but that does not include entertaining you in my bedroom while I am trying to get some sleep. So if you wouldn't mind pushing off...'

His gaze roamed up and down the body he could see beneath the sheet. 'To do this job, you will need my help.'

'If that becomes obvious, I'll ask for it.'

'Rowena says you intend to set up some kind of watch system to keep people off the island.'

'That does seem to be the simplest way to make sure no undesirable comes calling.'

'You'll need me to help you do it. These

people work for me. You are right that the island actually belongs to Rowena, but she is very much an absentee landlady. The day-to-day running of the cay is my province, and my people know that.'

The door opened. 'Oops!' Felicity said. 'Shall I come back later?'

She was also wearing only her towel wrapped round her waist, and carried her bikini in her hand; Lucian's attention was entirely distracted, as Jessica's body remained invisible.

'Not at all,' Jessica said. 'Mr Lenghurst was just leaving. We'll discuss your proposition later, Mr Lenghurst.'

Lucian shuffled past Felicity, endeavouring not to touch her.

'Close the door,' Jessica said. 'I see you couldn't resist following fashion.'

'Well, everyone else was doing it. You should see that fellow Arnie. Is he hung!'

'I suppose I will have to, eventually.' Jessica threw back the sheet and swung her legs out of bed. 'I may as well get up, as sleeping around here is a difficult business.'

Felicity draped the towel over a chair and went into the bathroom. 'Did that old geyser really proposition you? Him?'

'We're just good friends,' Jessica assured her.

'Now, JJ,' Rowena announced, as they gathered in the lounge for cocktails, served by a white-jacketed Truman, before dinner. The

120

group was wearing a wide assortment of clothes, Lucian being in a tuxedo and patent-leather shoes, Jeremy in shorts and a brightly coloured striped shirt and sandals, and Arnie in the khaki shirt and slacks he had worn for flying; he had apparently not brought a change. The women were no less disparate. Rowena matched her husband with a low-cut evening gown; obviously she kept a full wardrobe on the cay. Theresa had clearly not had the time properly to replenish her ward-robe, and wore trousers and a loose shirt, while on Jessica's recommendation both the policewomen wore summer dresses. The two dogs lay on the floor, panting. 'You must tell us what you want us to do.'

'And why you didn't come swimming,' Jeremy said.

'I need my sleep,' Jessica said. 'Not that I got a lot.'

Lucian drained his glass.

'As for what comes first...' That was to get the truth out of Theresa, but she didn't want to blow that wide open in front of the servants and, even more, Arnie, whom she still had no reason to trust, and who pre-sumably would be returning to Nassau in the morning. 'As you know, my idea is to keep anyone who isn't well known to you off the cay. We can work on a defensive system tomorrow, Rowena, when you show me over the island. But it is equally important for us to have advance warning of anyone *trying* to get on to the cay. Here's where you come in,

121

Arnie. You need to keep your ears open in Nassau, make inquiries about any suspicious characters that may turn up.'

'In Nassau? Just about everyone is a suspicious character.'

'But you know most of them already, I'm sure.'

'Well, if they're locals, sure. But visitors...'

'There aren't that many visitors at this time of year, are there?'

'Well, it ain't high season, that's for sure.'

'There you go. What you are looking for is anyone who may be making inquiries about Tiger Cay and how to get here. As you are well known to be Mrs Lenghurst's pilot, he, or they, will almost certainly be directed to you for information.' She drank from the glass that had been placed at her elbow. 'That's rather good. What is it?'

'That's a yellow bird, ma'am,' Truman explained. 'I got some more here.' He offered the cocktail shaker.

'Well...' She allowed her glass to be refilled; everyone else was doing the same, and she reckoned she had a stronger head than most. 'But we also need to keep our eyes open nearer to home. What are your relations with the people in Arthur's Town? Have you friends over there?'

She looked at Rowena, who looked at her husband. 'I wouldn't say we have any social friends,' Lucian said. 'The whole idea of having this cay is that we keep to ourselves.'

But you don't necessarily do that, Jessica

122

thought, and again had to decide not to pursue that subject, at the moment. 'But you shop over there.'

'I go across once a week, yes, for food and mail.'

'So you're known in the supermarket. Wouldn't they be prepared to inform you if any strangers were asking for a way to the cay?'

'They might.'

'When next did you mean to go across?'

'The day after tomorrow.'

'I'll come with you. Don't worry, I'll keep a low profile.'

'That ain't gonna be easy,' Arnie said. 'You'll be the hottest thing they've seen over there for ten years.'

'More like fifty,' Lucian suggested.

'You are all so sweet,' Jessica said.

'Dinner,' Rowena decided.

They were all so tired that the meal was brief, and they were in bed by ten, which was actually three in the morning from their point of view.

'Do we need to take any kind of precautions?' Felicity asked, as they shared the bathroom. 'Like we did in London?'

'I still think we're all right for a day or two.'

'Um.' This time she did not bother with a nightdress; clearly this hedonistic lifestyle was growing on her. 'Am I coming with you to this town?'

'Let's decide that at the time.' Jessica switched off the light.

* ★ *

Having been awakened by the strangely harsh cawing of the peacock and his two hens, as well as some noisy but apparently irrelevant barking from the dogs, they breakfasted on the back verandah overlooking the beach and the sea, being joined by the three birds, the cock spreading his immense, brilliantly coloured tail as he strutted to and fro. It was another glorious day, not yet hot, with acres of blue sky and a light breeze, although away to the south there were huge white clouds seeming to be piled one on top of the other.

'They call those tropids,' Lucian explained. 'They look important, but they aren't really. They seldom bring rain.'

'What's the word on this Brigitte female?' Jeremy asked.

'According to the news, she's due to make a landfall on Puerto Rico, this morning,' his father said.

'Where is that in relation to us?' Felicity asked.

'Something over a thousand miles. It's not a threat, right now.'

'What happens if it does come up here?'

'No problem, once we know it's coming.'

'But this house is made of wood.'

'It'll take a hurricane, unless we let the wind get it. We have shutters for every window, and every exterior door, too.'

'Where?' She looked left and right.

'Oh, we don't keep them in place all the time. They're sheets of plywood, which the

124

boys put up when necessary.'

Arnie stood up. 'Well, I guess I'll be heading back. See yuh around, ladies.' He headed through the house.

Jessica finished her coffee. 'Maybe we should take our walk now, Rowena, before it gets too hot.'

'Surely.' Rowena got up. Today she was wearing shorts, to reveal very good legs. Jessica had chosen jeans. 'Five minutes. And you'll need a hat, even this early.'

'Oops! I didn't bring one.'

'No problem. I have lots.'

'I'll come with you,' Lucian volunteered.

'Ah...'

Rowena got the message. 'I think JJ is thinking of some woman-to-woman talk, darling.'

'You can make up a four for tennis, Dad,' Jeremy said, and looked at Felicity.

Who looked at Jessica.

'I think that's a good idea,' Jessica said. 'One of us should stay close to him at all times.'

'I like the sound of that,' Jeremy said.

'But I don't have any gear,' Felicity almost wailed.

'I said we'll fit you out. But you're halfway there. And how.'

Like Rowena, Felicity was wearing shorts, and her legs were even better.

'I'm sure you'll have fun.' Jessica was offered a selection of hats, varying from the baseball cap to the wide-brimmed variety, and went inside to their bedroom.

125

Felicity followed. 'I don't even like the guy.'

'That, sadly, is too often how the cookie crumbles in our business. I don't like any of them.'

'And the way he comes on at me, in front of his girlfriend...'

Jessica selected a white hat with a floppy brim. 'That's part of the plan.'

'We have a plan?'

'We always have a plan, and right now, our plan is to get Theresa so browned off that she'll be prepared to split ranks, so to speak. So flirt with the lout, whenever she's around.'

'And suppose he really comes on heavy? Do I have permission to shoot him?'

'Wouldn't that be counter-productive, as we're supposed to be protecting him? You'll just have to lie back and think of England.'

'Do I say anything about the report from the Yard?'

'No. Leave that one with me.' She went to the door. 'Enjoy yourself.'

'Hurry back,' Felicity begged.

'I hope Lucian hasn't been making himself a nuisance,' Rowena remarked, as they crossed the tennis court and took the path to the helicopter pad, where several people, mostly children, were watching Arnie, having completed his checks, climbing into his machine and starting the engines. The dogs were already there, barking excitedly.

Rowena and Jessica paused also to give him a wave as he lifted off. 'He's quite a character,' Jessica commented.

126

'Lucian?' Rowena was surprised.

'Perhaps. I was talking about Arnie. Where did you find him?'

'I advertised. He was one of several applicants for the job.'

'This was ten years ago?'

'That's right.'

'Felicity tells me he's, shall I say, well made.'

Rowena flushed. 'I like men who are men and look like men.'

'Point taken.'

'Oh, I know I made a mistake about Lucian, but...'

'He is also well made.'

Rowena shot her a glance. 'He didn't expose himself to you?'

'Let's say, he didn't conceal himself. Please don't let it bother you. I'm a big girl.'

'I was going to say that he begged for my help. Well, he was my husband, no matter what he'd done. I'd just bought this place, so I told him he could live here, providing he never left it.'

'And he accepted that?'

'He didn't have any choice. He doesn't have any money, and here he can live like a king.'

'And pursue his peculiar tastes?'

'Good heavens, no. I'd never allow that.'

'Ah.'

'I'm usually here for at least part of the winter,' Rowena pointed out.

'And the rest of the time?'

'Just what are you getting at?'

'That even more than a leopard, a man who

127

is so sexually active that he becomes deviant in his pursuit of pleasure never becomes celibate without castration.'

'What are you, a copper or a psychiatrist?'

'A good copper needs to be both.' They arrived at the dock, which faced east, accompanied now by the dogs, which promptly plunged into the water. There was a fresh breeze blowing, so that they had to hold their hats on their heads, while the ocean sparkled with whitecaps. The dock itself was a roughly four-hundred-feet-square concrete enclosure, with a single narrow entrance on the north side; alongside the south wall the motor cruiser was moored, but even she was rising and falling to the small swell that entered the enclosure. 'Isn't that very exposed?'

'She's quite snug, really.'

'Even in a blow?'

'You mean a hurricane? If one really comes close, Lucian takes her across to the mainland for shelter.'

'You mean Cat Island? When did you last have a hurricane?'

'We've never had one. Not since we've been here, anyway.'

'But don't the Bahamas get hit pretty regularly?'

'Surely. But there are nearly eight hundred islands in the group, so it's a bit of a lottery. Hurricanes don't like land, you see; they get their strength from warm water. So sometimes they hit the Windward Islands, bounce over them, and then get their strength back in the Caribbean and head up for Jamaica or into the Gulf of Mexico. Other times they turn back into the Atlantic and come up here; then they do often try to get through the northern islands to Florida, but usually north of us. Eleuthera gets hit more often than most, because it's on the edge of the deepwater shipping channel to Fort Lauderdale. It had a bad one about ten years ago. The strange thing was, it was called Andrew – that is, it was the first of the season, although it was quite late. I suppose that's why it was so bad.'

'Just like this Brigitte.'

'It's not coming our way. Yet. Shall we go across to the village?'

'Can we walk round by the beach?' The sand began right next to the dock.

'Of course. Come on, come on,' she called at the dogs, who obediently left the water. 'And don't shake.' This they promptly did, scattering sand and water over the two women. 'Naughty Hero! Naughty Leander!' Rowena shouted.

Jessica brushed what she could off her clothes, as did Rowena, and they walked down on to the sand. The sun was now quite high, the rays reflecting off the sea.

'Lucian didn't come on to you, did he?'

'Only in the sense that he invaded my privacy.'

'I'll have a word with him.'

'I don't think that will be necessary. It's not me, Jessica, that interests him, it's Detective-

Sergeant Jones. I suspect he has a hang-up about policemen, or women.'

'I don't suppose you can blame him.' They walked in silence for a few minutes, the dogs bounding in front of them, the land steadily curving to the north-west so that they rapidly lost sight of the dock. 'What do you think of my island?'

With the breeze onshore even the sound of the generator was lost. 'I suppose it has to be the nearest thing to paradise on earth,' Jessica said. 'But not necessarily from a defensive point of view. Is there a reef?'

'Indeed. You can't see it today because of the sea.'

'But presumably the locals know where it is.'

'Certainly. But it's only on this side, and they don't often venture out into the ocean.'

'You mean there's no reef between you and the mainland?'

'Well, there is. You could say that this island is part of it.'

'I get you. But there is nothing between your west coast and the mainland's east coast?'

'Just a lot of shallow water. Wow, it's getting hot. Would you like a swim?'

'What, here?'

'Why not? It'll be a bit boisterous, but invigorating.'

Jessica had not been considering the sea state. She looked left and right, and then into the coconut trees behind them. There was no

130

one about, but... 'We don't have swimsuits.'

'Oh, really, JJ; I could understand you not wanting to strip off in front of the men, and certainly Lucian, but here there's only us.' She took off her hat, kicked off her sandals, dropped her shorts and threw her shirt on the sand; she wore no bra and had a very good body. 'If it really does embarrass you, you can keep your knickers on.' Hers joined the rest of her clothes on the sand, and she turned away and walked into the water, being immediately buffeted by the shallow waves. The dogs were already in, splashing up and down.

Jessica gave another glance along the empty beach. She enjoyed being naked in private, and had never let it upset her in public, when the occasion called for it; she still had vivid memories of taking on the Touareg slave traders, in the company of the tragic Princess Claudine, when they had both been naked, while during her infamous kidnap she had spent a good deal of her time in the nude; but perhaps for those very reasons she had become an increasingly private person in her outlook. On the other hand, the water was tempting, and she knew there was no feeling of exhilaration to be compared with being naked, in the open air, even though she wondered if Rowena might have an ulterior motive. But she had coped with sufficient ulterior motives in her time.

She took off her hat, laid down her shoulder bag, undressed, walked down the sand and into the water, which was surprisingly cool.

131

Rowena was up to her shoulders, rising and falling with each surge, breasts seeming to float. Jessica advanced until she too was up to her shoulders, which was several yards closer in, while she experienced a tremendous feeling of cool cleanliness spreading over her body, occasionally spluttering as a larger than usual wave swept in, realizing that her hair was getting wet; the dogs had prudently remained in the shallows.

'You *can* swim?' Rowena asked.

'I can swim. But I prefer to stand.'

Rowena came back to her, to stand hardly more than waist deep herself. 'The boys are going to be *green*.'

'Will you tell me, what is this great desire to see me in the nud?'

'It's simply that you are the most exciting woman any of them has ever known.'

'You have got to be joking.'

'Fact. It's not just your looks, although ... well, no woman your size has any right to tits that big...'

'I find them a nuisance, from time to time.'

'You should be so lucky. And then there's your aura – your general air of both fitness and ... well, command.'

'There's no magic in that. I train, constantly, both mentally and physically. For the rest, I simply do my job to the best of my ability. You asked for me, remember?'

'And am I glad I did!'

'Well, don't expect miracles. Look out, here comes a big one.'

The wave was in fact several feet high. Rowena promptly ducked into it. Jessica couldn't make up her mind in time to follow her, and was picked up and rolled over, flailing her arms and legs in an attempt to regain control of her body, which was being driven forward by the tumbled water, making the memory of that huge wave which had carried her ashore on the Pacific atoll seem like yesterday. She had thought then that she was drowning. This time she was merely tossed head over heels, so that she landed on her feet, now in shallow water. Her knees gave way and she knelt, in only in a few inches, as the wave receded.

The dogs immediately rushed up to her and began licking her face, while she gasped for breath. Then Rowena knelt beside her. 'Are you all right?'

'Just a little winded.'

Rowena put her arm round her shoulders. 'I could eat you alive. I *want* to eat you alive.' Her hand slipped down to Jessica's breast.

'Let's keep it,' Jessica suggested. 'I'm on duty. Oh, my God!'

The dogs had stopped licking and were barking. Rowena turned her head to look at the half-dozen boys walking along the beach. Jessica hastily lay down in the shallow water, allowing the next wave to break over her, but Rowena merely shouted, 'Clear off!'

The boys goggled at her for several seconds, obviously also taking in the just visible head of yellow hair, then one said, 'Oh, yes, Mrs

Lenghurst. Sorry, Mrs Lenghurst.' They turned and made their way back along the beach.

'I do apologize,' Rowena said. 'I'd forgotten that they'd be on holiday.' She stood up and waded out of the water.

'Don't you think', Jessica said, 'that they're going to nip into the trees and watch us?'

Rowena shrugged. 'So we'll bring a little joy into their lives.'

Jessica waited a last moment until the youths had entirely disappeared, then hurried out of the water and dressed as rapidly as she could – regardless of the fact that her clothes became as wet as her body and clung to her like a second skin – crammed her hat on to her wet hair. 'You mean you have a school on the island?' she panted.

'Good Lord, no. They go to school in Arthur's Town.'

'How do they get there?'

'Why, by boat, of course.'

'You mean the cruiser?'

'Heavens, no. One of the men runs them across every morning during term time.'

'You mean these people have their own boats?'

'Well, of course they do. Several of them.'

Jessica picked up her bag and they walked together along the beach, now heading due west, the sun at their backs. 'I'm just trying to get an over-all picture,' Jessica said. 'Where are these boats kept?'

'The village has its own dock.'

'This gets more and more tricky with every minute.'

'Oh, come now. Our people are absolutely loyal. They know who butters their bread: free housing, electricity, water in return for some light duties; talk about paradise.'

'Can you put your hand on your heart and swear that if someone offered one of your boat owners a fair sum of money to bring him, or her, across from the mainland, they'd turn it down?'

'Well ... why do you say her? Do you think Abriga would employ a woman for a job like this?'

'No. I expect him to employ several men.'

'Several? Oh, my God!'

'But there is also a woman involved, and we have to find out who she is.'

'How do you know it's a woman, if you don't know who she is?'

'Just information I received from the Yard.'

'You mean to do with the fire? You mean they've found that lousy concierge?'

'They've found him, but they don't think he's lousy. He was in the wreckage.'

'Oh, good heavens. You mean he was burned to death?'

'He was certainly burned, but not to death. He was dead before the fire got to him.'

'You mean he was *murdered?*'

'A knife was sticking out of his chest.'

'And this woman you're talking about...'

'Was the last person seen entering the building before the fire.'

'You mean she went up too?'

'No. She was seen leaving again, but without the coat she had worn going in. Traces of the coat were found by the dead body.'

'Why should she take the coat off?'

'Because it would have had bloodstains on it.'

'So she just took it off and walked out? She had a nerve. But what's this got to do with the fire?'

'She needed to kill him so that she could set the bombs that started the fire.'

Rowena stopped walking and turned to face her. 'She started the fire? Deliberately? To kill us? Oh, my *God*!! You think she was sent by Abriga?'

'No. I can't believe he would want to incinerate his own daughter. But she certainly is connected to what happened in Florida, and I have to find out how. You with me?'

They rounded a last bend in the beach and came in sight of the dock and then the village. This dock was not a total enclosure like that on the other side of the island, but consisted of a single stone jetty, perhaps two hundred feet long, from which trailed the painters of several open boats equipped with outboards. Beyond the dock were a dozen houses, forming a street. The boys that had interrupted their bathe were gathered on the dock, but turned to look at them as they passed. In the village itself they were greeted respectfully by several women and one or two men, who came forward to pat the dogs. There were also several hens and a strutting cock, which did not seem the least disturbed by either the humans or the dogs. Rowena engaged the various people in conversation, asking after their health and their families, and Jessica observed that they seemed quite pleased to see her.

'Do they all work on the island?' she asked, when they continued their walk, now turning away from the shore to follow a path through the trees.

'No, no. Most of the men have jobs on the mainland, that's why they're not here at the moment. They go over first thing in the morning, and come back in the evening.'

'I take it these jobs are in Arthur's Town?'

'Most of them, yes. A couple work on the coconut plantations.'

'So they probably have friends over there.'

'And relations,' Rowena said.

'Do they ever bring any of these friends and relations over?'

'I imagine they do, if there's a party or something. I don't really know. I mean, I own the island, but I don't own them.'

'But you have the right to ask them not to bring any strangers over.'

'Well ... I suppose I do. But I've never done it before. I'm sure they'd be offended. Although ... perhaps if we told them the situation...'

'We'll need to think about that. Do those hens always run wild?'

'Why not?'

'Why not, indeed. Are they yours?'

'I suppose they are. I've never thought about it.'

'Are there any other animals on the island?'

'No. We get our milk and meat from the supermarket in Arthur's Town.'

'What about other dogs?'

'Certainly not. I wouldn't stand for that. It'd upset my darlings.'

With whom you only spend a few months in every year, Jessica thought. The noise was now quite loud, and a few moments later they came upon the generators, which, to Jessica's surprise, were housed in an open shed. One of the machines was working, the other lay silent; twenty yards beyond was the storage tank, connected by a thick length of plastic piping.

Jessica looked left and right. 'There's nobody here,' she shouted.

'There isn't any need. Urban – that's the man I was talking with in the village – is our mechanic. He checks the oil and water levels every morning, and switches over every week or so. They need very little attention.'

'But anyone can come here and turn them off. Or worse: wreck them.'

'Why should anyone want to do that? They supply the village as well as the house.'

'Someone who might want to plunge the whole island into darkness, and cut off your radio and Internet communications.'

'Oh, my God! But ... he'd have to get here first.'

'Or she,' Jessica reminded her. 'But from what you tell me, there are boats coming and going all night. Or there could be, and nobody would pay the least attention, even if they heard an outboard over the noise from the generator.'

Rowena looked quite shaken, and absently fondled the bitch, who had come nuzzling up to her. 'What are we to do?'

'We have to work it out, if we're not going to upset your people. But surely there is one measure we could take which wouldn't offend them.'

'Tell me.'

'Ask them to report any strange people turning up in Arthur's Town. It's not all that big, is it?'

'No, no, it's quite small. Any Hispanic would stand out like a sore thumb. Especially this time of year.'

'I don't think we're necessarily looking for an Hispanic, even if Abriga is a Colombian. If he's a big drugs dealer, he'll employ people of every race, creed and colour. We need to know about *any* strangers.'

'I'll have a word with Truman.'

'Then let's get back. I could do with a shower.'

Rowena grinned. 'Not a swim? You mustn't mind the boys, you know. They're really quite harmless.'

'I'll let you know,' Jessica said, enigmatically.

★ ★ ★

139

It was past eleven when they got home. The tennis game had been long finished, or abandoned because of the heat, and judging by the shouts and good-natured screams from the beach the participants were cooling off ... or heating up! The dogs immediately dashed through the play room, nosed open the screen door, and bounded across the verandah and down the steps to join in the fun. Rowena and Jessica followed more slowly.

Truman was laying the places for lunch.

'Whew!' Rowena said. 'That was some walk. What are we drinking?'

'I got punch on the back porch, ma'am.'

'Then that's for us.'

Jessica followed her into the play room. 'I'll be with you in a sec.' She went through the lobby and into the bedroom, threw her hat on a chair and stripped off her shirt and jeans. She was wet through. So, a shower, or a swim? And if a swim ... she took out her white one-piece. With its deep décolletage it was both revealing and provocative while preserving a certain amount of decency; there was certainly no one out there for whom she had any desire to display herself in the nude. Especially not Rowena, again.

She put on the suit, had just opened the door when her mobile buzzed. 'Jones.'

'JJ,' the commander said. 'Are you just out of bed?'

'It is nearly noon, here, sir.'

'That's what I thought, as it's four here. I

tried you earlier, but there was no reply.'

'I was inspecting the premises, with Mrs Lenghurst, so I left my phone here.'

'And all is well, eh?'

'No, sir, all is not well. This place is about as secure as a goal without a goalkeeper.'

'Well, I'm sure you'll put it right.'

'I could put it right if I had a team of six people.'

'Now, don't start that again. You must do the best you can with what you have. I have the utmost confidence in you.'

'Thank you, sir.'

'Now I have some news which you might find useful. The FBI really are quite a good lot. Very efficient. It seems they have a mountain of data on this fellow Abriga. They dream of one day luring him out of Colombia so that they can nab him. And the data obviously includes various of his people. We gave them the name Rodrigo. Well, obviously that's not an uncommon name amongst the Spanish, and there are several people named Rodrigo employed by this fellow, but one of them could be our man. His name is Rodrigo Garcia.'

Jessica sighed. 'You do know, sir, that Garcia is the most common of all Spanish surnames? It approximates to our Smith.'

'Or Jones, eh? Ha ha.'

'Ha ha, sir.'

'However, this one will interest you. Rodrigo Garcia is recorded as having landed at Miami Airport in September last year, together with his wife, accompanying Miss Theresa Abriga to stay with her aunt in Coral Gables.'

Jessica sat on the bed, frowning. 'Yes, sir, I am interested. Was he not picked up?'

'Well, no, they had nothing on him, although they know who he works for. He had a six-month visa, and he was officially on holiday, but it was understood that he was actually there to protect Miss Abriga.'

'With his wife.'

'Well, obviously there would have to be a chaperone, even if the girl was staying with her aunt.'

'And the FBI are certain that the woman was his wife?'

'It seems so. Is it important?'

'Well, sir, when we spoke with Mrs Lenghurst in your office, and we asked her who this Rodrigo was, she told us that, according to Jeremy and Theresa, Rodrigo was the man Abriga wanted Theresa to marry.'

'Good Lord! You're absolutely right. I'd forgotten that.'

'So do the FBI have the whereabouts of Mr and Mrs Garcia now?'

'As far as they know, Garcia is still in Florida. There is no record of his having left the country. Mrs Garcia did leave the country, a week ago, on a flight to Heathrow. Good God!'

'Yes, sir.'

'But wait a moment, JJ. That reasoning is flawed, on two counts. One is that this

142

woman, if bent on some kind of crime, would surely use a false name.'

'She travelled under her own name, sir, because she was in too much of a hurry to wait for a false passport. A week ago is two days after the elopement.'

'And you think Garcia sent her after Theresa? I suppose that's possible. But he would hardly have told her to blow up the apartment block. Anyway, where would she get the explosives?'

'From one of Abriga's business associates in England.'

'To blow up his own daughter? If they're working for Abriga?'

'I think we need to find out if they *are* working for Abriga, sir, or if there is another factor involved of which we know nothing.'

'Going after a fifteen-year-old girl? Anyway, I don't see how Mrs Garcia can be linked to the bomber. The description we have is that of a woman with long yellow hair. That hardly sounds like a Colombian.'

'With respect, sir, the hair could have been dyed. But in any event, do we know that Mrs Garcia is a Colombian?'

'Hm. I'll have someone work on it and come back to you.'

'Thank you, sir.' Jessica replaced the phone in her bag and went down the corridor to the back verandah, checking as she emerged. Rowena sat in one of the loungers, drinking a large glass of iced rum punch through a straw. The other four were in the water, still making a lot of noise. They were playing a game Jessica recalled from her youth as being known as 'cock-fighting', in which the girl sat on the man's shoulders with one leg on each side of his neck, held by his hands on her thighs, and wrestled her opposite number, the winner being she who remained seated longest. As indulged in by teenagers it had been sufficiently sexy, and kinky to be a lot of fun, but she had never played it in the nude. Now she watched Felicity, squirming on Jeremy's shoulders, her naked groin pressed into the back of his head while he grasped a thigh in each hand, grappling with Theresa, similarly situated on her prospective father-in-law, all four bodies pressed against each other.

'Aren't they having fun?' Rowena asked. 'Help yourself to a drink.'

A large jug stood on the table, together with several glasses. Jessica poured. 'I think I need this.'

'Now, you mustn't be angry with Felicity,' Rowena said. 'She's only enjoying herself.'

'She also happens to be on duty.'

'No one can be on duty all the time. I do like that suit. Why don't you go down and join them?'

'With or without the suit?'

'Oh, they'd prefer it without, I'm sure.'

'Unfortunately, I also am on duty, and I have work to do. With your co-operation.'

'Of course. What can I do?'

'I'd like you to relieve your husband of his
144

nymphet burden.'

Rowena giggled. 'He'll think I'm jealous.'

'If you're not, you should be. Then, having dislodged Theresa, send her up here. We urgently need to have a chat.'

The Tourist

Rowena undressed and went down the steps into the water, immediately being surrounded by the splashing dogs. Jessica could not hear what she said, but after a brief hesitation, and some obvious comment or query from Jeremy, Lucian allowed Theresa to slide down his back and wade to the beach. Jeremy indeed made as if he wanted to follow her, but Felicity, after a quick glance at Jessica, close her thighs on his neck encouragingly, and completely distracted his attention.

Theresa came slowly up the beach and then the steps, dripping water from her hair and down her body. 'Mrs Lenghurst said you had something to tell me.' She had gained enormously in confidence since arriving on the island.

'We do need to talk. Shall we go inside?'

Theresa looked back at the sea, but Jeremy was now totally preoccupied with Felicity as she began to wrestle with his mother. 'OK.' She poured herself a glass of rum punch, picked up one of the towels lying in a chair.

'Aren't you a little young to be drinking this stuff?' Jessica asked.

'Jerry says that if I'm old enough to fuck

I'm old enough to drink.'

'Interesting point. Your room or mine?'

'I need to shower.'

'That's fine.' Jessica followed her along the corridor and into the first of the bedrooms. 'Known Jerry long?'

'Long enough.' Theresa sucked half of her drink through the straw, placed the glass on her bedside table, went into the bathroom and switched on the shower.

Jessica stood in the doorway to watch her; the girl's movements were sinuous, like a cat's. 'And you love him?'

Theresa, face turned up to the water, did not answer for a moment. Then she switched off the flow. 'If I didn't, I wouldn't be here.'

'That's another good point. So, does the situation with your father bother you?'

'Well, of course it does.' Theresa stepped out of the shower stall and began to towel herself, vigorously.

'Do you think your father will carry out his threat?'

Theresa turned to face her. 'To have Jerry castrated? Yes. I told you: I believe he will want to hurt him very badly.'

'So you're scared?'

Theresa stepped past her, pulled on a pair of knickers. 'Not here. Not with you here. No one can get at us here. Can they?' She dropped a T-shirt over her head; she apparently did not wear brassieres. 'You'll stop them, won't you?'

'It's my job.' Jessica sat on one of the beds

while Theresa pulled on a pair of jeans. 'But I need to know who I'm up against. Do you reckon this man Rodrigo Garcia will be the one?'

Theresa's head turned, sharply. 'Rodrigo ... how do you know his name was Garcia?'

Jessica studied her for a few moments while her stomach muscles tensed, as they always did when her brain was assimilating an unpalatable truth. But she continued to speak quietly. 'I belong to an organization which knows most things, and can generally find out those things it doesn't know. So Rodrigo won't be the one coming after you. How did he die?'

Theresa stared at her with her mouth open. 'How ... you are a witch.'

'Just a detective. You said how did I know his name *was* Garcia. You should have said, how did I know his name *is* Garcia.'

'Oh, my God!' Theresa muttered, also sinking on to a bed.

'He was your bodyguard, right? He and his wife. What is her name?'

'Greta.'

'That's hardly a Colombian name.'

'She's Swedish.'

'That fits. And she's still alive.'

Theresa gazed at her.

'You're using the present tense,' Jessica explained.

Theresa licked her lips.

'Terry,' Jessica said, 'I have to know what happened to Rodrigo.'

Theresa burst into tears. 'He ... he didn't mean to do it. He just appeared, as we were leaving...'

'I think we need a little grammar here. Would the first "he" be Jerry? And the second, Rodrigo?'

Theresa's head moved up and down.

'So Rodrigo attempted to stop you leaving with Jerry. So they fought. And Jerry...'

'Rodrigo reached for his gun, and Jerry stabbed him. I didn't know he had a knife. I swear it.'

'Shit,' Jessica commented. 'Shit, shit, shit.' She looked up as the door opened to admit Jeremy.

He wore a towel, and was looking hot and bothered. 'So here's where you are,' he remarked. 'Shacked up together.'

'Having a little chat,' Jessica said. 'And now it seems that you and I also need to have a little chat.'

'About what?' He looked at Theresa, realized that she had been crying. 'What have you told her?'

Theresa sniffed. 'She knew. She worked it out.'

'How the fuck could she have worked it out? You bitch! You unutterable bitch!'

'Just simmer down,' Jessica said. 'I'm prepared to listen to your side of the story.'

He glared at her, his hands opening and shutting. 'I ought to...'

'Sit down and tell me what happened.'

He hesitated for a moment, then perhaps

remembered both her reputation and their encounter in the London flat. His knees seemed to give way, and he sat beside Theresa. 'He came at me. Theresa said he had a gun, so I drew my knife. We grappled, and he fell. That's all. I didn't mean to kill him.'

'Did he draw the gun?'

'His hand was still in his pocket.'

'But you thought he was going to shoot you.'

Jeremy again hesitated, briefly. 'Yes.'

Jessica knew immediately that he was lying, but this was not the moment to follow that line. 'If that is true, you have a possible plea of self-defence. What did you do with the body?'

'Well, we left it there.'

'Where?'

'On the lawn outside the house.'

'Was anyone else present?'

'Of course not.'

Jessica looked at Theresa. 'Do you support that story?'

'Yes. Yes, that is what happened.'

Oddly, Jessica thought, *she* was telling the truth, at least so far as she knew it. 'Right. So Garcia's body was left lying on the lawn, where presumably it was found the next morning. But it was never reported to the police. Why?'

'Haven't a clue,' Jeremy said.

'Aunt Luana would have hushed it up. She would have known Papa would not wish the

Florida Police investigating his affairs.'

'OK. So presumably the body was buried or dumped by your aunt's people, and as far as the police are concerned Garcia is still living with her, just as presumably your disappearance has not been reported either. You realize that the immigration authorities will start thinking about him when his visa expires? I suppose you reckon that is no longer your business. But there is one aspect of what happened that is very much your business. In fact, it is all of our business. Tell me about Garcia's wife.'

'Did he have a wife?' Jeremy asked.

Jessica looked at Theresa.

'Greta,' she said. 'Like I told you, a Swede.'

'Which is not a lot to go on. Describe her.'

'Tall. Blonde. Very good-looking. I mean handsome rather than pretty. But she had a great figure.'

Which entirely fitted the description of the bomber. 'Where did they meet?'

'She worked for Papa. But he let her retire when she got together with Rodrigo.'

'When you say, worked...?'

'Well...' Theresa looked embarrassed. 'She attended to people who, well ... Papa wanted attended to.'

'You mean she was a hit man? Or woman?'

'Well, yes. But like I said, she retired when she married Rodrigo.'

'Until you brought her back on to the scene.'

'You can't mean...' Theresa checked, staring

at her. 'Oh, my God!'

'Just confirm that. You've remembered that her speciality, when she was working, was blowing people up.'

'Papa always called her the best. But...'

'Just let me get this straight,' Jeremy said. 'You are saying that this woman Greta, or whatever her name is, is responsible for what happened in the Aspern Building?'

'That is correct. She murdered the concierge, and then planted two bombs: one to knock out the electrics and start the fire, the other to block the emergency stairs. Congreve may have had a point when he suggested that hell hath no fury like a woman scorned, but he never got around to considering the mood of a woman whose husband, whom it would appear that she loved, has been knifed to death. And once she discovers that she didn't get you, she is going to try again.'

'Holy shit! But she can't get at us here, can she?'

'She's a professional. If she's determined to get at you, she will.'

'Papa would never allow her to harm me,' Theresa said.

'I don't think she is working for your papa, any longer.' Jessica stood up. 'OK, Theresa, get your clothes and come with me.'

'What do you mean?' Jeremy demanded. 'Where are your taking her?'

'I gathered from your ma that there is another spare bedroom on this floor. She can

152

sleep in there.'

Jeremy also stood up. 'No way. She's my fiancée.'

'That does not give you the right to beat her up, as you know you are going to do the moment you are alone and get around to imagining that she has let you down by telling me the truth.'

'Look here, you arrogant little bitch, you're not running things here. This is my mother's house.'

Jessica shrugged. 'Have it your way. Then you'd better come along with me and discuss the matter with your mother. We'll have to put her in the whole picture, of course.'

Once again Jeremy's knees seemed to give way as he sat down with a thump. 'You mean if I play along with you, you won't tell her?'

'I will take the matter under consideration.'

'Oh, get out. Both of you.' He discarded his towel and went into the bathroom.

Theresa hastily gathered up her clothes – she didn't have all that many – crammed them into her suitcase, and followed Jessica into the corridor. 'I have some toiletries...'

'We'll get them later.'

'But what will we tell the old lady, when she asks why I have moved out? I'm only here because of Jerry.'

Jessica wondered what this girl thought of *her*, if she considered Rowena to be an old lady? 'You'll tell her that you are fed up with the amount of attention Jerry is paying Detective-Constable Hewitt. You are fed up, aren't

153

you?'

'Well...'

'You should be.'

'I'm not half so fed up as I am with that father of his. He was feeling me all up while we were playing that game.'

'That figures, although I would have said you're a little old for him.' She opened the door of the fourth bedroom, listened to a banging noise.

'What's that?' Theresa asked, nervously.

'Sounds like the lunch gong, no doubt being beaten by Truman. He's being a bit premature. But just dump your stuff in here and get in there.'

'You'll be there?'

'Of course. In a moment.'

She went into her own room, where Felicity waited, wearing shorts and a shirt. 'I thought I'd lost you. What an experience! I hope I am going to get a commendation.'

'You looked to me as if you were enjoying it.' Jessica peered at her face. 'Even if you have got a touch of the sun.'

'I always burn easily.' Felicity giggled. 'You told me to act as if I was. Enjoying myself, I mean.'

'Then you have an alternative profession waiting for you if you ever get fed up with this sort of thing.'

'But what have you been *doing*?'

'Finding things out. I simply have to shower and get this salt out of my hair, and various other places. I see you've done that. Go along and hold the fort for ten minutes. I'll put you in the picture after lunch.'

Which was a sticky meal, apart from the food, which was a mixture of steaks from the freezer and local vegetables, principally avocado pears, which apparently grew almost wild on the island. Theresa had returned to her state of nervous tension, Jeremy glowered at his plate, and their joint behaviour both mystified and irritated Rowena. By contrast, Lucian was in the best of humours. 'I've been listening to the weather forecast,' he announced. 'Brigitte is coming our way.'

'What did you say?' his wife demanded. 'You said it wouldn't happen.'

'Well, it seems she hit Puerto Rico last night, and instead of passing over it into the Caribbean, bounced back into the Atlantic and turned off, making north. At a good speed too. Something like twenty knots.'

'Should we evacuate?'

'What for? She's still a thousand miles away from us. At twenty knots, that's about two days. She could do anything in that time. Anyway, she's not very big: her winds are only just over a hundred miles per hour.'

'That sounds pretty strong to me,' Felicity ventured.

'Aw, that's big enough to knock down a few trees and push up a bit of a storm surge. Big deal. While if she continues on her present course, she'll miss the Bahamas altogether, and just fizzle. There's no need to panic.'

Though, from the way in which he looked

around their faces, Jessica deduced that he would be delighted if they did. Especially her. But Felicity rode to the rescue. 'You've been in a hurricane, haven't you, JJ? Or was it a typhoon?'

'That's the same thing,' Jeremy said. 'Have you really been in a big storm, Sergeant?'

'Yes.'

'Sheltering in some big hotel, I suppose,' Lucian said.

'She was in a small yacht, in the middle of the ocean,' Felicity riposted.

'That must have been *terrifying*,' Rowena said.

'It was.'

'And the boat you were on was sunk,' Felicity said.

'It was wrecked, and sank later.'

'But you survived.'

'Well, obviously.'

'Is there anything you haven't survived?' Jeremy asked.

'If there had been something I didn't survive, I wouldn't be here. Right?'

Lucian snorted.

'What are we going to do this afternoon?' Jeremy asked.

'Anything you like,' his mother said.

'Well, how about going snorkelling? Maybe pick up a conch or two.'

'I'll tell Truman to have one of the boys from the village take you out. JJ?'

'I'm afraid I have some calls to make. You'll have to go, Felicity.'

156

'Me? I don't know anything about snorkelling.'

'I'll teach you,' Jeremy said.

Felicity stared at Jessica with her mouth open.

'You coming, Terry?' Jeremy asked.

'I'd rather stay and sunbathe.'

It was Rowena's turn to stare, with her mouth open.

'Suit yourself,' Jeremy said. 'Half an hour, Filly?'

'I just can't do this,' Felicity declared, when they returned to their bedroom.

'One of us has to be with him. And make sure you take your pistol. Not that I anticipate any trouble this early.'

'You don't understand. He'll have me naked before I can draw breath.'

'Stop salivating. And you don't have to strip off just because he asks you to. Although, if you're wearing that apology for a swimsuit, I don't see why you're bothered. Anyway, you'll have the boatman with you, so he won't be able to do anything more than look.'

'Both of them.'

'Remember that it is in the line of duty.'

'But I don't even know what's going on.'

'Well, you will know everything if you listen very carefully to what I am about to tell the commander.'

'About lunch? That was an atmosphere you could cut with a knife.'

'So listen.' She punched the numbers. 'Still there, Mrs Norton? Is the commander in?'

157

'He left an hour ago.'

'Then I'll call him at home. Have a nice night.'

'I wouldn't do that, Jones.'

'Don't tell me: he's going to another cocktail party.'

'He is going to the opera.'

'Which cannot start before eight thirty, and I make it seven fifteen, your time. I'll catch him.'

'I don't think he will be at all pleased.'

'Well, you can't win them all. Do have a nice night, but don't do anything I wouldn't do.' She winked at a scandalized Felicity – who, as far as she knew, had never met Mrs Norton – and punched some more numbers.

'Yes?'

'Hello, Mrs Adams. May I have a word with the commander, please.'

'Don't tell me ... Sergeant Jones.'

'Spot on, ma'am. You have a marvellous ear for voices.'

'I thought you were out of the country.'

'I am, ma'am. Several thousand miles out of the country. Which is why this call is costing the department a fortune.'

'Oh...' Mrs Adams made a noise which could have been a raspberry, but the conversation had apparently attracted her husband, who now took the phone.

'JJ? I have told you time and again not to call me at home except in an emergency.'

'I'm sorry, sir, but the fact is that nothing much starts to happen here until around midday, and by then it's gone five in your part of the world. And this could be an emergency.'

'Well, go on. What is it?'

Jessica outlined her conversation with Theresa and Jeremy, as succinctly as she could. Felicity listened with her mouth open.

'Hm,' the commander commented when she was finished. 'Tricky. But, you know, none of this happened on British soil.'

'It did happen, sir. Aren't we obliged to inform the Americans that we have information on a possible murder?'

'We don't know it was a murder.'

'We don't know that it wasn't – only Jeremy's say-so, and frankly, I wouldn't trust him further that I could throw him, and he's a big lad.'

'But you say his story is supported by the girl?'

'She isn't actually sure what happened, but she accepts that Jeremy thought he was going to be attacked. That doesn't alter the fact that we are engaged in protecting a man who is guilty of a suspicious death.'

'From the Colombians, not the Florida police.'

'That is exactly my point, sir – though, if I am right about Mrs Garcia, the Colombians are certainly involved. Have we any further information on her?'

'Oh, indeed. She left the country the same day as you, on a later flight.'

'Just like that?'

159

'Well, there was no reason to hold her. There is no evidence to connect her with that fire. The CCTV images were, as usual, blurred. As you yourself said, they could apply to a million women in this country.'

'Yes, sir. What is my brief, supposing she turns up here?'

'Do you think she is likely to do that?'

'If what Theresa Abriga told me is true, I think she is extremely like to do that.'

'Well, then, you'll have to see her off.'

'Suppose I can positively link her to the fire?'

'In that case, hand her over to the Bahamian Police to await extradition. But how do you intend to do that while fending her off the Lenghurst boy?'

'I think I may be able to think of a way, sir – if she turns up, as expected.'

'Now, JJ, no funny business. If you do anything outside the law in the Bahamas, you are outside the law.'

'I understand that, sir. Just to confirm: it is your official decision that we do not inform the Florida Police that there may be a dead Colombian lying around a house in Coral Gables, and that we know who killed him.'

'Are there any Florida policemen in your immediate vicinity?'

'Not to my knowledge, sir.'

'Then just let's cope with one problem at a time. I will get on to the Foreign Office and see what they think, and call you back. What is Mrs Lenghurst's attitude to this?'

'I don't think she has an attitude, sir; because I don't think she knows the truth of the matter.'

'Are you going to tell her?'

'I'd like your advice on that, sir.'

'I can't possibly advise you, JJ, as I do not know the situation on the ground. However, as your remit remains the protection of the Lenghurst boy, and by projection his mother, it would surely be counter-productive to antagonize them, certainly by suggesting you may be thinking of running them in. Remember that if this comes out, Mrs Lenghurst could be done for perverting the course of justice by protecting her son, even if she has done so inadvertently.'

'And Lord Blandin might just withhold further funding. I take your point, sir. Have a nice opera.'

'Wowee,' Felicity remarked. 'That bastard! Now I have to go fishing with a murderer!'

'You heard the man. As far as we are concerned, nothing has changed.'

There was a knock on the door. 'Are you in there, JJ?'

'Come in, Rowena.'

The door opened. 'I'd like a word. In private.'

'Ah...'

'I'd better get going.' Felicity gathered her shoulder bag and bikini, and hurried off.

'Barrier cream,' Jessica said. 'Use lots of barrier cream.'

'I have it,' Felicity assured her.

'What a sweet girl,' Rowena remarked.

'Just remember that she is also on duty.'

'Are you always on duty?'

'As long as we're protecting your son, yes.'

'You're not protecting him now.'

'I am assuming he knows what he's doing, and that there are no strangers involved.'

Rowena sighed, and sat on Felicity's bed. 'I wish to know what is going on.'

'In respect of what?'

'Your girl is going off with Jerry, and Theresa isn't.'

'My girl, or I, have to be with Jerry whenever he leaves the house.'

'But Theresa should be there too.'

'I agree with you. But Theresa feels that Jerry has taken a shine to Filly, and is jealous.'

'Oh, the silly girl. Surely she realizes that ... well...'

'Jerry can't keep his hands off anything with breasts and a backside?'

'Well, that's better than if he went for boys, isn't it?'

In view of Rowena's performance on the beach that morning, Jessica found that a somewhat ambiguous statement, although she reflected that living on this island, especially if one owned it, might slightly unbalance a far more balanced personality than Rowena. So she contented herself with saying, 'It's a point of view.'

'So what are you going to do about it?'

'There is nothing I can do about it, Rowena. I repeat, either Felicity or I have to be with Jeremy at all times outside this house. You set that up when you asked for protection. If it's any comfort to you, and if you won't take offence, Felicity does not go for him.' She fervently hoped she was telling the truth, for all Filly's protests.

'Hm. I suppose I'll have to have a word with Theresa. You know what these Latins are like – so emotional and hot-tempered.'

'But if she's in love with Jerry, she'll get over it.'

'Ha! How do we know she *is* in love with him?'

'She ran away with him.'

'But she has admitted that was to escape being forced to marry this character Rodrigo.'

'Ah,' Jessica said. 'I'd forgotten that. Well, we're stuck with her, tantrums and all. Have you considered sending her back to her father?'

'I don't think she would wish to do that and be beaten and locked up and then forced into marriage. Anyway, Jerry would never allow it What a fuck-up.' She got up and went to the door. 'I'm so glad you're here, JJ. You're so ... so reassuring. As well as so...' She licked her lips. 'What are you doing this afternoon?'

Jessica had intended to sunbathe, but now she decided that would probably be unwise. 'I thought I'd have a siesta, and then, when it's cooler, take a walk down to the village. It's there we're most vulnerable.'

'Oh, right. I'll come with you, shall I?'

'If it's all the same to you, I'd rather be on

163

my own.'

'Why is that?'

'Simply that people are always likely to say what they reckon the boss – that's you – wants to hear, rather than what she might not want to hear.'

Rowena considered this. 'Are you going to tell them who you are? What you are?'

'Heavens, no. I'm just an inquisitive tourist.'

She slept soundly, showered again, and set off along the path through the trees; her hair remained damp and she tied it up in a bandanna beneath her sun hat. It was delightfully primeval in the middle of the island, apart from the constant growl of the generator. But she hadn't got very far when she realized someone was following her. She turned, her hand resting on her shoulder bag, and watched Lucian coming towards her. 'Rowena tells me you're going to the village.'

'I intend to do so, yes. Do you have any objections?'

'None at all. But you're going the wrong way. The village is that way.' He pointed to the left.

'I know. I wanted to look at the reservoir first.'

'Oh. Right. I'll come with you.'

Jessica sighed, but she couldn't tell him what to do on his own island.

He fell into step beside her. 'I have the impression that you don't like me.'

'Are you asking as a person, or as the

husband of my employer?'

'Well ... both.'

'I do not like you as a person, Mr Lenghurst, as you know, just as you know the
reason. As the husband of my employer, I
have no feelings about you at all.'

'But you're here to protect me.'

'I am here to protect your son, and his
mother, if necessary. If you are around,
should a crisis arise, I will protect you as well,
remembering always that your wife and son
come first.'

'And you think a crisis is going to arise.'

'I sincerely hope not. But it is my business
to assume that it will, and prepare for it. As
here.' They had reached the large stone
troughs that held the water. There were two
of these, each about a hundred feet long, and
each roofed, but otherwise open to the
elements. Jessica went up to the first one, and
looked into the vat, which was perhaps six
feet deep and about a third full of stagnant
water. 'This is what we drink?'

Lucian grinned. 'And we're none of us
dying of typhoid, you mean? We add chlorine
every so often, and the water is filtered when
it reaches either the house or the village.'

'I'll believe you. But you have to admit that
it's pretty vulnerable.'

'Vulnerable to what?'

'Vulnerable to anyone who might mean you
no good and has a pocketful of, shall we say,
sarin.'

'Who would do that? He'd stand a chance

of killing everyone on the island. Just about all our people are related.'

'Suppose he, or she, didn't belong to the island?'

'He'd have to get here, first.'

'Is that impossible?'

Lucian gazed at her for several seconds. 'You want me to talk to them? Telling them what? Rowena says we need to keep this business under our hats.'

'We do. But aren't you on good terms with Urban, the headman?'

'We don't have anything like a headman here, save me. Urban is our senior citizen. I'd have to have a reason for asking him to keep an eye out for strangers.'

'Because they come across regularly, socially.'

'But none of them stays the night,' Lucian said, brightly. 'Well, not as a rule.'

'They wouldn't have to stay the night, Mr Lenghurst. Just disappear from the party for half an hour.'

'You seriously think someone might come across from Cat Island to poison us? All of us?'

'I seriously think we have to take every possibility into consideration. Let's take a walk into the village.'

'What are we going to tell him? Urban?'

'I have an idea. If you'll co-operate.'

'You mean we're going to be friends?'

'Allies, Lucian, allies. I'll tell you how we're going to handle this as we walk.'

166

They located Urban easily enough, sitting on the dock working on the outboard for his boat, wearing a tattered pair of shorts and an even more tattered straw hat. But then, seen without a T-shirt, he looked pretty battered himself; even the hair on his chest was white.

'Afternoon, borse,' he remarked. 'Afternoon, ma'am. Nice day for it.'

'Nice day for what?' Jessica asked.

'For whatever you want to do, ma'am.'

'This is Mrs Jones,' Luciant said, obeying Jessica's instructions. 'She's staying at the house.'

'I did see her this morning,' Urban said. 'With the madam.'

'That's right,' Jessica said, in apparent surprise. 'I remember you.'

'Mrs Jones wants your help,' Lucian explained. 'All of your help.'

Urban looked genuinely surprised.

'She has left her husband,' Lucian went on.

Now Urban looked vaguely alarmed.

'And she is afraid he might attempt to follow her here, or send someone to harm her.'

'That wouldn't be good, borse.'

'You're absolutely right. So what we want you – all of you – to do, is report to us any strangers who might wish to come to the cay, and not, under any circumstances, bring any stranger over without checking with us first.'

'I'd be ever so grateful,' Jessica said, fluttering her eyelashes.

'You got it, ma'am. You leave that with me.

167

I going tell them boys.'

'Thank you.' Jessica held out her hand, and after a moment, looking more surprised still, he took it.

'You are one hell of a woman,' Lucian remarked as they walked back along the beach to the house, the sun now drooping in the west. 'But I guess you know that.'

'I'm a professional, Mr Lenghurst. And I've been around a bit.'

'I admire you enormously.'

'Thank you.'

'So what's the secret of your success?'

Jessica considered. 'In one word?'

'Why not?'

'I'd have to say, concentration – on the matter in hand.'

'Which, at this moment, happens to be us. That is very reassuring. But surely self-confidence is as important?'

'I suppose that plays a part.'

'Based on your supreme skills.'

'Based upon the fact that a lot of people who have, from time to time, reckoned that I shouldn't be here, aren't here themselves, whereas I am. Still.'

'Touché.' His hand brushed hers, and he caught her fingers. 'You know, JJ, I...'

'Just don't say it, Mr Lenghurst.' Jessica freed her hand.

'Your prejudices, and your memory, run that deep, eh?'

'What you need to remember, Mr Lenghurst, is that you have a wife who has loyally supported you, above and beyond the call of duty, for more than fifteen years.'

'Ha,' he commented. 'I'm her slave. She made me her slave, and she keeps me locked up.'

'In rather pleasant surroundings, wouldn't you say? I can think of a lot of men who would give a great deal to enjoy this kind of slavery. The sun, the sea, all you can eat and drink, the use of that swish cruiser, all the sex even you can manage...'

'Sex? From her? You have to be joking. Don't you know she's a dyke?'

'My best friend is a dyke. Sometimes.'

'Shit! Don't tell me...'

'My private life is my private life, Mr Lenghurst. Anyway, don't you have ample other sources of supply? At least when Rowena isn't here?'

He tuned his head, sharply. 'Just what do you mean?'

'I'm speaking of your normal summer activities.'

'How do you know about that?'

'I'm a detective, remember.' They came in sight of the house.

Rowena was sitting on the back verandah drinking tea, the dogs at her feet. 'Join me.'

'That sounds a brilliant idea.' Jessica sat down, taking off her hat. Lucian wandered off.

'I had no idea that he followed you,' Rowena said. 'I hope he behaved himself?'

'His behaviour was exemplary,' Jessica said,

169

carefully.

'And did you accomplish anything?'

'I think so.' Jessica related their conversation with Urban.

'But that's brilliant,' Rowena said. 'You are a genius, JJ.'

Here we go again, Jessica thought.

'So now all we have to do is sit back and see what, or who, turns up,' Rowena said.

'Yes,' Jessica said thoughtfully. 'What's that boat doing there?'

The open boat had just come round the headland and was approaching the private beach.

Rowena squinted into the setting sun. 'That's Jerry and Felicity being dropped off.' She giggled. 'If it hadn't been, would you have got your gun and shot them up?'

'I would have requested them to remain offshore, if necessary at the point of my gun, until they had identified themselves.' She watched the boat nose into the shallows and Jerry jump over the bow, then hold up his hands for Felicity. They splashed in together and came up the slope from the beach. Jessica frowned. Felicity was carrying her bag rather than, as was usual, slinging it from her shoulder.

'Did you get any conch?' Rowena called, as they reached the steps.

'A couple,' Jerry said. 'We left them with Bartholemew. But we have a problem.'

'I'm all right, really,' Felicity protested.

Jessica stood up. Felicity was wearing her

bikini, which, as she approached, stood out in startling whiteness against the glowing red of her skin.

'God almighty!' Rowena remarked. 'You could have a second-degree burn.'

'Aloes,' Jerry said. 'We should use aloes.'

'I'm just a little sore,' Felicity said.

'Have we got aloes?' Jessica asked.

'It grows in the garden. Jerry, go and cut some.'

Jeremy went off.

'And you, come with me,' Jessica said. She led the way along the corridor.

'Please don't be angry,' Felicity asked. 'I didn't know the sun was so hot.'

'It's my fault,' Jessica conceded. 'I shouldn't have let you go, after the burn you got this morning. But I did tell you to wear barrier cream.'

'I did. But it all washed off.'

'And where is your hat?'

'Well, I didn't actually take a hat, as I knew we were going swimming.'

'Jesus!' Jessica opened the bedroom door. 'Take off that apology for cover and lie on the bed, on your face.'

'Can't I shower first?'

'I think, if you attempt to towel yourself, all your skin is going to come off in strips.'

'Shit!' Felicity took off her bikini and lay on the bed.

Rowena arrived, with Jerry, carrying several stalks oozing liquid. 'Here we are.'

'Great,' Jessica said. 'Do you mind, Jerry?'

Jeremy hesitated.

'Out,' his mother commanded.

He closed the door.

'Now let's see.' Rowena rubbed the end of one of the stems on Felicity's shoulder, and some more liquid trickled out.

Felicity jerked. 'Ooh!' And then she cried, 'What a terrible pong.'

'It does smell a bit strong,' Jessica agreed, using one of the stems herself to start coating Felicity's thighs and buttocks.

'How soon can I wash it off?' Felicity inquired.

'You can't.'

'What?'

'Well, not until tomorrow. Some of this skin is so burned it's broken...'

'You mean I'm going to be scarred?'

'Hopefully not.' Rowena was working down Felicity's back. 'The aloes will form a protective layer, allowing it to heal. But you must leave it on for twenty-four hours.'

'I'll smell like the devil's armpit.'

'You are already smelling like the devil's armpit,' Jessica pointed out.

'And you should stay in bed,' Rowena said. 'Certainly, under no circumstances must you leave the house and expose yourself to any more ultra-violet rays. Otherwise you could wind up in hospital.'

'Shit!' Felicity commented again.

Rowena went to the door, and looked over her shoulder. 'Such a pretty girl,' she remarked, and closed the door behind herself.

'Just what did she mean by that?' Felicity asked. 'That I *am* scarred for life?'

'No, no,' Jessica said reassuringly. 'Just that she fancies you.'

'She what?'

'Don't panic. She fancies me as well. But she's really of the closet variety.'

'Suppose she comes out of the closet?'

'Be tactful. Now, we have to somewhat review our plans, at least for the next day or two.'

'Oh, JJ, I am so terribly sorry.'

'There's no point in looking over your shoulder, save to remember not to let it happen again. Actually, it's not too bad a situation. I had intended us both to go into Arthur's Town tomorrow, as I have a pretty good idea that Jeremy and probably Theresa will be along. But you'll have to stay here and mind the fort.'

'But can you cope? The way things are they're unlikely to stick together.'

'I'll sort something out. Tell me, how did the snorkelling go?'

'Oh, it was great fun. Once Jerry taught me what to do, it was quite simple, really. And the underwater scenery ... it was out of this world.'

'And did he attempt to teach you anything else?'

Feliity giggled. 'I was tactful. Anyway, with that boatman chap, Bartholemew, there, I was chaperoned.'

'Well—' Jessica's mobile buzzed. 'Jones.'

'I tried to get you earlier,' the commander said in an aggrieved tone. 'But as usual you weren't there.'

'I was inspecting the island, sir.'

'You said that the last time.'

'It's bigger than it looks. How was the opera?'

'Lousy. Do you know what time it is?'

'Ten to six.'

'It is ten to eleven, Jones. And I am still working. Before I went out I called the Home Secretary and asked for instruction. After all, he set this whole damned thing up. He decided that the Florida Police *should* be informed of this development.'

'Won't this upset Lord Blandin?'

'He's going to have a word with him tomorrow, and explain the potential seriousness of the situation. Anyway, I immediately called the Yard and told them to get on with it. When I came home half an hour ago there was a call waiting for me. They have got through to Florida, and the Americans have decided to take the matter seriously. I suspect that they are anxious to find anything that might give them a reason to bring charges against Abriga, or any of his people. Now, JJ, nothing has changed from your point of view, save that they are sending a couple of their people to the Bahamas to interview the boy. He is, of course, out of their jurisdiction until and unless he sets foot on American soil, or until they ask the Bahamian government for his extradition. All of this will take a great deal of time, so, as I say, nothing will change, as far as you are concerned, for the immediate future.'

'Except that we are going to be visited by a couple of Miami detectives.'

'Is that a problem? You can consider them as reinforcements, should you need them.'

Jessica sighed. 'There are two problems, sir.'

'Oh, really, JJ. Are you sure you're not nit-picking?'

'One is that, if they are Miami policemen, they are extremely likely to be of Hispanic origin and appearance. As will Abriga's hit man, or hit men.'

'But these fellows will have their warrants and badges to show you.'

'Yes, sir. But to present their credentials they will have not only to be allowed to land, but also to come within arm's length of me and our clients. I am setting up a system whereby all strangers are excluded from the island.'

'Can you do that?'

'With Mrs Lenghurst's permission, yes. And I have that permission.'

'Hm. Can't have you shooting up a couple of Yankee coppers, eh? Ha ha.'

'Ha ha, sir. I don't think any Florida native would care to call himself a Yankee.'

'Is that a fact? Well, I know what we'll do: we will contact the Miami Police force again, give them your mobile number, and tell them to call you before travelling to Cat Island, so that they may be given access to the cay. How

175

does that take you?'

'The idea of giving my mobile number to a foreign department does not take me at all, sir. However, if there is no alternative. But there is the second problem.'

'What second problem?'

'In accordance with your instructions, sir, I have not told Mrs Lenghurst the true story. But that will now become necessary, in view of these new circumstances.'

'Hm. Yes, I suppose you're right. Well, handle it tactfully. I am now going to bed. Keep me abreast of developments, but not before tomorrow morning. I know you can handle it, JJ. Good night.'

'That,' Jessica remarked, 'is just about all I need.'

'Still, it must be nice to have someone like the commander with so much confidence in you,' Felicity said. 'Do you think I'll ever achieve that position?'

'Possibly,' Jessica said. 'If you remember to keep out of the sun.'

The evening, predictably, was somewhat grim. Theresa appeared only for dinner, and then went straight back to her room; her already well-browned complexion did not appear to have suffered any ill-effects from her afternoon's sunbathing. Lucian also appeared only for the meal, apparently preferring to spend his time in his office, which was on the upper floor next to the master bedroom. 'He has his computer and his Internet connection up there,' Rowena explained.

'Using what?' Jessica asked. 'Do you have telephone connection with Cat Island?'

'No, no. He has several mobiles.'

Jeremy was also uncommunicative, beyond inquiring after Felicity, who had her meal in her room. 'She is going to be all right?' he asked.

'I think so,' his mother said. 'Although she's almost certain to have a bad reaction tomorrow. But it was very naughty of you to allow her to expose herself for so long.'

'It just never crossed my mind. I was diving. She was just floating around on the surface with her back up. I figured that if she felt she was burning, she'd get back into the boat and put a shirt on. It was only when I packed it in after a couple of hours that I realized she didn't have a shirt. I gave her mine, of course, but I suppose by then the damage had been done.'

'Yes,' Jessica said.

'May I see her?'

'No.'

Jeremy looked at his mother.

'I think the sergeant is right,' Rowena said. 'Why don't you go and make it up with Terry?'

'It's her business to make it up with me,' he remarked, coldly.

'So, what are we going to do with our evening?' Rowena asked after supper. 'I know: Chinese checkers. I adore Chinese checkers. Don't you, JJ?'

'Ah...' Jessica had already decided not to

bring Rowena up to date regarding her son's real problem until she heard from the Miami Police, but the idea of spending the evening closeted with her did not appeal.

Fortunately she was saved by Lucian. 'Just don't stay up too late,' he recommended, rejoining them for a nightcap. 'We're making an early start in the morning. Eight o'clock on the dock. Right?'

'Well, in that case,' Jessica said, 'I think I will turn in, if you don't mind, Rowena. Actually, I've had a bit too much sun myself, so a good night's sleep won't do any harm.'

Rowena looked disappointed, but kissed her goodnight.

'How do you feel?' JJ asked Felicity, back in their bedroom.

'Like shit.'

'Well, you did bring it on yourself. And it can only get better. Would you like an aspirin?'

'I'd like two aspirins,' Felicity said.

Despite the sedatives, she spent half the night in the bathroom.

'Which end?' Jessica asked.

'Both,' she groaned. 'And my head is gonging. Oh, JJ, I feel such an idiot.'

'You're ill. I would say you have a severe case of heatstroke. It'll clear in a day or two. But until then, stay in bed and drink as much liquid as you can stand. I'll tell Millie. But absolutely no alcohol.'

'Big deal.'

'Just remember that you're no use to me unless you are a hundred per cent fit. So it's your duty to get fit again just as rapidly as possible.'

'Yes, ma'am.'

Jessica showered and put on a dress to look as feminine as possible. 'So, I'll see you later. Millie will bring you some breakfast.'

'I couldn't eat a thing.'

'I'll tell her to bring you a jug of coconut milk. That's both food and drink, and it tastes nice, as well.'

'Ugh! And you're off to Arthur's Town?'

'When I've breakfasted. Don't worry, I'll be back for lunch.'

'Is Jerry going with you?'

'As far as I know. Just have a restful morning.'

Jerry was going with them, but Theresa apparently was not. 'She's breakfasting in her room,' Rowena said, clearly irritated. 'She really is turning out to be a sulky little witch. She's your responsibility, you know, Jerry.'

'I'll have a word with her when we get back. You look good enough to eat, JJ.'

'You say the sweetest things,' Jessica replied.

'But he's absolutely right,' Rowena agreed, 'I think you should wear a dress all the time. It's a crime to hide those legs.'

'Thank you, but it's not entirely convenient if I have to undertake any action. Wouldn't you agree, Mr Lenghurst?'

Lucian, seated on the other side of the table, finished his coffee and stood up. 'Time

179

to go. We want to be back before it gets too hot.'

But for all his efforts it was past nine before they actually left the house. Jessica walked beside him on their way to the dock. 'Is there any word on your friend Brigitte?'

'She's on her way, and strengthening. Winds of a hundred and ten.'

'But you're not worried?'

'I still think she'll miss us. But if she doesn't change course by tomorrow morning I'll put up the storm shutters, just in case.' He glanced at her. 'Don't tell me you're scared, JJ?'

'I'm wondering if she can be used in a defensive capacity. What happens if she gets too close?'

'I get your drift. If she shows any signs of turning in towards the islands, they'll shut down, at least along this eastern fringe.'

'Transport too?'

'Definitely. All planes will be grounded, and all boats will take shelter.'

'Sounds interesting.'

'You have me thinking you actually *want* this thing to come ashore.'

'Every little helps,' Jessica agreed.

The cruiser was as luxurious inside as it had appeared from outside, with a spacious saloon over a sound-proofed engine room – housing a pair of hundred-and-twenty-five-horsepower diesels, as Lucian proudly showed to Jessica – a master cabin aft and two more staterooms forward, and a comfortable dining saloon-cum-galley immediately down a short ladder forward of the wheelhouse. Jessica had supposed the yacht on which she had, willy-nilly, spent several months a year previously had possessed the last word in navigational equipment, but she had to admit that this little ship – called, predictably, *Rowena* – surpassed it.

It also, naturally, possessed a flying bridge with an upper steering position, on which they gathered as Lucian started the engines. 'What sort of range do you have?' Jessica asked.

'If I'm hurrying, two hundred miles. At half-speed, she'll get us to Miami. Let her go, Bartholemew,' he shouted.

The boatman freed the mooring warps and reeled them in, then busied himself shipping the fenders, and Lucian used his thrusters to move the ship away from the dock. He certainly handled her to perfection, Jessica thought, as he turned her, one engine slow ahead and the other slow astern, towards the narrow entrance, and then gunned both ahead.

It was a superbly dramatic day. The clouds were building ahead of the storm, but remained white, piled one on top of the other up to a height, Jessica estimated, of several thousand feet. Between these immense pillars the sky was blue. There was again a fresh breeze, whipping up the sea into a considerable chop; no sooner were they outside the little harbour and steering into the wind than a cloud of spray came over the bow, quite a lot of it flying far enough aft to scatter across the bridge.

'Bugger this,' Rowena growled, and went below.

Jessica found it exhilarating, although she had to sit on the steering bench, beside Lucian, to keep her skirt under control. 'It'll be better when we turn off,' he said. 'Say fifteen minutes.'

'I'm enjoying it.'

'I'd forgotten that you are an old sea … ah, hand.'

I simply must not let myself like this man, Jessica told herself. And in fact the island, viewed from the sea, was intensely interesting, though she was surprised at how small it actually was. They were already abreast of the place where she and Rowena had bathed the previous day, and in front of them was a considerable area of broken water. 'That looks like a reef,' she remarked.

'It is. But there's a passage.' He pointed at the aircraft circling over the mainland. 'The Nassau plane.'

Which must mean they aren't bothered about the weather, Jessica thought. But she was more interested in the broken water in front of them – which Lucian clearly knew well, as he turned the cruiser away from the wind and through the tumbling waves. Jessica could not suppress a quick intake of breath as she saw the coral heads to either side, just beneath the surface but uncovering with each trough. Not wanting to distract him, she waited until they

182

were in the calm water beyond, then asked, 'Does that mean that anyone wishing to get to the windward side of the island has to know that passage?'

'That's right, if they don't want to wind up swimming.'

'Well, that is the most encouraging thing I've heard since arriving here. It means we don't have to protect the east coast.'

'I wouldn't get too euphoric. All the local fishermen know this passage.'

They were now cruising along the east coast of the main island. 'Where's that aircraft?' she asked.

'Oh, it'll be down by now.' He reduced speed and Jessica stood up to watch the harbour and town unfolding before her. 'Have a look.'

There was a pair of binoculars lying on the console. Jessica picked them up and levelled them, picking out a bank, and a supermarket, more than one church, and an obvious hotel, with three taxis just arriving, presumably from the airport – out of one of which there was stepping a woman who wore a smart pale-green trouser suit and carried a small suitcase; she was tall, slim, and had long yellow hair.

The Guest

Jessica sat down, replacing the glasses as she did so. She felt quite breathless. Even if she had known this had to happen, she had not expected it so soon. But then she reflected that she was over-reacting; there was no certainty that this was Greta Garcia, and if it were, this was the best possible moment for her to show up, when *she* had the initiative. The question was: what was she going to do about it? She wished Theresa had come along, to provide positive identification.

She glanced at Lucian, but he was concentrating on entering the harbour, and had not noticed any of her reactions. Feet sounded on the ladder and Rowena and Jeremy emerged. 'What do you think of our metropolis?' Rowena asked.

'From here, quaint. Do I get to explore?'

'Surely. I leave the shopping to Lucian and Bartholemew.'

'I thought you wanted to talk to the supermarket people about strangers,' Lucian said, expertly bringing the cruiser alongside the dock.

'Perhaps you could do that,' Jessica suggested, 'using the same formula as we did with

Urban yesterday.'

Bartholemew, having put out the fenders, tossed the after mooring warp to a waiting pair of hands, and now he hurried forward to deal with the other one.

They stepped on to the dock, and she gazed at the blonde woman, who was standing about twenty yards away, speaking with one of the men who had helped moor them, and undoubtedly asking about the cruiser. That she should be interested in the obviously expensive craft was not remarkable – quite a few onlookers were staring at it – but she was the only one asking about it; the locals all knew both her owners and where she had come from.

'What a whopper,' Jeremy said. 'Do you reckon she's on her own?'

'I don't see anyone with her,' Jessica said, and had an idea. 'Why don't you invite her to visit on the cay?'

Jeremy glanced at his mother, who did not look amused. 'Really, JJ, haven't we got enough problems?' She clearly did not connect the woman with what Jessica had told her of the Aspern bomber.

'You be here in an hour,' Lucian told them. 'Come along, Bartholemew.'

Jessica came to a decision: 'Is there some place we can have a drink and a chat?'

'Of course there is. But I thought you wanted to explore?'

'I've changed my mind. I'd rather sit and talk with you.'

'Oh.' Rowena looked perplexed for a moment, but also pleased. 'Right. That's great. You coming, Jerry?'

'Ah ... not right now. I've a little shopping to do.' He followed his father and Bartholemew towards the supermarket.

'He's such a dear boy,' Rowena said. 'So tactful. We'll go to the hotel bar.' She led the way, and they found themselves walking behind the blonde woman. 'She is well built, isn't she?' Rowena remarked, somewhat wistfully. 'Did you have something specific you wanted to talk about?'

'Her.'

'Eh?' Rowena stopped walking and turned towards her.

'Let's have that drink.'

The little hotel was not far, and they settled themselves in the small lounge bar, from which they could see into Reception, where the blonde woman appeared to be checking in. A waiter brought rum punches. 'I hope you are going to tell me what this is all about?' Rowena asked.

'I think it would be a good idea to invite that woman to visit with us on the cay.'

Rowena all but choked on her drink. 'I thought you were joking. I've never seen her before in my life. You said we shouldn't allow strangers on to the cay.'

'I said, "allow". I didn't say we shouldn't invite them.'

Rowena stared at her. 'You fancy her! You little devil! And I thought...'

'There's no need to be jealous: I'm not meaning to leap into bed with her. But I would like to have her somewhere close by and under my control.'

'You have completely lost me.'

'OK. I promise to tell you exactly what's on my mind, when we get back to the cay, providing we have this lady with us. Think how happy it'll make Jerry.'

'She's a bit old for Jerry, wouldn't you say?'

'She's no older than me, and he had a go at me, remember? Is it a deal? She's coming over.'

'Oh, all right.'

The woman had left Reception and was entering the bar. She smiled at Jessica, placed her case on a vacant table and made for the counter.

Jessica wondered just what was in that case, but she intended to find out. She got up and went to the bar herself. 'Hi.'

The woman turned to look at her more closely. Her face was too strongly aquiline for beauty, but was undoubtedly handsome, while there could be no arguing with the beauty of her hair, or the attractiveness of her clearly long legs and full figure. Her blue eyes were the coldest Jessica had ever seen, even when she smiled. But she was clearly reflecting that to have someone from the cay to which she needed to gain access actually making advances meant that this had to be her lucky day. 'Hi,' she responded.

'I'm Jessica Jones,' Jessica said. 'And that is

187

my friend, Rowena Lenghurst.'

'My pleasure.' Greta Garcia spoke with a faint American accent. 'I'm Gloria George.'

This choice as obviously dictated by the initials on her case, 'G.G.'.

'Are you up here on you own?'

'Island-hopping. I'm looking for a place to buy.'

Jessica seized the opening. 'Rowena owns that cay offshore. She may be able to advise you. Join us.'

Greta Garcia hesitated just a moment, then said, 'Why not?'

Jessica did the introductions.

'I saw you coming over on that terrific motor cruiser,' Greta said. 'You own that?'

'That's right,' Rowena said.

'Then I guess you're out of my class when it comes to buying a beach hut.'

'You have to start somewhere,' Rowena said, waiting for Jessica to take the lead.

She opted for the easy way first. 'Why don't you come across and look at the cay, anyway. Might give you some ideas.'

'I couldn't possibly impose.'

Obviously, if she knew Theresa was in residence, she couldn't risk a casual visit. On the other hand, if she had come here to complete her revenge for the death of her husband, she could surely be tempted into seeing if she could complete the job in one fell swoop, as it were. But she was not a fool. It would have to be done the hard way. What had the commander said? That if she broke

188

the law in the Bahamas, except in the line of duty, she would have to suffer for it. But surely it would be a grave abandonment of duty to have this woman sitting on their door-step, making plans, and do nothing about it. 'What a shame,' JJ said, and made a face. 'Isn't this rum punch dreadful? I'm sure we could make a better one on the boat. Don't you think so, Rowena?'

'Ah...' Rowena was clearly in a complete fog. 'We could try.'

'Why don't you come down to the boat with us, Miss George? We could show you over her, make you a proper drink, and then you could meet Jeremy.'

Greta's eyes gave the slightest flicker. 'Who is Jeremy?'

'Mrs Lenghurst's son. He's a great guy. And I know he'd love to meet you. Wouldn't he, Rowena?'

'Ah ... I suppose he would.'

'So ... shall we go?'

Greta hesitated but, as Jessica had hoped, the temptation was too great; she could never have met Jeremy, as he had never heard of her until yesterday, and as there had been no mention of Theresa, she had to presume, accurately, that she was not with them on this visit to the mainland. Nor could she possibly find anything sinister in this cute little blonde who was so over-enthusiastic about her com-pany. 'Sure,' she said. 'I'll just fetch my case.'

'You're bringing your case?' Rowena asked.

'I think that's a better idea than leaving it

here,' Jessica said. 'Unless you'd like to take it up to your room, first.'

But again, as she had expected, Greta was not going to be separated from her bag. 'It's not heavy,' she said.

Rowena paid for the drinks with a gold credit card and they strolled along the now brilliantly sunlit street towards the dock.

'What part of the States are you from?' Jessica asked, chattily.

'Miami. And you're British, right?'

'Absolutely.'

'Miami?' Rowena asked. 'That's where...'

'We have another guest,' Jessica said. 'A girl from Florida. Theresa Abriga. Do you know her?'

'Florida is a big state,' Greta said.

'I suppose it is. I've never been there. Here we are.'

They stood on the dock before the cruiser. 'Some ship,' Greta said. 'I reckon you could go down to Nassau in that.'

'Nassau?' Jessica scoffed. 'This boat will take you direct to Miami.'

She could just about hear the tumblers falling in Greta's brain as they climbed on board and Rowena unlocked the saloon door. She might still not be able to believe her good fortune at being taken into the very heart of the family she intended to destroy, but the way she was being presented with the means to complete her self-appointed mission and be back in Florida before anyone could even suspect what had happened had to be irresistible; she would be telling herself that if she did not seize this opportunity she might never get another.

Greta entered the saloon. 'Some ship,' she said again.

'It is, isn't it?' Jessica agreed, closing the door behind them. But the saloon had huge windows to left and right, and was clearly visible from the deck. 'It's even better below,' she said. 'And that's where the booze is – right, Rowena?'

Rowena was actually standing by the short ladder leading down to the galley. If she was still evidently totally mystified by the situation, she was loyally prepared to continue accepting Jessica's lead. 'I'll just see what we have.' She went down the ladder.

'After you,' Jessica invited.

Greta had to duck her head before reaching the full headroom of the galley. Rowena was opening a cupboard. Jessica stood immediately behind Greta. 'I'll take the suitcase, shall I?' she asked.

'I'd rather keep it by me.'

'I said, I'll take it,' Jessica said, dropping the dulcet tones she had been using this far. 'Greta.'

Greta turned, sharply, and found herself looking into the barrel of the Skorpion.

'It doesn't make a lot of noise,' Jessica said. 'But it does make a big hole.'

Rowena had also turned. 'Oh, my God!' she gasped. 'JJ...'

'Step aside,' Jessica said.

191

Rowena hesitated, and Greta acted, lifting her suitcase to block any shot, and kicking violently. Jessica had expected some reaction, but Rowena's being in the line of fire prevented her from using the pistol, and the speed and violence of the movement surprised her; she stepped back, her knees hit the seat by the table, and she sat down. She was handicapped by not really wishing to kill this woman, or even seriously hurt her, at this time, but she immediately realized that the latter at least might be necessary, as Greta swung the suitcase to hit her on the shoulder and tumble her off the seat and on to the deck. Before she could recover, Greta had kicked her wrist, and sent the Skorpion flying.

Jessica gasped, as much with fury as with either pain or concern; it was a very long time since anyone had treated her like that – she had forgotten that this woman was not just an outraged widow but also a professional assassin.

But Greta too could suffer from overconfidence. Considering Jessica immobilized, she placed the suitcase on the table, flipped it open, and took out an old- fashioned Browning automatic pistol, a weapon quite capable of blowing a hole in the side of the yacht.

Rowena screamed. Jessica propelled herself along the deck, kicking off her sandals as she did so, her skirt riding up to her thighs to give her legs maximum freedom of movement, and slammed her toes into Greta's knee.

'Bitch!' Greta turned, dropping the silencer she had been about to fit to the pistol. But Jessica was now on her knees, throwing her arms round Greta's legs and twisting with all her highly trained strength. Greta fell over, her gun exploding as she did so; the bullet smashed into the flying-bridge deck above their heads and went right through, blasting a gap in the fibreglass.

Rowena screamed again.

Jessica had now reached her feet and, as Greta turned towards her again, she swung her arm in a hammer blow, hand held rigid, its edge slamming into Greta's forearm with paralysing force. Greta yelped and dropped the gun, but Jessica, standing above her, was not prepared to take any more risks. She swung her hand again in another devastating chop, striking Greta where her neck joined her shoulder. Greta gave a gasp and slumped against the cushions.

'You've killed her!' Rowena gasped.

'I don't think so.' Jessica checked the unconscious woman's pulse. 'She'll live.' She retrieved her shoulder bag, rolled Greta on to her face, pulled her arms behind her back and handcuffed her wrists. Then she straightened her own dress.

'I wish you'd tell me what's going on,' Rowena said. 'This woman—'

'In a moment. Go outside and make sure no one heard the racket.'

Rowena hesitated, then obeyed. Jessica replaced her pistol in her bag, then checked the contents of Greta's case, and was relieved to discover that she had not made a mistake. She listened to Rowena talking to someone on the dock, and braced herself for some awkwardness, especially as Greta was beginning to stir. She pulled her into a sitting position against the cushions, her head lolling.

Rowena reappeared. 'There were some people who heard.'

Jessica straightened Greta's shirt and jacket. 'What did you tell them?'

'That a light bulb exploded and I screamed.'

'Brilliant. Now all we have to do is get out of here.'

Rowena stared at Greta. 'This woman ... have we kidnapped her?'

'We have arrested her.'

'You mean we're going to hand her over to the police? What are we going to charge her with?'

'First of all...' Jessica said, and looked at the companionway as the little ship rocked to heavy feet coming on board.

'That's the boys,' Rowena said.

A moment later Lucian appeared at the steps. 'What the hell is going on? Some chap said there was an explosion. God damn!' He was looking at the splintered hole in the overhead deck. 'Who the fuck did that?'

'This lady,' Jessica explained.

He gazed at Greta, and his jaw dropped.

Jeremy was behind him. 'Holy shit!'

'Where's the crew?' Jessica asked.

'He's in the cockpit with the groceries. He'll be down in a moment.'

'Then can we return to the cay?'

'I'd like to know what we're doing, first.'

'Then keep Bartholemew out for a moment.'

Lucian looked at his wife.

'I don't know anything more about this than you do,' Rowena said. 'But I'm prepared to go along with JJ.'

He went up the companionway.

Jeremy stared at Greta. 'What happened to her?'

'JJ laid her out,' Rowena explained. 'I've never seen anything like it.'

Jeremy looked at Jessica. 'But...'

Lucian retuned. 'He's hanging on. Now tell us what this is all about.'

'Close the door,' Jessica said.

He obeyed.

Greta was now definitely waking up. Her eyes opened, her head moved. 'God!' she muttered. 'What happened?'

Jessica sat beside her. 'You and me fell out. Now listen very carefully.'

Greta turned her head, slowly. 'I am in such pain.'

'And you are going to be in a lot more pain if you attempt to move or make a sound unless requested to do so. Understand, Greta?'

Greta blinked at her.

'I thought her name was Gloria,' Rowena said.

'It had to be "G" because those are the

initials on her case. Her name is Greta Garcia. Ring a bell?'

'Holy shit!' Jeremy said again. 'That was...' He bit his lip.

'Spot on. Rodrigo Garcia was her husband, until you stuck a knife into him.'

'What?!' Rowena shrieked. 'How can you say such a thing?'

'Ask him.'

'It was him or me,' Jeremy said.

'Oh, my God!' Rowena sank on to the seat beside Jessica.

'Bastard,' Greta remarked.

'Remember what I said,' Jessica told her.

'Let me get this straight,' Lucian requested. 'You killed some character, Jerry?'

'It's not true,' Rowena wailed. 'It can't be true. Say it isn't true, Jerry.'

'He came at me with a gun! What was I to do?'

'My Rodrigo had no gun,' Greta said. 'You murdered him.'

Rowena gave another shriek.

Jeremy stared at Greta. 'Terry said he had a gun...'

'So this female...' Lucian said.

'She wanted to avenge her husband,' Jessica sad. 'So she went to England, ascertained where Rowena and Jerry were staying, murdered the concierge, and used explosives to set fire to the building.'

'But she could've killed everyone in that block.'

'I don't think that would have bothered her

196

all that much. Blowing up people is her profession. Or was, before she temporarily retired to be a housewife.'

'We'll have to get hold of the police. I take it you can prove all this?'

Jessica delved into the suitcase, held up the roll of semtex. 'This is not normal gear for a holiday in the Bahamas.'

'Right. I'll go ashore and tell the local bobby.'

'I don't think that would be a good idea, right this minute, for several reasons. One is that if she is taken to Nassau by the local police I would bet my last penny that she would be out of there on bail in twenty-four hours. I'd prefer to take her back to the cay, where we can keep her out of mischief until I can sort things out. I would also like to have a chat with her.'

'What for? Isn't she the one you're protecting us against?'

'Actually, not in the first instance. I told you, she no longer works for Abriga. But she did once, and she knows how his people work, and probably even who are the ones who will come after you.'

'You mean there's more?' He gazed at his wife, accusingly.

'I didn't know all this was going to happen,' Rowena wailed.

'Look, will you please play it my way for the time being?' Jessica requested. 'Get us back to the cay.'

A last hesitation, then he nodded. 'I suppose you know what you're doing. What am I to tell Bartholemew?'

'Nothing, until we get back to the cay. We'll put her in one of your staterooms.'

'Good idea,' Jeremy said enthusiastically. 'I'll help you.' He grasped Greta's arms. 'Up you get.'

Lucian went on deck, while Jessica and Jeremy half-carried Greta forward into the first stateroom. 'Now, you sit on the bunk and behave yourself,' Jessica suggested.

Greta sat down. 'Can't you take these cuffs off? My shoulder is in agony.'

Jessica listened to the engines starting up. 'We'll be back at the cay in half an hour. We may be able to take them off there.'

'I'll stay here and keep an eye on her,' Jeremy said.

'I don't think that will be necessary. She can't throw those cuffs.'

'Well, don't you think we ought to search her? She may have a concealed weapon.'

'You,' Jessica said, 'are a singularly nasty young man. Clear off.'

'Only trying to help.' He left the cabin.

'And close the door,' Jessica commanded. He obeyed.

'Although, you know, he has a point,' Jessica said. 'I'll be as decent as I can.'

'Who *are* you?'

'I work for an institution called the Metropolitan Police, Scotland Yard.'

'You're a *copper*? Shit!'

'Not your day, is it? Now sit still.' She felt in

Greta's jacket pockets, and then her trouser pockets. 'Clean. Now, I'm terribly sorry, but it is possible that you may have a knife hidden away somewhere, like friend Jeremy said. Spread your legs.'

'I have rights, and you have no jurisdiction here.'

'Been studying law, have you? The only rights that matter at this moment are that you are helpless and I am in control. I don't think the Lenghursts would offer a word of objection if I suggested that the best thing to do with you would be to toss you overboard once we get on the far side of the cay, where we can't be seen from the mainland.'

Greta panted. 'What do you want of me?'

'Right now I'm trying to make sure you do not have a concealed weapon. If you won't co-operate, I'll get Jeremy back and tell him to take over. He'll have you stripped naked in a second, and what would happen after that I wouldn't care to imagine. So give.'

Greta spread her legs, and Jessica ascertained that there was no knife beneath the material of her trousers. 'There we go. Now just relax.'

'You have not told me what you wish of me.'

'Well, having got over that hurdle, my main objective is to stop you carrying out your wish to avenge your husband's death, at the expense of my clients.'

'Do you have a husband?'

'Right this minute, no.'

'But if you did, and he was stabbed to death

199

in cold blood, would you not wish to avenge him?'

'If you are referring to my husband, and not being theoretical, the answer is that I would probably have shaken the assassin by the hand. However, one murder is never solved by another, unless it's judicial. I won't talk about your previous crimes, but you *are* guilty of the murder of the night porter at the Aspern Building.'

'You cannot prove that.'

'I think we can have a go.'

'You mean to take me back to England?'

'I'm going to take advice on that,' Jessica said.

She closed the cabin door behind her. Jeremy was waiting in the galley. 'Do these things lock?' she asked.

'Not from the outside. We've never had a reason before.'

'Well, being handcuffed, I don't think she can possibly get out, but I'd like you to stay here and keep an eye on it. From here, mind. I don't want you to go inside.'

'Yes, ma'am,' he agreed, with facetious subservience.

Jessica went up to the bridge, hanging on in the breeze, which, as they were now steering into it, was quite fresh, sending clouds of spray over the bow.

Rowena was seated beside her husband on the bench. 'What have you done with her?'

'Nothing, yet.'

'We ought to bust her ass,' Lucian growled.

'Look at that hole.' It was actually situated between his legs. 'A few inches further forward, it would have smashed into the console and wrecked it.'

'Always look on the bright side,' Jessica recommended. 'It didn't.'

'But what *are* we going to do with her?' Rowena asked.

'Keep her under wraps, at least for a while. Doing that, we've removed one factor from the hostile equation. And I'm still pretty sure I can persuade her to give us some information – which may be vital – on Abriga's methods: how he may try to get at us, in what numbers, and so on.'

'Supposing he even knows we're on the cay,' Rowena said, optimistically.

'If she could find out so easily, he can do it even more easily.'

'So you mean to keep her on the cay? What are we going to tell the servants?'

'How trustworthy are they?'

'Well, Millie and Truman know who butters their bread.'

'Then just tell them we have another guest. If they don't see too much of her – well, they're not seeing too much of either Theresa or Felicity, at the moment.'

'And Bartholemew?'

'Same thing.'

'He's bound to notice the hole in the deck, if he hasn't already.'

'Tell him I was showing you my gun, and it went off accidentally.'

'Does he know you have a gun?'

'Rowena,' Jessica said patiently, 'nothing in this world is perfect. You will have to do the best you can.'

'When you say, "persuade"...' Lucian ventured, flushing as he glanced at her.

'Down, boy,' Jessica said. 'Mrs Garcia is now the property of the Metropolitan Police.'

He concentrated on conning them through the reef, ears still glowing, and a few minutes later they were tied up at the dock, where Truman and two other men were waiting, with a handcart to transfer the shopping to the house.

'Here's a problem,' Rowena said.

'Leave it with me.' Jessica slid down the ladder and into the saloon, then went below.

Jeremy was still sitting at the table. 'How do we handle this?' he asked. 'Getting her ashore, I mean.'

'Go talk to your mother,' Jessica said, and opened the stateroom door.

Greta was still seated on the lower bunk, wedged against the bulkhead. 'God, that was dreadful,' she said. 'I feel quite sick.'

'Well, you'll be on dry land in a moment. If you promise to behave.'

Greta looked at her.

Jessica sat beside her. 'You see, I would like to release your wrists, so as not to excite the natives. Now, I should point out that this is not a matter of life or death. These people all live on the cay by courtesy of the Lenghursts, and most of them work for the family in some capacity or another. So you see, if it comes to making a decision whether to support you or the family, it will be no contest. I am merely trying to save you the embarrassment of being taken ashore in handcuffs. You with me?'

Greta continued to stare at her, face expressionless, but Jessica could tell she was thinking very hard, weighing the odds ... and, hopefully, deciding that her chances would be greater if she was patient, and waited for her captors to lower their guard. There was no harm in encouraging that line of thought. 'I should also point out,' she went on, 'that you took me by surprise just now. That will not happen again. And if I have to deal with you again, I will break something.' She smiled. 'Of yours, not mine. Just remember that while you have made a career out of shooting people, knifing them and blowing them up, I am pretty good at all of those things too, and also at taking them apart with my hands. So please be sensible. Right?'

Greta inhaled, slowly and deeply. 'I will not cause trouble.'

'There's a good girl. Turn over.'

Greta obeyed, and Jessica unlocked the handcuffs and took them off. Then she stepped away, resting her hand on her shoulder bag, which now contained both guns, just in case her prisoner had a rush of blood to the head. But Greta merely straightened her suit. Jessica opened the door and stepped into the passage, waiting for Greta to pass her.

Jeremy was just returning from the deck. 'Hey! You've taken off the cuffs.'

'Greta has promised to co-operate.'

'Oh.' He looked disappointed.

Jessica escorted her on deck and they stepped on to the dock. The waiting men merely glanced at them, and they walked up the path, past the helicopter pad to the tennis court. 'Pretty good,' Greta remarked.

'Isn't it?' Jessica agreed, and waited for Rowena to catch them up.

'What are we going to do with her?' Rowena asked.

'Put her in the spare bedroom, if that's OK with you – the one used by Arnie.'

'Oh. Right. I'll leave that with you, shall I? About lunch...'

'Again, if it's all right with you, she can lunch with us.'

'Oh,' Rowena said again. 'If you think that's proper.'

'Well, we have to feed her, and she's promised to behave.'

'Yes, but she tried to blow us up, to kill us.'

'I remember reading in Winston Churchill's memoirs,' Jessica said, 'that the day after the Japanese attack on Pearl Harbour, the Japanese ambassador, having received his marching orders, called on the Prime Minister to take formal leave. The two men bowed to each other. When the ambassador had left, Churchill was criticized for having shown so much courtesy to a detestable foe, whereupon he replied, "When you are going to hang a man, you should always be polite."'

'Brilliant,' Jeremy said from immediately behind his mother.

'You can't hang me,' Greta declared.

'Sadly, no. But before too long you may wish we had. Come along.'

They approached the front verandah, and the dogs emerged from the house and bounded towards them. Greta stopped walking and tensed.

'Relax,' Jessica said. 'They'll only eat you if Mrs Lenghurst tells them to.'

Behind the dogs, Theresa appeared. She wore a bikini, and looked in a good enough humour until she saw Greta. 'Oh, my God!' Now she looked ready to run back into the house.

'Easy,' Jessica said. 'At the moment, she's harmless.'

'You mean they know each other?' Rowena asked.

'Well, of course they do. They're out of the same stable. Say hello, Greta.'

'Bitch,' Greta remarked.

'Do you think this is going to work?' Rowena asked.

'Of course it is. Apologize, Greta.'

'I apologize,' Greta said in a low voice.

'But what is she *doing* here?' Theresa wailed.

'Being kept out of trouble. I'll take the suitcase,' Jessica told Truman. 'It's through there.'

Greta went into the lounge.

'Keep going,' Jessica told her.

She went into the games room.

'Through here.' Jessica indicated the door into the lobby, then escorted her, first of all, to her bedroom. 'How are you feeling?'

'Like shit.' Felicity lay on the bed, on her face, in the nude. Her skin still glowed, and despite the application of aloes was starting to peel. 'I suppose you've been living it up.'

'Trying to. By the way, this is Mrs Greta Garcia.'

Felicity rose to her knees with a startled squawk, twisting round to look at the intruder, and grabbing a pillow to hold against herself. 'What did you say?'

'Fact. Our handsome bomber-cum-murderess herself.'

'Shit! In our bedroom?'

'Don't panic. At the moment she's co-operating. Greta, I'd like you to meet my partner, Detective-Constable Felicity Hewitt.'

Greta looked Felicity up and down. 'Nice perfume you're wearing. Are you always this colour?'

'Why, you...'

'Easy,' Jessica said. 'And you want to be careful, Greta. She hits even harder than I do.'

'You mean you hit her?' Felicity asked.

'It seemed a good idea at the time. Now, Greta, come with me.' She showed her into the fourth bedroom. 'Here you have a very pleasant bedroom, en suite, where I am sure you will be comfortable for a few days.'

'A few *days*?'

'Or however long it takes.'

'What takes?'

'Whatever it is.' She placed Greta's suitcase on the bed. 'I'll just have a look through here.' She took out the box of cartridges. 'As I've confiscated your gun, you won't be needing these. And I'm sure you won't be needing this semtex. Now, Greta, I suggested you have a wash and brush up. I will return for you in half an hour, and we will have lunch. And please, no funny business. Or it's back in the cuffs. Right?'

Greta sat on the bed.

Jessica closed and locked the door, then carried the cartridges and the explosive into her bedroom.

Felicity was still kneeling on the bed, her internal discomfort momentarily forgotten. 'My God! Isn't that semtex?'

'Our friend believes in being prepared for every eventuality.'

'What are we going to do with it?'

'Keep it as evidence.'

'Where?'

'I think right here would be safest.'

'You mean we're to sleep with that stuff under our pillow?'

'Under the bed would be better.'

'Will you *please* tell me what's going on? Where'd she come from? What is she doing here?'

'As before, just listen.' Jessica closed the bedroom door and called London. 'Why, Mrs Norton, what sort of day are you having?'

'It is raining, Jones.'

'What a shame. We have wall-to-wall sunshine here. In fact...' She regarded Felicity, who was cautiously pulling a shirt over her shoulders. '...for some of us there is a shade too much. The boss still around?' She knew it was just after five in England.

'Of course he is. I suppose you wish to speak with him.'

'We'll make a detective of you yet, Mrs N.'

The commander came on the line. 'What is the problem now, JJ?'

'Whether it is a problem is up to you, sir.' She smiled at Felicity as she related the events of the morning.

'Good God!' was his predictable comment. 'You do realize that you have no legal grounds for what you have done?'

'I was sent here to protect our clients, sir. This woman arrived on our doorstep armed to the teeth.'

'That is circumstantial. You don't actually know what she intended.'

'I mean to find out.'

'Now, JJ...'

'I will behave properly, sir. But she did try to burn DC Hewitt and myself to death. And our clients. Supposing I can prove, as I am sure I can, that she is the woman who murdered the concierge and then destroyed the Aspern Building, what course will we take?'

There was a brief consideration. Then he said, 'Very well, JJ, it will be all systems go. I will contact the Bahamian police and inform them of the situation, and that we require them to place the lady under arrest pending extradition.'

'Is that absolutely necessary, sir? Wouldn't it be possible just to get her back to England? My concern is that the Bahamian Police may not be able to hold her once a clever lawyer gets to work. Equally, if she starts to talk, it is Jeremy Lenghurst who may find himself under arrest for murder, awaiting extradition to the States. Surely that would be counter-productive?'

'Really, JJ, sometimes you do worry me. I understand that you have strong feelings about this woman, but we simply have to play these things by the book. You have already torn out a couple of pages by placing her under illegal arrest. Now I must straighten that out with the Bahamian authorities, and hope that they don't arrest *you*.'

'Yes, sir. May I ask what the situation would be if I had done nothing about this woman, and she had gained access to the island and approached the house with the intention of blowing it up?'

'Well...'

'My colleague and I would have been re-quired to stop her, if necessary by shooting her. Is that not correct, sir?'

'Well, I suppose...'

'The way I have handled it, sir, if a bit of red tape may have been torn up, no lives have been lost, or even threatened.'

'JJ, I have often considered that us having

you has been the legal profession's loss. I will sort this mess out. All you have to do is sit on this woman for the next few days. I am not speaking literally. However, if you are required to hand her over to the local police, you must do so. That is an order.'

Jessica sighed. 'Yes, sir. Thank you for your co-operation.' She switched off.

'You'd think the old bastard would congratulate you,' Felicity remarked.

'His way of congratulating me is to keep employing me, no matter how often I bend a few rules. You up to joining the family?'

'I'll have a go.' Felicity inserted herself into a pair of shorts. 'How are they taking this?'

'They're in a state of shock. Let's wake them up.'

Jessica prudently left Greta in her room until she saw how the land lay, which was just as well. The family had already woken up, principally Theresa. 'I will not stay on this island a moment longer, with that woman here,' she declared.

They all looked at Jessica. 'As long as she's in our custody, she can't harm you, or anyone,' Jessica told them. 'I've called London, and steps are being taken to have her extradited back to England to stand trial. Just be patient, and trust me.'

'Anyway,' Jeremy said, 'if you leave, where are you going to go?'

'Oh...' Theresa got up and flounced out of the room.

'I think you need to mend that bridge,'

Jessica said. 'Otherwise this whole exercise is totally meaningless, and you will have killed a man for nothing.'

Jeremy looked at his mother.

'Why, oh why, did you have to do it?' Rowena asked.

'I told you: it was him or me.'

'Oh, go and speak with her.' She watched her son go to the back of the house. 'What is going to happen?' she asked. 'About Jerry?'

'I'm afraid he will have to defend himself in a court of law.'

'But ... you mean you're going to turn him in?'

'I have made a full report of the situation As I was bound to do.'

'You came here to help us.'

'I came here to protect you from Abriga's hit men and, as it turned out, Rodrigo Garcia's widow. I did not come to protect your son from the results of his own folly.'

'In that case, why are you here? We don't want you. You can leave now.' She glared at a petrified Felicity. 'Both of you. I'll have Lucian call for the helicopter to take you back to Nassau.'

'You are being hysterical. From Abriga's point of view, nothing has changed – which means that Jerry is in as much danger now as he ever was. If he is telling the truth about what happened in Florida, he has a legitimate case of self-defence. But he has taken a human life, and he must justify his action in a court of law. In any event, my instructions have been confirmed from London, and they are to remain here until arrangements can be made to extradite Mrs Garcia, and until a Florida detective gets here to interview Jerry.'

'A Florida policeman? Coming here? Suppose I refuse to let him land?'

'I don't think that would be a very wise thing to do.'

'Oh...' Rowena burst into tears. 'What a mess. What a fucking awful mess.'

Jessica squeezed her hand. 'Just remember that Felicity and I are here to help.'

'But this detective...'

'Is coming to interview Jerry. He will have no powers of arrest here in the Bahamas. If he indicates that he is going to seek extradition – well, you will have ample time to get hold of the best lawyers and let them sort it out.'

'I've half a mind to take Jerry back to England.'

'I think he's safer here, for the time being.'

'Oh, well ... isn't anyone coming in for lunch?'

'I'm here,' Felicity said brightly.

Rowena gave her a dirty look.

'I think she's feeling better,' Jessica explained.

'It's just that if I drink any more coconut water, it'll be coming out of my ears.'

'What about Mrs Garcia? If Theresa really has gone into a sulk, she may as well eat with us.'

'Maybe Jerry can fill us in,' Jessica suggested. He was at that moment entering the room.

'Well?' his mother demanded.

'Says she's not hungry. Actually, my guess is that she's been drinking rum punch all morning.'

'Stupid girl. All right, Truman,' she bawled. 'Let's have lunch.'

'I'll fetch Mrs Garcia,' Jessica said.

'Do you need a hand?' Felicity asked.

'I don't think so.'

She went to the bedroom, opened the door, cautiously; but Greta, having taken off her jacket and shoes, was lying on one of the beds looking perfectly relaxed.

'I've been thinking,' she said. 'I checked in at that hotel. When I don't turn up this evening, they'll start to wonder where I am.'

'They'll know where you are,' Jessica pointed out. 'Almost everyone on Cat Island saw you walk down to the dock and board the cruiser, entirely of your own free will. Then the cruiser returned here. They will assume that, having been offered free accommodation for the duration of your stay on the cay, you have gone for it. You won't be very popular at the hotel, but I shouldn't think anyone is going to get very excited about it. Anyway, that's what we'll tell them next time we go across.'

'You have it all thought out.'

'That's my business. You hungry?'

'I'd prefer a drink.'

'I'm sure even that can be arranged. Just

213

remember: any funny business, and you get chained to that bed. Now, use the bathroom and come along.'

Their reception in the lounge was rather frosty, but Jessica gave them all a bright smile. 'As Greta is here willy nilly, I think we should all be civil.'

'Will she tell us how many people she has murdered?' Jeremy asked.

'Jerry!' his mother remonstrated.

'Well, I'll bet it's not as many as Jessica.'

Greta turned sharply, to look at Jessica.

'It goes with the job,' Jessica explained.

Greta looked at Felicity.

'And her,' Jessica agreed, stretching a point.

'Only none of yours were actually murdered,' Jeremy said. 'She kills people, Greta, to stop people killing her. Or her clients. That means us, at this moment.'

Greta drank some of the rum punch Truman had thoughtfully provided.

'So, any advance on a dozen? But of course, you've killed more than that, JJ. The dozen was all at one go. Can you beat that?'

'Jerry!' his mother snapped. 'We are about to have lunch.'

'I just thought she should know what she's up against. And the dozen she did with one shot were Colombian druggies, too.'

'You?' Greta asked. 'You were that one?'

'You heard about that?' Jessica was equally surprised. 'Don't tell me they were Abriga's people?'

'They were not Señor Abriga's people. But

214

everyone in the business heard about it.'

'Well, there you go,' Jeremy said. 'Hi, Dad. We're just bringing Greta up to date.'

Lucian ignored him, looked from face to face. 'I've had a phone call from Nassau. From Jessop.'

'Who's Jessop?' Jessica asked.

'Our lawyer,' Rowena said. 'Don't tell me: he's got some Miami policeman there, asking questions.'

'No,' Lucian said. 'No. He's got a lawyer there, who says he's representing Jose Abriga. He wants to come to the cay, to discuss the situation.'

The Catastrophe

'Hallelujah!' Rowena exclaimed. 'Oh, hallelujah. I knew he'd come round. Well...'

'Could we hold the celebration for a moment,' Jessica suggested. 'Has this man got a name?'

'Bridge,' Lucian said.

'And he is known to your man...?'

'Jessop. No, Jessop didn't know him. I mean, there must be thousands of lawyers in Florida.'

'But Jessop is satisfied that he's a genuine attorney?'

'Oh, JJ,' Rowena complained. 'You are so *suspicious*.'

'It's my business to be suspicious. Well, Mr Lenghurst?'

'He didn't seem to have a problem.'

'So what did you tell him?'

'That we'd be pleased to meet with him.'

'Where?'

'He's flying up to Cat Island tomorrow morning. I'm to pick him up and bring him over.'

'You have invited this man *here*? Sight unseen, and knowing nothing about him?'

'Now, really, JJ,' Rowena protested. 'This

216

man has come here, in good faith, on behalf of Señor Abriga...'

'How do we know he has come in good faith? What do you think, Greta? Do you know this man?'

'No. But Señor Abriga employs many people.'

'Give me your opinion as to why he is coming here. Will he be the assassin?'

Rowena snorted.

'I do not think he will be,' Greta said. 'Not if he is coming to you by the courtesy of a Nassau lawyer.'

'There,' Rowena said, triumphantly.

'But I do not think he is genuine, either,' Greta said.

Rowena glared at her.

'He will have been sent to reconnoitre,' Greta said calmly. 'Find out the situation here on the cay, count heads, see what defences you have, lay the groundwork for whatever actual plan Señor Abriga has in mind.'

'I refuse to believe that,' Rowena declared. 'He is coming here on behalf of Señor Abriga. If we meet him fair and square, and discuss the situation in a civilized manner, what reason will he have to resort to violence?'

'What are you going to discuss?' Jessica asked.

'Well...'

'He made a demand. Suppose this man has come to require your compliance with that demand? Are you going to agree?'

'Well, of course not.'

'May I ask what was this demand?' Greta inquired.

'Well...' Rowena looked at Jessica.

'He made two demands,' Jessica said. 'The first was for the return of his daughter.'

'Will she agree to that?'

'She seems to feel that if she goes home she's going to get a bashing.'

'May I assume that she has lost her virginity?'

Everyone looked at Jeremy.

'She wanted it,' he declared. 'Oh, how she wanted it.'

'Jerry!' his mother admonished.

'Then she will be severely punished, yes,' Greta said. 'And the other demand?'

'Mr Abriga requested, along with the return of his daughter, that he be given possession of a certain part of Jeremy's body. Or I suppose you could say three parts, closely connected.'

'JJ, please!' Rowena said.

The two men were clearly horrified.

'You mean he wanted Jerry to have the chop?' Lucian demanded.

'And you never told me?' Jeremy was clearly finding it difficult not to grab his genitals, protectively.

'I didn't want to upset you,' his mother said defensively. 'Anyway, it was obviously pure rhetoric.'

'Do you think it was rhetoric?' Jessica asked Greta.

'No. If Abriga said he wanted the boy castrated, he meant it.'

'Oh, don't be ridiculous,' Rowena snapped. 'This is 2005. Not the dark ages.'

'Señor Abriga doesn't look at life like that. You could say he is still living in the eighteenth century. He doesn't talk about things like virginity and indiscretions. He speaks of maidenheads and his family honour. In his eyes, your son has committed a far more serious crime than murder.'

'So you don't think this guy is coming to negotiate?' Lucian said.

'He is coming, as I said, to check out the lie of the land.'

'But you don't think he is actually coming to get me?' Jeremy asked.

'No. The hit squad will be waiting for his report. But I would say they are already in the Bahamas.'

'How can you listen to this creature?' Rowena demanded. 'She is a self-confessed murderess. She tried to blow us up, for God's sake. She came *here* to blow us up. Now she's simply trying to frighten us.'

'It would still be very unwise of us to allow this man on to the cay,' Jessica said. 'I'll come across with you tomorrow morning, Mr Lenghurst, and we'll interview Bridge together.'

'I beg your pardon,' Rowena said. 'Do you happen to own this cay?'

'I was sent here to protect it,' Jessica said quietly. 'To protect you.'

'And now that I – we – no longer need protecting, you're suffering from sour grapes.

You're paranoid.' She glared around their faces. 'All of you. Abriga wants to negotiate. I always knew he would climb down. I intend to see this man, and hear what he has to say. And if you don't like it, you can clear off. Both of you. And take that bitch with you.'

'If you are dispensing with our services,' Jessica said, still speaking quietly, 'I would like you to put it in writing. I will also need to contact my superiors, to inform them of the situation, and make it perfectly plain that neither we, nor the department, can be held responsible for anything that may happen in our absence.'

'Oh ... let's have lunch,' Rowena said.

After the meal she took Jessica aside. 'I apologize,' she said. 'I understand that you are only doing your job. Of course I want you to stay, until ... well, it is safe for you to go. But you must understand how anxious I am to have this business resolved. If there is the slightest chance ... I mean, surely we can hear what this man has to say?'

'Yes, we can. All I wish to do is not allow him on to the cay.'

'But if he insists...'

'We insist otherwise.'

'But you won't antagonize him, as you did with that Garcia woman.'

Jessica smiled. 'As I don't want him on the cay, there'll be no reason to kidnap him, if that's what you mean.'

'That was a bit grim,' Felicity remarked, when they had returned Greta to her room and regained their own.

'The poor woman is scared stiff,' Jessica said. 'Now you. How are you feeling?'

'Better for that lunch.'

'Are you up to the job?'

'Oh, yes. Well, I think so.'

'Let's see your pistol.'

Felicity raised her eyebrows, but took the Ingram from her shoulder bag.

'Level it.'

Felicity obeyed, and Jessica stood behind her to look along her arm and watched the barrel move. 'Try both hands.'

Again Felicity obeyed. This was better, but still the gun was far from steady.

'I think it's back to bed for you.'

'I'll be all right, really.'

'I'm sure you will be. Tomorrow. That's when it may matter.'

Felicity made a face, but lay down. 'What are you going to do?'

'Relax while I have the chance.' She changed into her white one-piece, slung on her shoulder bag, and went next door. 'Care to come out?'

'You bet.' Greta sat up, took her in. 'You going swimming?'

'Perhaps.'

'May I?'

'Certainly.'

Greta got off the bed and changed herself – into a green bikini, which concealed somewhat more than Felicity's; but then there was a great deal more to conceal.

'Out the back,' Jessica said.

Greta led the way on to the back verandah, which was deserted save for Theresa, who was lying on a lounger at the foot of the steps, nude. She opened her eyes at the sound of feet on the wood above her, gazed at Greta, muttered, 'Shit!', got up, and went past them into the house.

'I don't see why she's being so anti,' Greta complained. 'Her man whacked my husband. I haven't whacked her man.'

'But you did try. You tried to whack us all, as you put it.'

Greta's head turned, sharply. 'You were in that building?'

'Both Felicity and I were there. Doing this job.'

'Shit! I'm sorry. I didn't mean to kill any policeman. Or policewoman. But you got out. There was a miracle.'

'It was a job of work. In you go.'

'Aren't you coming in?'

'After you. Just remember two things: keep at least twelve feet away from me at all times, and stay above the surface, again at all times.'

'You afraid of me?'

'I just don't want to have to hurt you. Again. Oh, and one more thing: if you try anything, you'll be cuffed to that bed for the rest of your time here. Got that?'

'Yes, ma'am.' Greta went into the water. 'You really the one who brought down that chopper? The word is that you're dead. They reckon that, after you escaped into the jungle,

222

you and your pals got eaten by snakes or something.'

'Everyone makes mistakes.' Jessica waded up to her neck, and enjoyed the cool, at the same time becoming aware that there had been a change in the general atmosphere. The air was even hotter than usual, almost soporific, and while the scattered clouds above were still white, there was a line of black above the southern horizon.

'Looks like we might have some rain,' Greta remarked.

'Yes,' Jessica said thoughtfully; she had seen this sort of scenario before.

They soaked for half an hour; then Jessica said, 'Long enough. We're both too fair-skinned for too much sun. I'll go first.' She back-waded to the beach, followed by Greta. The Swedish woman was carefully keeping several feet behind her, but as Jessica sat down in the shallows, she suddenly accelerated and splashed into the shallow water. She made no attempt to attack Jessica, but ran past her and up the beach, making for the steps ... and the shoulder bag.

Jessica scrambled up, but realized she had been overconfident again, all because she had wanted to treat the woman as a human being. She dropped to her knees, hastily gathered a large handful of wet sand, which she rolled and packed into a ball, stood up, and hurled it with all her strength. It burst on Greta's back as she reached the steps, and she staggered and went down to her knees. Jessica raced behind her, but before she could reach her, or Greta could regain her feet, they were both arrested by the sight of Lucian, coming round the house, and accompanied by two men from the village carrying large sheets of plywood. 'You girls having fun?' he inquired.

'Lots of fun,' Jessica panted, passing Greta to get up the steps and reach her bag. Then she could sit down and relax. 'You expecting trouble?'

'Better to be safe than sorry. I had a weather update after lunch. Brigitte is within five hundred miles of us.'

'Coming this way?'

'She's still well out in the Atlantic, but moving north-north-west, so you could say she's converging. I don't think we'll get anything more than some heavy rain, but like I say: better to be safe than sorry.'

'What about the cruiser?'

'She'll be OK. If the storm does turn towards us, there'll be time to run her across to the mainland and the hurricane harbour.'

'So you'll still be going across tomorrow to meet this man Bridge.'

'That's what I said I'd do. But listen, JJ, I'm happy to take your instruction on this.'

'Thank you. I think Rowena is too. Come along, Greta. Time for bed.'

Greta had remained kneeling. Now she pushed herself up and came up the steps. Jessica indicated the door into the house, and she went into the corridor. Jessica closed the door behind them.

224

'I had to try it,' Greta said. 'You know that. You would have done the same.'

'Perhaps. But having been warned what the consequences of failure would be I would accept them.'

'You're going to cuff me to the bed?'

'That's right.'

'For how long?'

'Until someone arrives to collect you, either from England or Nassau.'

'And when will that be?'

'Keep your fingers crossed. My boss is working on it.' She saw her into the bedroom. 'Don't worry. You'll be fed and allowed to use the bathroom. You'd better take off that wet swimsuit.'

'I wish to shower and wash my hair.'

'Be my guest.'

By the time Greta was sorted out the entire ground floor of the house was blacked out, as regards daylight. It was all very efficiently done. Jessica had not noticed it before, but every window was fitted with the necessary metal eyelets, both inside and out, into which the bolts on the shutters slid, again both inside and out; the upstairs windows had permanent shutters, with bolts on the inside, and these could be closed in seconds; so Rowena, who had been resting, did not discover the situation until she came downstairs for cocktails. 'Oh, really, Lucian,' she complained. 'Do we have to have them up? I thought you said it wasn't going to hit us?'

'Like I said to JJ: better safe than sorry.

225

Don't worry, they'll come down again the moment it's clear.'

'So how many are we tonight?' Jeremy seemed to have regained his nerves. 'I see no tame murderesses.'

'Greta won't be joining us,' Jessica said.

'Don't tell me she's come down with something?' Rowena asked.

'No. But I have confined her to her room. I'll take her meal in.'

'You mean she tried something on?' Jeremy asked. 'And you busted her again?'

'So that's what you were doing,' Lucian remarked.

'You came along at a very appropriate moment,' Jessica agreed. 'So, is Theresa coming in? Seeing as how Greta isn't.'

'Champagne,' Rowena said. 'Let's drink champagne. Truman!'

Jessica reckoned they were all a bit hysterical, faced with a situation they had not experienced before, and had determined, not unnaturally, that the solution was to get drunk. Theresa did join them and the evening got quite jolly, although Jessica limited Felicity and herself to two glasses. But she took one in to Greta with her dinner.

'Sounds like you're having fun,' Greta said, wistfully.

'They're trying,' Jessica agreed. 'Have a good night.'

'How am I supposed to do that with one wrist chained to the bed head? I'll get cramp.'

'I'll stop by again before we go to bed,'

Jessica promised.

But before she could do that, it started to rain. There was no wind, and the big drops came straight down, drumming solemnly and loudly on the roofs.

'Is this good, or bad?' Felicity asked.

'Rain before wind means trouble,' Jessica said.

'It means Brigitte is out there,' Lucian said. 'But I still think she'll miss us. In the short term, it's very good, for us. The catchments were getting a little low. But a couple of hours of this will bring them up.'

It rained all night, and although it slackened towards dawn, it was still drizzling when Jessica awoke. She swung her legs out of bed, went to the bathroom, then stood above the faintly snoring Felicity. 'Officers' call.'

Felicity opened one eye and then the other. 'Whatsa matter?'

'It happens to be morning, and we have a lot to talk about. I want you to get up, wash your face, clean your teeth, and when you are fully awake, come back in here and listen.'

'Yes, ma'am.' Felicity slowly got out of bed and padded into the bathroom. But she looked brighter when she returned.

'Sit beside me,' Jessica said.

Felicity obeyed.

'Now listen very carefully: I am going to Arthur's Town this morning, with Mr and Mrs Lenghurst, to interview this man Bridge. I have to go, otherwise they are going to let him persuade them to bring him back here, which we can't allow. You with me?'

Felicity nodded, slowly. 'You mean...'

'You got it.'

'Oh, my God! But...'

'There is absolutely no need to panic. We are not going to be gone more than two hours, at the outside. I am going to take in her breakfast now, and immediately before we leave I will see that she goes to the loo and does whatever else she needs to do, so there will be no reason for her to need any attention until I return. Right?'

'Right,' Felicity said solemnly.

'Now, you sure you're all right?'

'I'm fine, really.'

'Good. I just want you to remember that Greta is a professional assassin, to whom life – or other people's life, anyway – is totally irrelevant. You should think of her as a violently venomous snake, and keep your distance. She is almost certain to try something the moment she feels sure I am off the island. Just do not go to her, no matter what. OK?'

Felicity nodded, looking at once determined and apprehensive.

Jessica kissed her. 'And it's your first independent command.'

'But only for two hours, you said.'

'Two hours. Now let's get dressed and get this show on the road.'

'I think Theresa should accompany us,' Rowena announced over breakfast.

'Me?' Theresa cried.

'Well, this man has come here to discuss your situation, and as Jessica will not allow us to bring him to the cay...' She cast a glance at Jessica, having apparently undergone another of her mood swings. 'I think you should at least be there in person to listen to what he has to say.'

'What you mean is,' Jeremy said, 'you hope that Theresa will be sweet talked into going back to Papa, thus letting us off the hook.'

'I did not mean that at all,' Rowena snapped, her flush giving her away.

'Perhaps Jerry should come as well,' Lucian suggested.

'Not my scene, Dad. Anyway, surely someone has to stay here and keep an eye on friend Greta?'

'Oh, I'm doing that,' Felicity said.

Everyone looked at Jessica.

'Felicity is perfectly competent,' she said.

'And you'll only be gone a couple of hours,' Felicity said, revealing that she did not feel as competent as Jessica had asserted.

'I still think it would be a good idea if I stayed with you,' Jeremy said.

Theresa snorted.

'I think you're right,' his mother decided.

'Can you handle it?' Jessica asked in the privacy of their room.

'I can handle him.'

'OK. Just remember I'm at the other end of your mobile.' But she used her own to call London and bring the commander up to date.

'Interesting,' he said. 'But you don't think this man is a genuine lawyer?'

'He may well be a genuine lawyer, sir, but I don't think he's here in a legal capacity.'

'Hm. But you think there is a chance that he might persuade this girl to return to her family?'

'I doubt it. But Mrs Lenghurst thinks there may be.'

'Now, JJ, you are not to interfere. If we can get this thing peacefully sorted out, and quickly, that would be ideal.'

'Yes, sir. I will not interfere in the negotiations. But I hope you agree that it is essential to keep this man off the cay.'

'Well, I suppose that would be prudent.'

'Thank you, sir. Now, what have you got for me?'

'Am I supposed to have something for you?'

Jessica sighed. 'You were going to arrange the formal arrest and extradition of Mrs Garcia, sir.'

'Ah, yes. That's in the hands of the Foreign Office lawyers. They have to handle it carefully, because of course her arrest was not strictly speaking legal. Was it?'

'As you say, sir.'

'Now, what about that other matter? Have you seen the Florida detectives, yet?'

'No, sir. But the weather here is a little uncertain.'

'In the Bahamas?'

'I'm afraid so, sir. It's raining. You should

230

tell Mrs Norton. I'm sure it would interest her.'

'Then I will do so. Have a nice day, and tell me how you get on with this lawyer.'

'So here we go,' Jessica told Felicity.

Who giggled. 'Guess what we didn't think to bring?'

'Raincoats.'

'Or umbrellas.'

'I'm sure Rowena will be able to fit me out.'

Rowena produced an armful of cagoules, into which they inserted themselves. The dogs had already been out in the rain and were shaking water over everything. 'Think of the catchment,' Lucian said, as his wife complained.

'Do I really have to go?' Theresa asked, plaintively.

'We have to find out what this fellow wants,' Rowena said. 'Don't worry. JJ will protect you. Won't you, JJ?'

'That's why I'm here,' Jessica agreed. Even though it wasn't, actually.

They trailed down the path to the dock, pausing to gaze at the rollers dashing themselves against the concrete arms, despite the fact that there was no wind. But there was a huge swell rolling in from the Atlantic.

'That's our girl,' Lucian said, 'reminding us that she's there.'

'You're sure this is safe?' Rowena inquired.

'A swell never hurt anybody, on the open sea. As long as it isn't breaking.'

Jessica, who had rounded the Horn under

231

sail, knew he was right. But one had to get to the open sea, and the water rushing past the entrance looked formidable. She had, however, by now realized that, whatever his faults, Lucian was a good seaman and an even better helmsman. He carefully lined up the cruiser, then gunned both engines and charged the gap. It was the bottom of a trough as they shot between the narrow pierheads, and they were clear before the next swell picked them up. But then he was putting the helm to starboard, so that they soared over the top and down into the following trough, while spray flew, and Theresa, whose first outing in the cruiser this was, uttered a shriek.

She had elected to be on the bridge to watch the departure, but now she gasped, 'How do I get down from here?'

'Use the ladder,' Lucian suggested, never taking his eyes from the seas as he negotiated the next swell.

'I couldn't do that. I'd fall off.'

'I'll help you.' Jessica went down the ladder; today she was wearing trousers. She reached the cockpit deck, braced herself. 'Come along. I'll catch you.'

Theresa cautiously moved from the seat the few feet to the ladder. 'What do I do?'

'Face the ladder, and come down step by step, sliding your hands down the rails. It's only six feet.'

With the utmost care Theresa came down the ladder, watched indulgently by Bartholemew, who was seated on the transom, while the cruiser rolled to and fro. She had got to the last two steps when the little ship gave a bigger lurch than usual and she let go of the rail with a shriek; but Jessica caught her easily enough and set her on her feet. 'Now go inside and lie down,' she recommended, and rejoined Lucian on the bridge.

'I don't suppose,' he said, 'that if I divorced Rowena you would marry me?'

She seated herself beside him. 'I don't suppose.'

'I'd like to tell you about it.'

'Didn't you tell the judge?'

'He didn't understand. Nobody understood. They all got hysterical about it.'

'You're lucky it happened so long ago. Nowadays you'd be down for life, no matter who your father-in-law was.'

'I was so lonely. Married to Rowena was like being married to an iceberg...'

'Mind this big one,' Jessica suggested.

He sighed, and concentrated.

The reef was spectacular, with spray being flung high in the sky, but for that very reason the passage was easy to see, and once they were through, the swell was entirely dissipated. But still the rain fell with steady determination.

'Will the flight from Nassau be delayed?' Jessica asked.

Lucian squinted at the sky. 'Probably. But I would say it can get down in this.'

'I wouldn't like to be away from the cay for more than a couple of hours.'

He glanced at her. 'You worried about your girl?'

'It's the first time she'll have been on her own.'

'But she's trained, right? Is she armed?'

'She is both trained and armed. But the first time is always nerve-racking.'

'She'll be OK. How do you want to handle this meeting?'

'Straight up. Be courteous, listen to what he has to say, tell him you'll let him have a reply as soon as possible. But under no circumstances allow him on to the cay.'

'And you? He's going to be interested in you.'

Jessica considered, briefly. But the tenets of the department were ingrained: prevention is always better than cure. 'You should tell him who and what I am. But don't do it in public.'

'You got it. Bartholemew!' he shouted.

Bartholemew hurried forward and a moment later they were moored up.

'It's all right for you two,' Rowena complained, emerging from the saloon. 'This child has been bringing everything up.'

Theresa certainly looked pale.

'She'll be all right once she gets on dry land,' Lucian said reassuringly.

Arthur's Town looked dismal in the rain, especially as most of the shops and some of the houses were boarded up; but they found a taxi without difficulty for the ride of a few miles to the airstrip.

'You reckon this storm going hit us, borse?'

the driver inquired.

'No, I don't think so,' Lucian said, squeezed in the back between Rowena and Theresa; Jessica sat in the front. 'Now you tell me: is the plane coming in today?'

'Oh, it must come in, borse. Some time.'

'Cheer us up,' Jessica suggested.

The airstrip looked even more desolate in the rain than the town. It reminded Jessica very much of the strip in north Eleuthera where she had landed with Brian on their honeymoon, being a single long length of tar-macadam with a couple of sheds to one side; there was no control tower nor indeed any officials, although inside the larger hut there was a counter with a bored woman sitting behind it. Behind her a CB radio crackled on a shelf.

'You going?' she inquired.

'We're meeting the Nassau plane,' Lucian explained.

'Oh, yes. You're Mr Lenghurst, from Tiger Cay.' She looked at the three women with a sceptical expression. Perhaps, Jessica thought, she knew something about his usual summer guests, and they did not fit the bill.

'So, do you have anything on it?' Lucian asked.

'It left. It going be here.'

'Great. Anyone feel like a beer?'

Jessica looked around her. At the far end of the hut there were several chairs, arranged in two rows, and half a dozen people sitting, smartly dressed and obviously waiting to catch the plane to the metropolis. But there was no sign of a bar.

'It's next door,' Lucian explained.

'Well, may as well get wet inside as well.'

They trooped next door.

'Now you understand why we have our own transport,' Rowena remarked.

'Absolutely.'

But the beer was good, and a few minutes later they heard the drone of an aircraft. They went outside and peered up into the grey.

'You reckon he'll be able to find us?' Jessica asked.

'He's done it before,' Lucian said.

The aircraft appeared through the clouds, banking to line up the strip, and came down, a flurry of water flying away from its wheels. It taxied to just in front of the two huts, the doors were opened, and the dozen passengers disembarked. Most of them were obviously Bahamian, but one was a short, slight middle-aged man, who wore a toothbrush moustache and a fedora together with an expensive suit beneath a raincoat, and carried an overnight bag as well as a briefcase.

'You ever seen him before?' Jessica asked Theresa.

Theresa shook her head; she was again in a highly nervous state.

'It has to be him.' Rowena started forward.

Jessica caught her arm. 'Let him find us.'

She studied the little man as he went up to the counter. Apart from his clothes, he moved easily and confidently, had big-city operator written all over him.

'I'm expecting to be met,' he told the woman behind the counter, revealing that he also had an American accent. 'Name of Lenghurst.'

'Over there,' she suggested.

'Now,' Jessica said.

Bridge turned, and Lucian went forward. 'Mr Bridge? Lucian Lenghurst. Welcome to Cat Island.'

Bridge shook hands. 'Some weather you guys got.'

'It's the time of year. This is my wife, Rowena. And Miss Theresa Abriga.'

'Well, say, am I pleased to meet you,' Bridge remarked. 'Who's been a naughty girl, then?'

'I think that is something we should discuss in private,' Lucian said, as heads turned.

Bridge was looking at Jessica. 'And who is this lovely lady?'

'I'll introduce her in the car,' Lucian said, as instructed. 'It's waiting.'

'Someone special, eh?' But Bridge followed them outside. 'I hope the ground transport is better than that plane. Gave me the jumps, it did. That your only way off this cay?'

'We use our helicopter,' Rowena said.

Oh, the stupid bitch, Jessica thought.

But the damage was done. 'Your own a chopper, eh? Now that's what I call style. Yes, sir. Style. You keep it on the cay?'

'No, no,' Rowena said. 'It's based in Nassau. We call for it when we want it.'

In another moment, Jessica thought, *she'll*

237

give him Arnie's name and address.

'Man,' complained the driver. 'this car only licensed to carry four passengers.'

'You can squeeze another one in,' Lucian said. 'For, shall we say, twenty dollars over the fare?'

'Well ... but if I hit something...'

'Were you planning to hit something?'

'Well, no, borse, but in this rain...'

'Drive carefully. Now, let's see: you and Mr Bridge are the smallest, JJ, so you had better get into the front.'

Jessica got in, moved up almost against the driver; she kept her shoulder bag on her left side, so that any entry to it could not be impeded by Bridge, who moved up far enough to have his hip wedged against hers.

'This is how I like to travel,' he confided. 'So what's your name, sweetheart.'

'Jessica.'

'Say, that's nice.' The others had by now settled themselves in the back, and the taxi had moved off.

'Her full name,' Lucian said, 'is Detective-Sergeant Jessica Jones, of the Metropolitan Police Special Branch, and she is with us as our bodyguard.'

Bridge looked Jessica up and down, as well as he was able, sitting beside her. 'I ain't gonna laugh,' he said. 'I swear. But this little lady is gonna protect you ... From what?'

'You never know your luck,' Jessica agreed.

'Well, I'll be...'

'Where are you staying?' Lucian asked.

'There won't be another plane until tomorrow – if then, with this storm about.'

'Well, seeing as how we have a lot to discuss, I thought maybe you'd give me a bed on your cay for a couple of nights.'

'I'm afraid that won't be possible. But I'm sure there'll be room at the hotel. You'd better drop us here,' Lucian told the driver. 'Then we can have our meeting, and you can spend the rest of the day enjoying Cat Island.'

'That ain't very sociable of you,' Bridge complained. 'After I've come all this way to talk with you guys.'

'That's the way it's going to be,' Lenghurst said. He really was doing very well, Jessica thought, appearing very masterful. She could not help but suppose that he was inspired by the knowledge that he had her to back him up, if need be.

Bridge was still digesting this when they arrived at the hotel and hurried in out of the rain. Lucian escorted him to the desk, where the clerk looked past them at Rowena and Jessica. 'That lady who came in yesterday,' he said. 'She checked in, and then left and didn't come back. Someone said he saw her getting on your boat to go across to the cay.'

'That's right,' Lucian said. 'We invited her to stay with us, and she accepted. Didn't she let you know? That was naughty of her. I'll have a word. But we've brought you this gentleman for the night.'

'Now wait a moment,' Bridge protested. 'You invited some dame to stay with you, but

239

you don't have room for me?'

'I didn't say we don't have room for you, Mr Bridge,' Lucian said pleasantly. 'I said we didn't wish to entertain you on the cay.'

'That sounds like you have something to hide.'

'Don't we all? You check in, Mr Bridge. We'll wait for you in the bar.'

'Congratulations. You handled that very well,' Jessica said, as they took off their cagoules and ordered rum punches.

'Thank you.'

'Do we have to be so antagonistic?' Rowena asked. 'We haven't even heard what he has to say.'

'We are about to,' Jessica said, as Bridge came towards them.

He had obviously decided to keep his cool, accepted his drink and sat down with a smile. 'So tell me why you need a bodyguard?' he asked.

'Tell us why you are here,' Lucian counter-ed.

'I'm from Mr Abriga. I thought you knew that. I've come to see the señorita. Your dad is very disappointed in you, Theresa. And the boyfriend. Where is he, by the way?'

Theresa looked at Rowena.

'My son is on the cay, Mr Bridge.'

'Scared, eh?'

'He has nothing to say to you,' Lucian said. 'So what have you to say to us?'

'Well, the fact is, Mr Abriga reckons you guys are quite out of court. Your boy not only

240

ran off with the señorita here, but whacked one of our people in doing it. That ain't acceptable behaviour. Mr Abriga doesn't want to go to law about this. He believes in washing his own dirty linen. So he wants his daughter back.'

'And suppose she doesn't want to go?' Lucian asked.

'Well, now...'

'Surely the decision as to whether she returns to her family must be left to Theresa?' Rowena snapped.

Everyone looked at Theresa, who licked her lips.

'I think it would be helpful if Mr Bridge told us exactly what will happen to Theresa if she returns,' Jessica said, quietly.

Bridge glared at her. 'You got any right to ask that question?'

'Yes.'

'What the shit...?'

'I'm here to protect Miss Abriga,' Jessica said. 'That protection even extends as far as from her father's wrath.'

'Now, really, Jessica,' Rowena protested.

'Be quiet, Rowena,' Lucian said.

Rowena stared at him with her mouth open; Jessica had to suppose he had never spoken to her like that before.

'Well?' Jessica asked.

'You protecting the boy, too?'

'That is correct.'

'You...' Again he looked her up and down. '...aim to protect these two kids? From Mr

241

Abriga? You know who you're dealing with?'

'Does Mr Abriga know who *he* is dealing with?' Lucian asked.

Bridge looked from face to face. 'You're putting me on. This pretty little chick...'

'Happens to be the most deadly operative in the British Police Force.'

Bridge stared at him for several seconds, then looked at Jessica, who gave him an encouraging smile.

'And,' Lucian added, 'on the cay there is her sidekick, who is only a little less deadly than she is.'

'Another dame?'

'A lady, yes.'

Bridge snorted.

'Well, now that we have sorted that out,' Jessica said, 'you will understand that I cannot permit Miss Abriga to return to her father unless I can be assured of her safety. We will also require an assurance from Mr Abriga that no retaliatory action will be taken against Mr Jeremy Lenghurst.'

'You sure have a high opinion of yourself.'

'I do,' Jessica said, as arrogantly as she could.

'Well, shit!'

'I think,' Rowena said, 'that Theresa should be allowed to offer an opinion. Do you wish to go home to your father, Theresa?'

Another quick lick of the lips. 'He will beat me. And lock me up.'

'The ball is in your court, Mr Bridge,' Jessica said.

Bridge considered for a moment, then appeared to make a decision. It was the one Jessica had anticipated, but she was also certain that the decision had been taken long before he ever landed on Cat Island: she had only made it easier for him. 'Well, hell,' he said. 'He's your daddy. He's entitled to be mad as hell. Sure he'll take the skin off your pretty little ass. And sure he's gonna lock you up. You sure ain't no use to any other man now, right? As for that boyfriend of yours, when Mr Abriga says he's gonna wind up singing alto, that's what's going to happen.'

'Oh!' Rowena looked about to faint.

'Would you like to add anything to that, Theresa?' Jessica asked.

'I would like to go back to the cay.'

'Right.' She stood up, her right hand resting on her shoulder bag. 'It hasn't been a pleasure meeting you, Mr Bridge, but have a nice day. Oh, and by the way: if I see you on the cay I am going to blow your head right off.'

'Well,' Rowena remarked as they returned to the dock, 'you made a right mess of that, Sergeant.'

'If you can't see that he came up here simply to get on to the cay, then you're suffering from myopia. As for telling him about your helicopter...'

'What was wrong with that? I do have a helicopter.'

'He didn't know that until you told him. If you'd told him that you always use public transport, he'd have gone away believing you.'

243

'And what harm can his knowing about the helicopter do? I didn't tell him Arnie's name.'

'Everyone at Nassau Airport knows Arnie, right? And what he does when he's not mixing drinks. All Bridge has to do is go back to Nassau tomorrow and ask who runs Mrs Lenghurst's helicopter. In fact, as he will certainly have a mobile, he is probably on the phone now to his contact in Nassau, telling him to find that out.'

'And then what? Arnie would never carry a man like that, or any man, without my say so.'

'I'm sure you're right. As long as he is capable of making that decision. But I think you should call him and tell him what could be happening. You can use my mobile.'

'Let's get back to the cay.' Rowena went below when they got on board.

'Now you've got her all upset,' Lucian said. 'She'll be impossible to live with for the next twenty-four hours.'

Jessica looked out to sea. 'That's building.'

The swell was now enormous, breaking on the reef and sending clouds of spray into the air.

'I reckon you're right,' he agreed. 'We'll use the public dock.'

Even inside the reef the water was turbulent, but the waves were small, and they made good time; in twenty minutes they were tied up alongside the jetty.

'We'll lie here for the next day or so, Urban,' Lucian said, as Bartholemew secured the mooring lines.

'That is the best thing, borse,' Urban agreed. 'You reckon that storm going hit us?'

'I'm going to find out as soon as I get up to the house.'

'After we've called Arnie,' Jessica reminded him. 'Let's go.'

They stepped ashore, followed immediately by Theresa, and more slowly by Rowena, and hurried along the beach. Now the entire eastern sky was black, and the roar of the surf even obliterated the growl of the generator. Then they approached the house and saw Millie, seated on the sand, her head in her hands.

'Millie?' Lucian shouted. 'You ill?'

She raised her head. 'Oh, Mr Lucian, thank the Lord you is back. I ain't knowing what to do. When it happen, I am saying we should tell Urban, but Truman say we must wait for you to come home. But I couldn't stay in the house. Not with...' She burst into tears.

Jessica felt as if she had been kicked in the stomach. 'Not with what?' she asked. 'What happened?'

'That woman...' Another flood of tears.

Jessica began to run, scattering sand as she reached the steps. The dogs were on the beach, barking excitedly. She brushed past them, and faced Truman, standing on the verandah.

'Oh, Miss Jones!' At least he wasn't weeping.

Jessica panted up the steps, saw that there

245

was blood on his white tunic. . 'What's happened?'

'She's dead,' Truman said. 'Dead. I didn't know what to do. And Mr Jeremy...'

Jessica drew her pistol, stepped up to the door to the bedrooms, conscious of the dogs panting at her heels, and peered through but saw nothing. 'Felicity!' she shouted, not allowing herself to consider what might be the response.

'JJ! Oh, thank God you're back. Please keep the dogs out.'

Jessica pushed the door in, closed it in the faces of the two eager retrievers. The first door on the left – that leading to Jeremy's bedroom – was open. She looked in. Jeremy lay on his bed, and the sheets were soaked in blood. Felicity was kneeling beside him, her hands and bikini also bloody as she tried to cope with the wound in his thigh.

'What happened?' Jessica demanded.

'He would ... Oh, my God!' She also looked ready for tears.

'Where is Greta?' Jessica snapped.

'She's dead. I shot her.'

Visitors

Jessica stared at Felicity in horror.

'I had to do it,' Felicity said. 'She had shot Jerry, and was turning the gun on me. You said if we had to shoot, it must be to kill.'

Feet pounded on the wooden floor, and Lucian arrived, gasping for breath, with Theresa at his shoulder. Fortunately, Jessica thought, Rowena had lagged behind.

'Jesus Christ!' Lucian said. 'Jerry? What the fuck...?'

'Jerry!' Theresa screamed, shouldering Felicity out of the way to reach the bedside.

'Be careful,' Felicity snapped. 'He's in pain.'

'God, I'm in agony,' Jeremy groaned. 'I'm going mad.'

'Where is he hit?' Jessica asked.

'Just above the knee. I think the bone is shattered.'

She moved the cloth she was holding against the wound, and Jessica peered at it. 'Have you a first-aid kit?' she asked Lucian.

'A small one.'

She opened her bag and took out her own. 'There are some strong analgesics in there. Give him a couple. And then get this wound bound up. We must stop the bleeding. Oh, shit!'

Rowena had arrived.

'What is happening?' she boomed. 'The servants are quite hysterical.' She stood in the bedroom doorway. 'Jerry? Jerry!' Her voice rose an octave. 'Jerry!' she screamed, and in turn thrust Theresa aside.

'I'd be careful,' Jessica recommended. 'He's badly hurt.'

'He's dying,' Rowena wailed. 'Oh, my God, he's dying! He's been shot!' She raised her head to stare at Felicity. 'You shot him!'

'Of course I did not shoot him,' Felicity snapped. 'I shot *her.*'

'That woman?' Rowena tuned her gaze on Jessica. 'You brought her into the house! You caused this to happen!'

Jessica decided to lose her temper. 'While you are having hysterics, Mrs Lenghurst, your son is both in agony and bleeding to death. Lucian, you will have to take charge. Give Jerry the analgesics, and get that wound properly bound up. Then use your mobile and get on to your doctor in Nassau ... you do have a doctor in Nassau?'

'There is a chap...'

'Can he be trusted?'

'To keep his mouth shut? I doubt it.'

'Right. So just tell him there's been a serious accident, and will he come up here right away. Then call Arnie and have him bring the doctor up in his helicopter.'

'Jerry has to go to hospital,' Rowena declared.

'For once I agree with you. But we have to

248

get him there. And if he's going to travel in your helicopter, it might be a good idea to have a doctor with him.'

'There is a nurse who runs a clinic in Arthur's Town,' Lucian said. 'The doctor comes up twice a week.'

'Is today one of the days?'

'No. He comes on Mondays and Thursdays, and today is Tuesday.'

'And we can't wait that long. We want to get hold of Arnie anyway. I'll leave that with you.'

'What about ... ah...'

'I intend to sort that out now. Come with me, Filly.' She led the way to the fourth bedroom.

'I guess I'm a catastrophe,' Felicity said.

'Let me be the judge of that,' Jessica suggested, and opened the door. The atmosphere was heavy, and Greta Garcia lay on her back across the bed. Her shirt front was bloodstained, and her right hand held the Browning. The handcuff dangled from her wrist, but was no longer secured to the bed.

'You said I should keep it on single shot,' Felicity said.

'I did. And thank God you did, otherwise this would not be liveable. But, a single shot...' She peered at the shirt. 'Through the heart?'

'I'm a markswoman.'

'I don't think anyone is gong to argue with that. So what happened?'

'Well ... I didn't go near her, like you said. Even when, like you said, she started screaming that she was in pain. Truman and Millie came to me and suggested we should do something about it. I told them to forget it, that you would soon be home and know what to do. I could see they weren't happy. Neither was Jeremy, who was on the back verandah with me. So I guess I got fed up, and went down to the beach for a dip.'

'Leaving your bag behind.'

'Well, I couldn't take it into the water, could I? I just never thought he'd touch it.'

'So what happened next?'

'Jerry had been making his usual advances, and talking about Greta too, saying how she was built, and asking me what was going to happen to her. I said she'd probably go down for a long time. He said that was a damned shame for such a woman. That made me more fed up, seeing she'd tried to kill us all; so like I said, I went for a swim. I thought he'd follow me into the water, but he didn't, and when I looked round a couple of minutes later, he wasn't there. I suppose I didn't react quickly enough. I thought he'd gone to the loo, or to get some more rum punch. Then I heard the shot. I dashed up the beach, picked up my bag, and went along the corridor. I realized that he had taken not only the key for the handcuffs but also the Browning. Thank God he hadn't touched the Ingram.'

'What do you suppose he had in mind?'

'I think probably sex. I think he thought he could control the situation, with the gun. He had no idea who he was dealing with.'

'So what did you do?'

'I drew the pistol and went along the corridor, opened the door. That distracted her. She'd already shot him once, but she missed her target the second time. I got the impression she had meant to shoot him in the balls. Anyway, she swung round when the door opened. She was still holding the gun, looking at me, so I fired first. Oh, JJ. What else was I to do?'

'You did what you had to do,' Jessica said.

'But it's still a fuck-up, isn't it?'

'The fuck-up is mine,' Jessica said, 'for trying to be too smart, bringing her here in the first place. Now, have you touched anything in here?'

'I had to get Jerry out.'

'But you didn't touch her, or the gun?'

'No.'

'There's a good girl.'

'What are we going to do?'

'From here on, play it by the book.'

Jeremy had been sedated and bound up, and was lying peacefully enough. Theresa sat beside him, but Rowena had retired to the lounge with a drink. Both the servants had returned to the house, but no one was discussing lunch. They would have to be dealt with, but first things first.

Jessica went upstairs to where Lucian was chatting into his mobile. He waggled his eyebrows at her and gave a thumbs-down sign. 'OK,' he said. 'Tell him to call me the

251

moment he gets in. The very moment, mind.'
He switched off.

'Arnie's out, and Clarissa doesn't know where he is. He never was a very reliable character.'

'Did you raise the doctor?'

'Yes. But apparently all flights out of Nassau have been closed for the time being, until they see which way this storm is going. Actually, they should resume tomorrow. Apparently Brigitte is already past us and making north. They reckon she's headed for Bermuda.'

'But at this moment flights out are still cancelled. What about flights in?'

'Oh, they'll accept those to the last moment. But the plane out of Cat Island will have left by now.'

'That's not relevant; we couldn't possibly have got Jerry over there in time.'

'But at least Bridge is stuck in Arthur's Town.'

'That's not relevant either. Like I said, he'll have contacted his friends by mobile.'

'To tell them what?'

'I suspect to tell them about Arnie, and a back door into the cay.'

'Arnie would never let us down.'

'Everyone keeps saying that. He wouldn't have much choice with a pistol at his throat.'

'Holy shit! You serious?'

'I'm pretty sure they are. What did you tell the doctor?'

'That there'd been an accident with a gun,

and my son was hurt.'

'Excellent. Is he prepared to come up by helicopter, when you raise Arnie?'

'Actually, no.'

'Eh?'

'He said he can't spare the time, once I'd told him Jerry's life wasn't in danger.'

'He does realize that, if that leg isn't operated on pretty soon, Jerry could lose its use?'

'I explained that, and he pointed out that he couldn't operate up here anyway. Our business is to get Jerry down to Nassau the moment it can be done. As I said: even if I can't raise Arnie, they expect the planes to be flying again tomorrow, now that Brigitte has moved on.'

'You're quite sure of that?'

'The met boys are. Right now she's stalled about seventy-five miles north-east of us.'

'Stalled?'

'They do this from time to time, over the ocean. Sort of gathering strength before moving on.'

'And they never come back?'

'Not as a rule. It has happened, mind. There was one called David that doubled back and did a lot of damage in the northern islands. But that was more than forty years ago.'

'I still think we should use the chopper if it's at all possible. You simply have to get hold of Arnie, and not only because of Jerry. But there's something else you have to do, right away.'

'What?' Lucian was starting to look rather tired.

'Get hold of the Nassau police and tell them there has been a fatal shooting on the cay. Don't go into any more detail than you have to, but tell them you need them up here as soon as possible.'

'Won't that land your girl in the cart?'

'We can prove it was self-defence.'

'How?'

'Greta is still holding her pistol. It will have been fired three times, and any forensic surgeon will be able to tell that it was her bullet shattered Jerry's thigh. Felicity clearly fired in self-defence.'

'OK, but I thought, as far as anyone knows, that you guys were here as friends, not policewomen? There'll be some questions.'

'I intend to sort that out now. But you handle your end. Then you need to have a chat with your servants. Tell them that you have contacted the police and that they are to keep their mouths shut until they get here. It might also be an idea to have a late lunch.'

'You mean you can eat?'

'We have to eat, Lucian. Breakfast was a long time ago.'

'I'll do the best I can. But ... ah ... the woman...'

Jessica, already at the door, checked. 'She'll be all right for twenty-four hours, as long as the air conditioning stays on.'

'And if the police don't get here for twenty-four hours?'

'Then she'll have to go in your deep freeze.'

'That's full of food.'

'Lucian, life is full of little difficulties. If we have to use the freezer, the food will have to be taken out. Now get with it.'

At the foot of the stairs she met Truman.

'Please, ma'am,' he said. 'Can you tell me what is happening? Them boys...'

'If you mean the people in the village, Truman, we'd prefer it if they weren't immediately told what has happened. Mr Lenghurst is calling Nassau now, to inform the police of the situation.'

'Yes, ma'am.' He looked relieved. 'And the lady?'

'We'll leave her where she is for the time being. The police will wish to see exactly what happened. Now, Truman, we seem to have missed lunch. Do you suppose you could rustle up a substantial high tea?'

'Well, ma'am, I'll ask Mrs Lenghurst...'

'That may not be a good idea. Where is she?'

'She sitting on the front verandah, drinking rum punch and playing with the dogs.'

'Then I would leave her there and get on with it. Serve the meal on the back verandah.'

'She will make a fuss.'

'If she does, refer her to me.'

He looked doubtful, but went off.

Jessica went to her room, where Felicity was sitting on the bed, looking utterly disconsolate. 'Cheer up,' she suggested. 'It hasn't happened yet.'

'But what *is* going to happen?' Felicity moaned. 'I've killed a woman, JJ.'

'In the line of duty, protecting our client. Just keep telling yourself that. As for what is going to happen, I'm about to sort that out.'

As it was eight o'clock in London, she didn't waste her time with the office. 'Oh, really, Sergeant,' Mrs Adams said. 'Is it important? He's watching his favourite film.'

'Oh, I'm sorry, Mrs Adams. What film would that be?'

'*Captain Blood.*'

'You mean with Errol Flynn? That's seventy years old. The commander isn't seventy, is he?'

'Of course he isn't, you silly girl. It's still his favourite film. He's a fan of Errol Flynn.'

It occurred to Jessica that that explained a great deal about the commander she had never quite understood. 'And it's on the box.'

'No, no, Sergeant. We have it on video.'

'Ah! Then surely he can turn it off for a few minutes?'

'He won't like it. Can't you call back in a couple of hours?'

'This is actually rather urgent, Mrs Adams.'

'Oh ... very well.'

A few moments later, Adams came on the line. 'What on earth is the matter now, JJ?'

Jessica outlined the situation with her usual succinctness.

She had certainly gained his attention. 'You say the boy isn't badly hurt?'

'He *is* badly hurt, sir. He may well be a

cripple for life. But I do not think he is in a life-threatening situation.'

'And you say you can't get him to hospital?'

'Not right this minute, sir. The weather is a bit dodgy. But we're hoping to do so tomorrow. What I want to know is how we handle the situation regarding DC Hewitt.' She gave Felicity, staring at her with enormous eyes, an encouraging smile.

'You say it was self-defence. You can prove this?'

'I can, sir. But I do not wish to have to do so in a court of law, which will entail Hewitt being arrested. She was doing her duty in protecting our client. There is also the matter that the Bahamian Police may be concerned about her carrying a weapon.'

'As you are also carrying a weapon.'

'That is correct, sir.'

'All right, JJ. I can't do anything about it at this hour, but I will get on to it first thing tomorrow morning. You have my word that if either of you, or both of you, are arrested, I will have you out on bail within twenty-four hours. What about the real business? Any sign of movement from the Abriga camp?'

'Yes, sir. I think they could be here the moment the weather improves.'

'They?'

'My instincts indicate that there will be more than one.'

'Can you handle it?'

'That depends on how many there are.'

'So you may be glad of the assistance of the

Bahamian Police after all, eh?'

'Not if they relieve us of our weapons, sir. There is also the point that if a couple of their people come up to interview us about a death that has been reported as accidental at this stage, they are hardly likely to be armed, and will therefore merely get in the way if it comes to a shoot-out.'

'Hm. Yes. I take your point. Leave that also with me. And JJ, do keep me informed if there happens to be a shoot-out.'

'Even if it interrupts your movie, sir?'

'Now, JJ, behave yourself.'

'I will keep you informed, sir. If it is possible to do so.'

'Thank you. Have a good night.'

'Has he ever been in a shoot-out in his life?' Felicity inquired.

'In his younger days, I believe. But that was some time ago. Let's eat.'

'I couldn't eat a thing. The thought of being locked up by a lot of men...'

'These men are policemen, trained in British traditions...'

'Oh, cheer me up.'

Jessica grinned. 'They'll love you.'

'That's what bothers me.'

But she followed Jessica from the room.

'We'll just check on lover-boy first,' Jessica said, and opened Jerry's door. Theresa sprang up like a startled stag. 'Oh!'

'How is he?'

'Every so often he twitches. And his breathing is so heavy.'

Jessica stood by the bed, peered at the unconscious man, then took his pulse.

'He'll do.'

'What do I do when he wakes up? Will he still be in pain?'

'Yes, he will. So you'll give him another of those pills. That'll put him out again.'

'What's in them?'

'Nothing you should know about, at your age. Now come and eat. Don't worry: if he wakes up, we'll hear him.'

'Eat? I couldn't eat a thing.'

'Don't you start. What use are you going to be to Jerry if you've starved to death?'

They went on to the back verandah, where Truman and Millie were laying out cold meat, bread and salad with jugs of coconut water.

'That looks splendid,' Jessica said. 'You've done ever so well.'

'What is going to happen, miss?' Millie asked.

'The police are going to come up the very moment they can – certainly tomorrow – and sort everything out. Meanwhile we should continue as normal. But no one is to go into the room where Mrs Garcia is. They want it exactly as it is.'

'Yes, ma'am.' But she was clearly unhappy.

Lucian arrived. 'God, how can you eat at a time like this?'

'Try,' Jessica recommended, between mouthfuls. 'Any joy?'

He sat down. 'The police aren't really

interested, at this moment. They say they'll be up as soon as they have the time and the manpower.'

'Is there trouble?' Felicity asked, also eating vigorously now that she had got into the habit.

'Not really, yet. They're uptight about Brigitte.'

'I thought she was going up north,' Jessica said. 'It certainly looks like it. The rain has stopped, and there's blue sky over there.'

'You're looking west,' Lucian pointed out. 'It's pretty black in the east. Trouble is, she's still stalled, and they don't know what she's going to do next. I wanted to get these shutters down this afternoon. They make the place seem like a tomb.' He received three old-fashioned looks, and flushed. 'I'm talking about the gloom.'

'I think we can stand them being up for another night,' Jessica said. 'You can't take them down by yourself, can you?'

'No, no. I'd get some boys up from the village.'

'That's what I thought. But we don't really want anyone up here right now, do we?'

'Good thinking. But you do understand that Truman and Millie live in the village and will be going home after dinner tonight. There is no way they're not going to tell people what happened here today.'

'What do you think they'll do?' Felicity asked. 'The people in the village, I mean.'

'I have no idea.'

'Well, they're not likely to do anything before tomorrow morning,' Jessica said. 'And hopefully the police will be here by then. Now tell me, did you get hold of Arnie?'

'I'm afraid not. Now there's no reply, even from Clarissa.'

'They run a bar, right? Did you try the bar?'

'There's no reply from there either. It must be shut.'

'Do bars in Nassau usually close when there's a storm about?'

'Hell, no. They're usually working overtime.'

They gazed at each other.

'Fuck it,' he remarked.

'That sounds appropriate. But he must have friends, if he's lived there for ten years. Can't you call one of them?'

'I have no idea who they are. When he's not flying for us, his life is his own.'

Rowena appeared in the doorway, swaying to and fro. 'What the fuck are you doing?' she demanded.

'Making up for missing lunch,' Jessica explained. 'Won't you join us?'

'I didn't instruct anyone to prepare a meal.'

'Do you usually do that?'

Rowena pointed. 'You can sit there, stuffing your filthy faces, while my son lies dying in his bed!'

'He's not actually dying,' Jessica said. 'But I expect he'd like a glimpse of his mother from time to time.'

'That is it!' Rowena said. 'You are fired! You

and that bitch can get off of my island. Now!'

Jessica looked at Lucian.

'Now, my dear,' he said. 'You are going a little bit over the top. Jessica and Felicity were doing their job – of protecting us.'

'They brought that woman here in the first place.'

'And she would still have been here,' Felicity said, 'alive and well and properly under restraint, if your son had been able to control his desire for sex.'

'Why, you...'

Jessica stood up. 'I've had enough to eat, and all of this I can stand. I think you need to bear in mind, Mrs Lenghurst, that we are not employed by you. We are employed by the Metropolitan Police, at your request, to protect you. This we are doing, to the best of our ability, and in most difficult circumstances such as not even knowing this woman Greta existed until after we arrived here. Now, you cannot dismiss us, because we are acting under orders from our superiors. If you are dissatisfied with the way we are doing our job, I suggest you contact Commander Adams and request that we be withdrawn and replaced. I will give you his telephone number. But until we hear from him, Felicity and I will continue to do our job. Filly.'

Felicity also stood up. Rowena stared at Jessica, her mouth opening and shutting like a stranded fish gasping for air.

'Meanwhile,' Jessica said, 'I suggest you keep trying to raise Arnie, Lucian. This could

262

really be very important.'

'But if he's not at home, and the bar is closed, for whatever reason...'

'Try the airport. The helicopter is parked there. We want to make sure that chopper stays there, until Arnie can bring it up to collect Jerry. But he must call us before taking off.'

He nodded. 'I'll have a go.'

Felicity followed Jessica into the bedroom, closed the door. 'Are our assignments always like this?'

'In varying degrees. People are inclined to call for protection without really understanding what it can mean.'

Felicity sat on the bed, hands dangling between her knees. 'I feel so wretched. I never thought...' Tears welled up in her eyes. 'I've killed another human being!'

Jessica sat beside her, put an arm round her shoulders, and gave her a hug. 'In the line of duty. Always remember that.'

Felicity sniffed. 'Was it like this for you?'

'Ah ... I was lucky. I was with another officer when I first had to shoot at someone. My partner was hit, so I just reacted. As did you.'

'Did your partner die?'

'No. He recovered.'

'But you got the gunman.'

'No. I missed. I wasn't as good a shot as you, then. Though I will say that the range was slightly greater. No, my first real shoot-out was a little later, when I was serving with the SAS.'

'They allowed a woman into the SAS?'

'Not so you'd notice. But I was the only one able to identify the man they were after – Korman the bomber, the man who had shot my partner. He'd had a face lift, you see. But we'd exchanged words when shooting at each other, and I knew his voice.'

'That must have been tremendous – serving with the SAS, I mean.'

'It was an experience, yes. But the real experience came before; they wanted me along, but they'd only have me if I was fully trained to their standards.'

'You mean you did the whole SAS training course?'

'It was abbreviated, because they were in a hurry. But it made me what I am.'

'Gosh! What did Sergeant Lawson say?'

'He didn't say a lot. I think his feelings were a mixture of pride and consternation. Now I'm going to sleep for an hour. I suggest you do the same.' Because there was nothing she could do, until Lucian located Arnie, or until the police got there.

She awoke just before five. Felicity was still fast asleep. She got dressed as quietly as she could, slung her shoulder bag, and went out-side.

The house was utterly quiet. The rain had stopped, and there was quite a lot of blue sky in the west. When she went on to the front verandah, however, she saw that the northern and eastern horizons were black, indicating that Brigitte was still not very far away. That had to be reassuring, as surely no competent pilot would risk flying up here with so much weather about. But were Colombian hit men concerned about the weather?

She had listened at Jeremy's bedroom door, and heard nothing. Obviously he had been drugged again, and as a glance into the room occupied by Theresa showed it to be empty, she had to conclude that she was sitting with her lover; Jessica had not supposed she would be that faithful, but the girl was clearly in a very confused emotional state.

There was no sound from upstairs either. Rowena was presumably sleeping it off, but Lucian did not appear to be using either the radio or his mobile, although, presumably, if he kept the office door shut she would not hear him. She had to assume that he would tell her the moment he had any news, and she had no desire to risk more unpleasantness by venturing up the stairs and perhaps encountering Rowena.

But where were Truman and Millie? She had not troubled to inquire what the servants did when they were not actually serving, but presumably they had to be somewhere around. She went down the steps and walked right round the house, being joined halfway by the dogs, which had been sleeping under the huge mango tree situated beside the house. 'Sssh!' she begged, as they started barking, but they ignored her.

There was still no sign of the servants; she realized that the temptation must have proved too great for them, and they had gone down to the village to regale their families and friends with the tale of what had happened. That was a nuisance, but it should not have any immediate consequences.

She crossed the tennis court and went along the path to the helicopter pad, then the dock, the dogs frisking around her and rooting in the bushes to either side. She stopped short of going on to the dock itself, for the swell seemed to be even higher than earlier, great waves she estimated at over twenty feet high smashing into the concrete, the spray coming down with a sound like the rattle of machine-gun fire, while to either side of the dock the sea crashed on to the beach. What made it most disturbing was that there was almost no wind, just the occasional fitful burst out of the north-east. But when she looked in that direction, she gasped. The entire sky was a blackish-purple, and she even thought she could see the white flashes of lightning.

She had seen a sky like that once before, in advance of the typhoon she had so narrowly survived in the Pacific.

'Come on,' she told the dogs, and turned back.

They had had more sense than to venture on to the beach, and readily trotted behind her. They walked back along the path, reached the tennis court, and saw Lucian standing on the front verandah.

'Don't look too good, eh?' he asked.

'It looks horrifying,' she said.

'Yeah. She's coming back. That's official.'

She went up to him. 'Aren't you glad you didn't take those shutters down. When will she get here?'

'Well, they don't know for sure where she's heading. Historically, she should move to the west, and strike Abaco, or maybe North Eleuthera. But if she were merely to double straight back, she'd be coming for Cat Island. The hurricane people in Miami have planes out monitoring her progress now, and we should get an update in a couple of hours. In any event, she can't get back here before midnight at the earliest.'

'And you plan to sit it out?'

'Well, it's a bit late to think of leaving, save for Cat Island. But you wouldn't think that's a good idea.'

'In our circumstances, no – not if you still feel the house will stand it.'

'Oh, no problem here, just as long as no one lets the wind inside. But I have to give our people the option of moving to the mainland; their houses aren't as solidly built as ours, or as high above sea level. I'm going down there now.'

'Would you like me to come with you?'

'Will you?'

'Surely. I'll just put Filly in the picture.'

Felicity was sitting on the back verandah, brooding at the sea. 'Waking up and not finding you there,' she said, 'I got the willies.'

'I was having a look at things, which aren't very good. That storm is coming back. It could be heading straight for us.'

'Oh, shit!'

'Look on the bright side. It should keep the baddies away.'

'But shouldn't we be evacuating or something?'

'Lucian seems to feel we'll be perfectly safe here, at least from the weather. But he's worried about the village, so he's going down there now. So hold the fort. We should be back in about an hour.'

'It'll be dark in an hour.'

'No, it won't.' She checked her watch. 'It's only half past five. It won't be dark until eight.'

She hurried back through the house to join Lucian and the dogs. 'You know that Truman and Millie have gone down there already,' she said.

'I thought they would.' He glanced at her. 'That's why I'm glad to have you along.'

'You expecting trouble?'

'I don't know what to expect. I, and they, have never been in this position before. If there were to be trouble, can you handle it?'

'I can handle it. But it could be nasty. There's a more important point. Are you expecting them to leave?'

'I would say so. As I said, they're only a couple of feet above water level. Any big storm surge would wipe them out.'

'But aren't they on the sheltered side of the

island?'

'After her stalls, Brigitte is generating winds of a hundred and thirty miles an hour. That's enough to push up a surge of maybe thirty feet. That could go clear across the island at the north end.'

'How high is your house?'

He grinned. 'Fifty feet.'

'That doesn't sound like too much margin for error. But the point I was going to make was: once these people get to the mainland, everyone on Cat Island will know what happened here.'

'I guess you're right. We'll just have to face it out until the people from Nassau arrive. Anyway, if Brigitte *is* heading back this way, they'll have more on their minds than a shooting up at the house.'

'So will the people in Nassau,' she pointed out. 'So tell me, did you manage to raise Arnie yet?'

'Not a sausage. I tried the airport, as you suggested, but they hadn't seen him. Nor did they know anything about his bar being closed.'

'But the helicopter is still there.'

'Oh, yes.'

'And if he was going to fly, he'd have to take on fuel, right?'

'I don't know about that. He normally keeps her fuelled up, certainly when Rowena is in residence. When she wants to go somewhere, it is generally *now*. Brace yourself.'

Although it was late afternoon, they had

been spared the worst of the sandflies as they had taken the path through the trees rather than go by the beach, but now the dogs were barking to announce their arrival, and it seemed that the entire village had turned out to welcome them. Or at least to receive them: Jessica saw very little welcome in any of the faces.

'Are you there, Urban?' Lucian asked.

'I am here, Mr Lenghurst.' Urban stepped out from the throng.

'I've come down to tell you that the storm has turned back, and could well hit us, probably before tomorrow morning. So if any of you want to go across to the mainland, now is the time. I can take all of you in the cruiser, if one of you will bring me back.' He grinned. 'And fetch me when the blow is past.'

'You staying here, Mr Lenghurst?' Truman asked.

'That is our intention, yes.'

'Because of what happen up at the house?'

'Partly. As you know, we are expecting the police to come up as soon as the storm is past, and we intend to stay here until they arrive. But we are not expecting any of you to do the same.'

There was some muttering. Then Urban said, 'I think it is best we go across, borse. We will come back the moment the storm is past.'

'Very good. We need to do this before dark, so will you please get your gear together and

270

go on board the cruiser.' They hurried off and he turned to Jessica. 'That went off better than I expected. You coming for the ride?'

'I'd love to, but I can't abandon Filly. She's still pretty upset about what happened. Can you really get those people over and be back before dark?'

'If they hurry. But I can make it in the dark if I have to. There are no obstacles inside the reef, and I know the waters. But I should be back around seven.'

'Well, just make sure that you are.'

'I never thought I would hear you say something like that.'

'Everything comes to he who waits. What about the hens?' Several of which were scratching at the ground around them.

'It would take too long to round them up. They'll have to take their chances. Well...' He made a move towards her, and checked. 'I'll see you.'

Jessica turned away: he had almost sounded as if he was saying goodbye. But not even Lucian Lenghurst could be such a rat. Surely. She snapped her fingers, and the dogs followed her as she decided to ignore the sandflies and take the quicker way back along the beach to the house. Before she got there it began to rain again, a steady drizzle, and she was no longer wearing her cagoule. There was no point in trying to run several hundred yards on the sand, so she allowed herself to be soaked.

Rowena stood on the back verandah,

271

wearing a dressing gown and looking de-
cidedly the worse for wear. 'Am I allowed to
ask what is going on?' she demanded.

'Lucian is taking your people over to Cat
Island.'

'Now? Why is he doing that?'

'Because they want to go. Brigitte has
turned back and may be going to hit us. He
also wants to put the cruiser on to a hurricane
mooring.'

'You mean he's just abandoning us? The
bastard! He could have taken us with him.'

Jessica went up the steps. 'He feels we'll be
better off here. And I feel we should stay here,
in view of what we've got in the spare room.'

Rowena sat down. 'What a fucking awful
mess.'

'It'll all look different this time tomorrow,'
Jessica assured her. 'I have to change.'

On the way she looked in at Jeremy, who
was lying absolutely still. His thigh had
apparently been bleeding, as the bandage was
pink, but it did not seem to need immediate
attention. Theresa sat on the other bed,
drinking rum punch.

'Who made that?' Jessica asked.

'I did. The servants seem to have disappeared.'

'That's right. They've abandoned ship.'

'What?'

'They've gone across to the mainland until
the storm is past. So we'll have to fend for
ourselves tonight.'

'I thought the storm *was* past.'

'It seems to have changed its mind. That's what comes from giving it a woman's name. Just relax. We're perfectly safe here. Lucian says so. And at least Jerry seems peaceful.'

'He's peaceful because every time he looks like waking up I give him one of those pills.'

Jessica picked up the bottle; it was half empty. 'For God's sake take it easy. You're either killing him or turning him into a drug addict.'

'I just don't like to see him in pain.'

'Moderation in all things. Now I'm going to have a shower. When I'm done I'll come back and we'll change that dressing.'

'He'll have to have another pill then.'

'We'll see.' She went into her bedroom, stripped off her wet clothes, and was in the shower when Felicity came in.

'I thought I heard the dogs barking. Thank God you're back.'

Jessica towelled. 'Problems?'

'No, no. Just the general ambience. When Mrs Lenghurst showed up I thought I'd better make myself scarce, so I went out front. Do you realize the servants seem to have disappeared?'

Jessica used the hairdryer and brought her up to date.

Felicity was aghast. 'Shit! You mean that bastard has pushed off and left us four women here with a corpse and a cripple?'

'He's coming back.'

'So he says.'

'Just relax. His being here isn't going to

keep that storm away.' She dressed herself, in jeans and a shirt. 'However, the situation does mean that we'll have to fend for ourselves for tonight. I don't think either Rowena or Theresa is going to be a great deal of help.' She looked at her watch: seven fifteen. 'The first thing we have to do is change Jeremy's dressing.'

'Ugh!'

'Don't you want to put your first-aid training to use? Better on someone else than on yourself, right? Let's go.' She took the first-aid box from her shoulder bag and they went to Jeremy's room.

Theresa had finished her jug of rum punch and was lying with her eyes closed, crooning softly to herself, while Jeremy was moving restlessly.

'See what I mean?' Jessica asked.

Theresa opened her eyes. 'You going to give him another pill?'

'Afterwards, if we have to.'

'He's going to holler.'

'Can't be helped.' Gently she pulled the sheet down to expose the naked body, the bloodstained bandage.

At her shoulder, Felicity gulped. 'Looking at that could put you off sex for life.'

'You'll be surprised at how quickly you'll recover, given the right bloke. Go round the top and be ready to hold his shoulders.'

She obeyed, while Theresa actually sat up. Carefully Jessica untied the knot and unrolled the bandage, having to push his legs apart to get underneath; his flaccid penis flopped against the back of her hand as his restlessness increased.

The wound itself was a bloody mess. Jessica used cotton wool to clean some of the blood away, and now he moaned. 'Hold him!' she snapped.

Felicity grasped his shoulders and pressed down.

Jessica could see fragments of shattered bone protruding through the mangled flesh, but there was nothing she dared do about it: even if she had had any but the most rudimentary surgical training, she entirely lacked the instruments. All she could aim to do was staunch the bleeding and keep him alive until help arrived. She did not even dare properly sterilize the wound; to use any strong antiseptic would be to induce pain he might be unable to bear. As it was, when she laid the sheets of lint smothered in antiseptic cream on his flesh he gave a sudden shriek and woke up.

'God!' he screamed. 'God!'

'Hold him!' Jessica shouted. 'Theresa, his legs.'

Felicity continued to press down on his shoulders while trying to control his flailing arms at the same time; even so Jessica received a clout on the side of her head that nearly tumbled her off the bed.

'Easy,' she gasped. 'Easy.'

Theresa was lying across his legs.

Rowena arrived. 'What are you doing to my

son?' she demanded. 'Jerry! Oh *Jerry!'* She screamed, and fell across the other bed in a faint.

Jessica realized this was the first time she had actually seen the wound.

'Shall I...' Theresa began.

'She can wait,' Jessica said. 'We have to finish this first.'

Jeremy continued to scream and moan and curse and attempt to thrash. By the time Jessica had finished bandaging him all three women were bathed in sweat.

'Now,' she panted, 'water and those pills.'

They got Jeremy to swallow the pill, but still had to hold on to him for several minutes while it took effect. But at last he was quiet.

'What about her?' Felicity asked. Rowena was showing signs of waking up.

'I would let her get on with it,' Jessica decided. 'You stay here with her, Theresa.'

'Why me?'

'Because she's your future mother-in-law.'

Theresa was clearly no longer certain of that.

'And when she comes to,' Jessica said, 'try to persuade her not to touch Jerry.'

Felicity followed her. 'I feel like a drink.'

'So do I. Go and mix some up.'

'While you do what?'

'See if I can get any sense out of Nassau.'

She went upstairs and into Lucian's office, a surprisingly tidy place, and a mass of equipment. She booted his computer. As she had expected in a situation where only he as a rule

276

had access to the machine, there was no password required. She clicked on 'My Documents', and found what she wanted: a list of addresses and telephone numbers. She used one of his mobiles to call, firstly, the home number given for Arnie. It rang a dozen times without reply. Then she tried the bar. But there also she could not get a reply. Thus Arnie had not been available since just after lunch, or just after Bridge would have had sufficient time to telephone his associates in Nassau and give them the information, and the fact that his wife had also become unavailable soon after that raised all manner of sinister possibilities.

She telephoned Nassau Airport, and after some toing and froing was put through to a man who said, courteously, 'May I help you?'

'I hope so. I am calling on behalf of Mr Lucian Lenghurst, of Tiger Cay.' She paused.

'Oh, yes.'

'Mr Lenghurst keeps his helicopter at your airport.'

'Yes.'

'He is anxious to contact his pilot, Arnold Pleass. Do you know if he has been to the airport today?'

'Oh, yes. Mr Pleass was here just now. But you know this.'

'Ah ... do I? Do you have any idea where he went after leaving you?'

'Miami.'

'Would you repeat that, please?'

'Arnie Pleass came out here about half an

hour ago and cleared for take-off. He said Mrs Lenghurst had called him and told him to take the chopper to Miami for safety until after this storm passes.'

'I see. Was he alone?'

'No, no. He had Clarissa – that's his wife – with him and six other passengers.'

Jessica swallowed. 'Did you say six? Men?'

'That's right.'

'Did you know them?'

'Well, I didn't get to meet them: they were kind of in a hurry. I guess they were all scared stiff.'

'But were they local?'

'No, no, ma'am. They were visitors. I reckon they must have been in the bar when Arnie got the orders to leave, and they begged a lift. You reckon Mrs Lenghurst is going to be uptight about that?'

'Probably. Thank you.' She switched off and remained staring at the computer for some seconds. Then she heard the guttural chatter of a helicopter engine.

The Storm

Jessica left the office, ran through the master bedroom – an oasis of utter luxury – and on to the upper verandah. It was still light enough to see the helicopter, slowly descending towards its landing pad. At just over half a mile away it was beyond the range of her Skorpion ... but could she bring it down, anyway, when it was almost certainly being piloted by Arnie? With his wife on board? She had to believe they were both under restraint.

Where the hell was Lucian? She turned her gaze the other way, but the little headland to the north-west prevented any sight of the village or the dock, or of the sea between there and Arthur's Town. For the moment, at least, she and Felicity were on their own. Even the weather had turned against them; the rain had stopped, and there was still no wind.

She ran back through the bedroom and down the stairs, into the lounge, where Felicity was mixing up a jug of punch, watched by the two dogs. 'Do you know,' she said, 'I could swear I heard the chopper just now. But it can't be, can it?'

'You heard the chopper,' Jessica said, closing the front doors. These had their own shutters, and these she closed as well.

Felicity had her back to her. 'You mean Arnie got up here after all? We'll be able to take Jerry out? Whoopee.' She turned. 'What are you doing?'

'Locking up. Thank God those storm shutters are still in place.'

'I'm not with you.'

'You did hear the chopper,' Jessica repeated. 'It'll be down by now. Unfortunately, it has on board six of Abriga's people.'

'Say again?'

'I've been in touch with Nassau, and they told me that Arnie took off, ostensibly for Miami, with his wife and six other passengers, all men. They are now on the cay, and as they are not known Nassau residents, such as policemen or doctors, we have to assume that Arnie has been nobbled.'

'Shit! Did you say six? What are we going to do?'

'Shut up shop, first thing.' She switched off the light in the lounge. Although it was not yet dark outside, the gloom inside the shuttered building was intense. Then she went through the games room to the back verandah, followed by the dogs, which had sensed an air of excitement. These doors she also closed, and then the shutters.

Felicity had followed her. 'Just you and me ... Don't you think we need help?'

'Yes, and I intend to work on that. But no help is likely to arrive within an hour, at the earliest.'

'I was thinking of Lucian.'

'So was I, although I'm not sure how much help he will be, if he comes back. Now listen: we each have a spare cartridge box plus the ones in our pistols, of which you have used one. That's a total of seventy-nine cartridges, which is more than enough to take care of six men, but not if we loose off whole magazines at a time. So, strictly single shots. Right?'

'Right. There's also the Browning.'

Jessica nodded. 'And another dozen spares. But I'd rather leave that in situ unless we really need it. However ... Why, Rowena. Just the woman I was looking for.'

Rowena stood in the inner doorway. 'Just what is going on?'

'We are about to be visited by Mr Abriga's people, so we are making sure they can't get in.'

'Abriga's people? Here on Tiger Cay? Don't be ridiculous. How could they get here?'

'Courtesy of your helicopter, and Arnie. Don't blow your top. I think he was coerced. But that doesn't alter the fact that we are probably going to need all the firepower we can get.'

'You mean to shoot at these people? Again?'

'Only if they shoot at us first. We do have an ace in the hole: Theresa. They won't want to risk harming her. However, I seem to remember Jerry telling me Lucian has both a revolver and a shotgun. Right?'

'Jerry! My God, Jerry! They're after him!'

'That's why we may need those guns,'

Jessica said patiently. 'Where are they?'

'They're in a cabinet in the office. But it's locked.'

'Which is as it should be. Where is the key?'

'It's on his chain, with all the other keys.'

'And this chain is...?'

'In his pocket, I suppose. It usually is.'

Jessica gave her an old-fashioned look, trying to determine whether or not she was attempting to be funny. But being funny was not one of Rowena's characteristics. 'OK,' she said. 'Filly, go upstairs and open that cabinet.'

'Right. Ah...'

'Use your pistol. But remember: single shots.'

'You can't go firing guns at my furniture,' Rowena protested.

'Put in an insurance claim.'

Felicity asked, 'Can I use the light?'

Jessica nodded. 'But switch it off again when you're finished. No use giving them targets.'

Felicity went upstairs.

'Now,' Jessica said. 'I assume Lucian travels with one of his mobiles. Would you give me the number?'

'I have no idea what his number is.'

Jessica kept her temper with difficulty. 'OK. Well, then, what's the number of the supermarket? The police station? The hotel? The airport? Anywhere in Cat Island? They do have telephones?'

'I don't know. I suppose they have a link with Nassau. But I imagine the telegraph

282

office has shut down by now.'

'But these people will respond to a satellite call, surely?'

'I suppose so. But I don't know any of their numbers.'

Jessica snapped her fingers. 'The PC. It has a list of phone numbers.'

From upstairs there came the sound of a shot, followed by another. The dogs started barking.

'Don't waste them,' Jessica muttered.

Theresa appeared. 'Someone's shooting. Why is someone shooting?'

'Explain to her, Rowena, there's a dear.'

She went to the stairs, and the dogs barked even louder. A moment later there was a knock on the door.

'Oh, my God!' Rowena moaned, and threw both arms round Theresa.

Jessica came back into the room, hand resting on her shoulder bag. 'Just be quiet,' she whispered. 'Let them make the running.'

There was another knock. 'You in there, Mrs L?' Arnie called. 'It's me, Arnie.'

His voice had certainly changed from the slow drawl Jessica remembered. Again she shook her head – violently – as Rowena opened her mouth.

'I heard you were trying to contact me,' Arnie called. 'So I reckoned I'd come up while it's still possible. I figured you guys want to get out before this storm gets here, and that's a damned sensible decision. Let me tell you, it's rough out there. But I made it up, so I can make it back. That's if we get a move on. The met boys say she'll be here in a couple of hours.'

Another pause. Felicity came down the stairs, carrying the shotgun, a box of cartridges and the revolver. Jessica touched her lip with her forefinger.

'What're you doing, Mrs L?' Arnie shouted, his voice becoming very agitated. 'We ... I know you're in there. I saw your lights when I was coming down. Now's no time to play silly buggers.'

When he stopped, the dogs also stopped barking. 'We must say something,' Rowena said. 'If he knows we're here...'

'They don't know who is in here or how many,' Jessica pointed out. 'The next move is up to them.'

'But if you're sure they're hit men...'

'I am sure, but I don't know what their orders are. If they have come here to negotiate, and we refuse to talk to them, they should go away again. The weather isn't very nice out there, and it's going to get worse. They'll hardly want to spend the night in the open, with a hurricane knocking about. If, on the other hand, they have come here looking for trouble, they are going to have to start it pretty soon. But they have to start it.'

'And you are sure you can handle it?'

Jessica smiled at her. 'If they give me the opportunity, yes.'

'Now, Mrs L,' Arnie called, 'you ain't being very friendly. And that after ten years? Come along now, don't let that yellow-haired bitch steer you the wrong way. Open up.'

'The bastard,' Felicity commented. 'I thought he liked us – you, anyway.'

'I think he's being told what to say,' Jessica pointed out. 'Now, I have to get to that computer and see who I can rustle up. You hold the fort down here, Filly.'

'What do I do?'

'Just don't let anybody in.'

She went to the stairs, and was checked by a tremendous bang on the front door.

'You in there,' shouted a new voice, one with a pronounced foreign accent, 'open this fucking door before we break it down. You can't fuck with us, lady, even if you are a fucking policewoman. Rile me, and I'll have your tits for dinner.'

'Well,' Rowena said. 'What terrible language.'

'I have a notion he's not going to survive the night,' Jessica said.

'That's my brother, Arturo,' Theresa said.

They all turned to look at her.

'I didn't know you had a brother,' Rowena said.

'I have four brothers, and two sisters,' Theresa said. 'My parents are Roman Catholics.'

'He doesn't sound in a very good mood,' Jessica suggested.

'He's never in a good mood. He's a thug.'

'Ah. So would I be right in supposing that you would not like to be handed over to him?'

'He'd probably kill me.'

'Now that's interesting. But it's not something that we can really risk putting to the test.'

'She has to be allowed to talk with him,' Rowena said.

'Do you want to talk with him, Theresa?'

'I have nothing to say to him.'

'Well, then...'

'All right, you stupid dames, you asked for it,' Arturo shouted.

There was a burst of automatic fire, and bullets smashed into the storm shutters. None actually got through, but the inside of the thick wood was splintered in places. Rowena and Theresa both screamed and again clung to each other; even Felicity gave a little shriek, but she also drew her pistol.

'Well, that's it, then,' Jessica said.

'What was that?' Felicity asked.

'I would say an AK Seventy-Four. Let's have a look at that shotgun.'

Felicity handed it to her; her hand was shaking. Jessica inspected the weapon. It was actually a Remington pump-action riot gun, which she knew would hold seven shots in its barrel magazine. This was presently empty, but when she checked the box of cartridges she discovered to her delight that while half were buckshot, the other half were solid slugs, each the length and size of a man's finger. They were called deershot in the States, and were capable of going through a wooden wall at several hundred yards' range.

She thrust four buckshot cartridges into the magazine, followed with three of the solid shot, and pumped once to fill the breech.

'You girls got the message?' Arturo called. 'We mean business.'

'Ah, but you see,' Jessica said quietly, 'so do we.' The blood was pumping through her arteries, as it always did at the prospect of action: but her brain was ice-cold, again as it always was in a crisis.

'So, you going to open up?'

'I think we should oblige the man,' Jessica said. 'If you ladies will retire from the possible line of fire...'

'You're going to open the door?' Rowena demanded.

'Just a little.'

'And shoot that gun?'

'I think it would be a good idea to let them know we're not about to lie on our backs with our legs in the air.'

'They're standing on the verandah. If you shoot that gun you're liable to hit someone.'

'I'd be a bit disappointed if I didn't.'

'But ... Theresa's brother is out there.'

They looked at Theresa, whose face was contorting. 'Let me speak with him.'

Jessica considered for a moment, but she knew she had to be reasonable, even if she had no doubt about the outcome. 'All right,' she said. 'Just stay away from the doorway.'

Theresa went forward, keeping to one side of the room. 'Arturo,' she called. 'This is madness.'

'I agree with you,' Arturo said. 'Open the door.'

'What do you want with us?'

'I have come to take you home to Poppa.'

'What will happen to me?'

'I do not know. I do know that Poppa is very angry. You have brought dishonour upon the name of Abriga.'

Theresa drew a deep breath. 'If I come with you, will you leave the island and these people alone?'

'She's got guts,' Jessica conceded.

'We will leave,' Arturo said, 'but your paramour must come with us.'

'But he has come here for a fight,' Jessica said.

'You won't let them take Jerry,' Rowena begged.

'That's what we're being paid to prevent, ma'am.'

'He cannot travel,' Theresa said. 'He is badly hurt.'

'Do not worry, little sister. We will carry him. Now open the door.'

Theresa looked at Jessica.

'I think you have done all you can,' Jessica said. 'I also think that we know the situation. He has come for Jerry as much as for you. So now will you permit me to take over the negotiations?'

Theresa looked at Rowena, whose shoulders were slumped. 'What are you going to do? What *can* you do?'

'Disburse a little information. Theresa,

288

come back here and stand against the wall. Or better yet, go into the bedroom and stay with Jerry. Maybe you'd like to do that as well, Rowena.'

'This is my house. I will stay with you.'

'OK. Then go behind the bar.'

Rowena obeyed.

'Now, Filly,' Jessica said. 'We want to open the left-hand half-shutter when I say the word. As you do so, stand aside.'

Face grim with determination, Felicity moved to beside the shutter. Jessica stood on the other side, with the shotgun. 'Are you still there, Señor Abriga?' she asked.

'Who the fuck are you?' Arturo demanded.

'I am the yellow-haired bitch Arnie referred to earlier. More correctly, I am Detective-Sergeant Jessica Jones of the Metropolitan Police, London, Special Branch.'

'Well, shit!'

'And in answer to your next question, I am here in an official capacity, to protect the lives of the Lenghurst family, and your sister, as long as she wishes to be protected. Do I make myself clear?'

'Listen, sister—'

'No, no,' Jessica said. 'I am doing the talking, and you are doing the listening. You are at present guilty of three offences. One, you are trespassing on private property. Two, you have uttered threats. Three, you have damaged private property by firing into this door. I suspect you are also guilty of carrying unlicensed weapons, and of kidnapping or

289

coercing Mr Pleass. My advice to you is to return to Nassau as rapidly as possible, and then leave the Bahamas as soon as you can, because as soon as this weather improves I am going to file charges against you.'

'Yeah? And suppose I tell you that if you don't open this door right now we are going to bust it down and then we are going to take you apart.'

Jessica gave an entirely false sigh. 'In that case, Mr Abriga, please do not say afterwards that you were not warned. You have fifteen seconds to evacuate this verandah and return to the helicopter.'

'You shitting bitch. You know what I'm going to do to you?'

'You told me,' Jessica reminded him.

'Now?' Felicity whispered, carefully drawing the bolts.

'He has another five seconds.' Jessica counted the numbers, drew a deep breath, and said, 'Now.'

Felicity pulled the shutter in, Jessica stepped into the aperture, the shotgun levelled. The glass doors had already been shattered by the earlier firing, but she removed some more as she thrust the muzzle through and squeezed the trigger. Before the storm of buckshot had even reached the tennis court, or the explosion begun to reverberate, she had pumped another cartridge into the breech, swung the gun to the right and fired again. Still in almost the same movement she again pumped, swung to the left and fired a third time.

The reverberations of the shots mingled with the shout of alarm and some shrieks of pain. Someone returned fire, but the bullet screamed over Jessica's head as she stepped aside, to smash into the ceiling. Rowena, crouching behind the bar, also screamed.

Felicity slammed the shutter shut and shot the bolt. 'I think you hit someone.'

'I hope it wasn't Arnie,' Rowena panted.

'So do I,' Jessica agreed. She still had some doubts as to his exact role in the invasion by Abriga's people; she would have thought he should have been able to give some indication of distress to the various officials at Windsor Field. But for the moment they could hear nothing from outside, except for the drumming of the rain, which had again become quite heavy. 'OK, Filly,' she said. 'Your watch. I'm afraid I am going to have to ask you to keep moving, from back to front, as we don't know where next they may try to get in.'

'You don't think they'll go away, after you shot one of them?' Rowena asked.

'I don't think I hit anyone very seriously,' Jessica confessed. 'I wasn't trying to. I just wanted to convince them we meant business. As to whether they'll go away, I have my doubts. So the sooner we arrange some support, the better.'

'Can you do that?'

'I intend to have a go.' She looked at her watch. 'Eight o'clock. Do you think you could rustle us up something to eat?'

'Well,' Rowena said. 'I suppose I could, if...'
She looked at Felicity.

'She is on guard duty,' Jessica reminded her.
'Do the best you can.'

'If only Lucian would come back ... He
should be back by now, don't you think?'

'If he was coming back, yes.'

'You don't suppose something has happened to him?'

'I really have no idea. But it's probably a
good idea for him to stay over there for the
time being, until and unless 'he can return
mob-handed. If he's on his own he might just
run into our friends.'

'Oh, my God! But...'

'I'm going to see if I can raise him now.
Start cooking.'

She went upstairs, surprised at how light it
still was beyond the unshuttered windows,
despite the fact that it was raining heavily.
She peered out but could see very little beyond the palm trees, still moving only gently
to and fro; from here she could not see the
beach or even the sea. She reflected that
Abriga's people were going to have a wet and
uncomfortable night, even if the weather did
not deteriorate as it was supposed to.

Despite her instructions, Felicity had left
the light on, as she had the computer, and she
recalled the picture, again opening the
various files in 'My Documents'. There were
quite a few Nassau addresses and telephone
numbers, but none for Cat Island. She toyed
with the idea of trying the police again, but

she doubted they would believe her, any more than the Lenghurst lawyer would; Lucian himself had not been able to get much reaction when he had tried earlier. So...

She used her own mobile to call London. It rang for several minutes before a sleepy voice muttered, 'Hello.'

'I really am sorry to bother you at this hour, Mrs Adams, but it is most urgent that I speak with the commander.'

There was a moment's silence, then the voice suddenly came awake. 'Sergeant *Jones*! This is really too much. Do you know the time?'

'I imagine it is just past one.'

'And you expect me to wake up my husband?'

Jessica listened to some background grunts. 'I would say he is already awake.'

'Give me that,' the commander snapped. 'Now look here, JJ; this is getting beyond a joke. I said I'd deal with the situation in the morning.'

'Yes, sir. Unfortunately, things have moved on. A good way.'

'What? Don't tell me the boy is dead?'

'No, sir. Jeremy Lenghurst is still alive. For the moment. But the house is under siege from six of Mr Abriga's people.'

'What? Be serious.'

'I am very serious, sir. They are armed with at least one AK Seventy-Four assault rifle, but I would estimate that they are all equipped with firearms.'

'Now look here, JJ...'

There was a whine and a crash. The windowpane shattered and Jessica found herself on her hands and knees, having dropped the mobile.

'JJ?!' Adams was shouting. 'Are you there, JJ?'

Sprawled on the floor, Jessica retrieved the mobile. 'I am here, sir. Can you hold on a moment. It appears that they also have a high-powered rifle.'

She crawled to the wall and the light switch. As she did so there was another crash, and another bullet smashed through the shattered window. This struck the computer, which disintegrated into flying fragments with a scorching smell.

'JJ?' Adams shouted. 'Are you shooting at someone?'

Jessica took a deep breath, stood up, and flicked the switch. The light went off, and there was another shot. The bullet entered the room, but where it went after that she had no idea. She slid back down the wall and sat on the floor. 'I am not shooting at anyone, sir,' she panted. 'But someone is shooting at me.'

'Are you all right? You sound very strange.'

'I am sounding strange, sir, because I am panting.'

The door burst open. 'JJ?' Felicity cried. 'Oh, God! JJ! Where are you?'

'On the floor,' Jesica said. 'Join me.'

Felicity crouched beside her.

'Who is that?' Adams demanded.

'Detective-Constable Hewitt, sir. My partner.'

'I demand to know what's going on.'

'I am trying to tell you, sir. The exact situation is that we have in this house four live women, one of whom is a fifteen-year-old girl, and another of whom is an on-going hysteric, one badly wounded man and one dead woman. That is to say, we have two effectives. Outside there are eight people. Six are gunmen. I am not sure whether the other two are hostile or not, but they cannot be assumed to be of much help to us.'

'But ... where is Lenghurst?'

'He is not on the island at this time, sir.'

'Well, hadn't you better call him back?'

'I am unable to contact Mr Lenghurst, sir.'

'Good God! Well, what about the village? You have a whole village there, haven't you? Surely they'll give you a hand?'

'I would like to think so, sir. But the villagers are also not on the island.'

'What? But they live there. Don't they?'

'Yes, sir. But they have evacuated the island.'

'Because of these gunmen? Good God!'

'They left because of the storm, sir. There is a hurricane calculated to hit this area by dawn tomorrow morning.'

'What a foul-up.' His tone, as so often, suggested that he considered the situation was entirely because she was involved. 'Right. Can you hold the situation until the Nassau police arrive?'

'I am sure we could sir, were the Nassau police *going* to arrive.'

'What? You mean you haven't called the police?'

'We did call the Nassau police, sir, several hours ago, when we reported both the injury to Jeremy Lenghurst and the death of Mrs Garcia. I'm sure you will agree that these are both very serious matters. However, we were informed that the police could not come up to the cay until this storm had passed on. Well, since then the weather has deteriorated considerably and, frankly, I doubt they would believe what I have to tell them. I thought that perhaps if you were to call the British High Commissioner, or perhaps the Bahamian Prime Minister, it might have more effect.'

'JJ, it is past one.'

'It is only just past eight here, sir. No one will have gone to sleep yet. I doubt they will even have had dinner.'

There was a brief silence. 'Do you consider your lives are in danger?'

'Yes, sir, I do. The only way we are going to survive is if massive reinforcements arrive within a couple of hours, or we kill all six of the villains. I am sure you would not wish us to have to go that far, sir.'

'JJ, you are going to be the death of me. I will see what I can sort out and get back to you.'

'Thank you, sir.'

'Do you think he'll be able to do anything?' Felicity asked.

'Keep your fingers crossed. How's Rowena doing?'

'When last I saw her she was crouching on the floor with her hands over her ears. We may have to get our own dinner.'

'Well, let's do that while there's a temporary lull. I think maybe they're hoping they hit me.'

'Don't you think they were just firing at the light?'

'You could be right. But we'll close the shutters. In fact, we had better close all the shutters up here. There may not be time later on.'

Once the floor was secure, they went downstairs, where the dogs, now in a highly excited state, were frisking around.

In the kitchen, Rowena was still sitting on the floor. 'All that shooting,' she wailed. 'What were they shooting at?'

'Me, mainly. Or perhaps the light in the office. I'm afraid up there is a bit of a mess.'

'Lucian will be *furious*.'

'Maybe he should have been here. Now do please get dinner. Filly, I have a job for you. We should've thought of it sooner. Go to every bathroom, put the plugs in, and turn on the taps. I have an idea we may soon be cut off from the reservoir.'

Felicity gulped. '*Every* bathroom?'

'OK, you can skip the spare room.'

'What about keeping watch?'

'They can't get in without making a noise.'

Felicity hurried off, and Jessica went into Jeremy's bedroom. He was lying quietly, and Theresa was on the other bed, but she sat up as Jessica came in. 'All that shooting ... I'm so scared, Miss Jones.'

'They were just trying to frighten us. Help is on its way.' She had to believe that. 'How is he?'

'He was so fretful. I gave him some more pills.'

It occurred to Jessica that Jeremy was probably in greater danger than any of them. 'Well, he seems quiet enough.'

Suddenly Theresa clutched her hand. 'Are you going to shoot my brother?'

'Not unless he makes me.'

'Do you think I should have gone with him? Saved all this trouble?'

'Perhaps. But as he wasn't accepting you without Jeremy, that's academic. Come on out of here and help Rowena get dinner together.'

'I couldn't eat a thing.'

'Force yourself. It may be your last meal for a while.'

The house was filled with the sound of running water.

'Whatever is causing that?' Rowena inquired. 'Have we a leak or something?'

'That's Filly filling the bathtubs.'

'The silly girl. She'll run the reservoir dry.'

'I shouldn't think so – not with the rain

298

that's falling, and the lots more that's on its way.'

She bullied them into finishing preparing the meal.

'What about Jerry?' Theresa asked. 'He hasn't eaten since breakfast.'

As if she had just remembered that she had a son, Rowena burst into tears. 'He's going to die. I just know he's going to die.'

'He won't die from missing a couple of meals,' Jessica said. 'But we'll get him to eat next time he wakes up. And no more sedatives,' she told Theresa.

'But he'll be in pain.'

'He'll have to grin and bear it for a while.'

Felicity joined them. 'All done. And boy, am I hungry. And...' She looked longingly at the jug of rum punch she had prepared before the Colombians had arrived.

'I think we could all do with one drink,' Jessica agreed. 'But just one.'

'What are they *doing*?' Rowena asked, as they ate.

'Perhaps they've gone back to Nassau,' Theresa said optimistically.

'We'd have heard the chopper,' Jessica said. 'I imagine they're exploring the island, finding out just what they can use against us. Does Arnie know the island well, Rowena?'

'Oh, yes. But...'

'Please don't start that "he'll never betray me" business again. I would say...' And as if she had said it, the lights went out, plunging the shuttered interior of the house into pitch darkness.

'Aaaagh!' Theresa screamed.

'For God's sake,' Felicity protested.

'It must be the fuse,' Rowena said.

'It's not the fuse,' Jessica said. 'Listen.'

The only sound was that of the rain drumming on the roof.

'Shit!' Rowena said. 'The air conditioning has gone off.'

'Because the generator has been switched off,' Jessica said.

'Oh, my God! We have to open some windows, or we'll stew.'

'I imagine that is the object of the exercise.'

'It's not only us are going to stew,' Felicity said in a low voice.

'You're right,' Jessica agreed. 'We have to move fast. I suppose you don't happen to know where your candles are kept, Rowena?'

'I don't even know if we have any candles.'

'Par for the course. OK.' She felt in her shoulder bag, found her torch, switched it on, looked round the anxious faces. Felicity did the same but Jessica shook her head. 'Save yours for the time being; mine will do. First thing, we empty the freezer.'

'But that's crazy,' Rowena protested. 'Left alone, the food in there will last forty-eight hours without power.'

'That's already frozen. But fresh meat should last twenty-four.'

Rowena stared at her in the glow of the torch. 'You mean ... Oh, my *God*!'

'It has to be done, Rowena. And it has to be

done *now*. Let's move it.'

She and Felicity opened the chest freezer and began dumping food on the floor. After a moment Theresa joined them. Rowena continued to sit at the table. It took them ten minutes to reduce the contents of the freezer by half. 'That's enough,' Jessica said. 'There's room for her body, and the rest of that frozen stuff will bring her temperature down. Come on, Filly.'

Felicity gulped, but faithfully followed her to the spare bedroom. Jessica paused outside the door. 'You OK?'

'I'm OK.'

Jessica drew a deep breath and opened the door. The air in the room was thick, but not yet unbreathable. In fact, Jessica realized as she shone the beam of the torch on the bed and the body lying there, thanks to the air conditioning, rigor mortis was only just setting in, thus disintegration and decomposition would hardly commence for at least another twelve hours, and it should be checked altogether for even longer once she was in the freezer.

'Take her legs,' she said. 'Lift from above the knees.'

'What about the gun?' It was still clutched in Greta's right hand.

'It comes with her.' Still holding the torch, Jessica got her arms under Greta's shoulders and then into her armpits and round in front, and they lifted the dead woman from the bed.

'God she's heavy,' Felicity commented.

'Dead bodies generally are,' Jessica pointed out.

'I didn't know. This is my first.'

Jessica realized that, for all her courage and devotion to duty, Felicity was as close to hysterics as either of the two other women. Gasping and stumbling, they carried the body along the corridor, through the games room, and into the kitchen, where Theresa gave another scream, as if she hadn't known they were coming.

Rowena remained seated at the table, and she had the jug of rum punch. 'I just can't look,' she said; 'I just can't.'

'Well, then, don't look,' Jessica suggested, somewhat brutally. She was thoroughly fed up with her client.

They laid Greta on the frozen food left inside the freezer, and then packed as much as they could of the stuff they had taken out around her and on top of her before closing the lid.

Rowena had after all got up to watch them. 'All that food,' she remarked. 'There must be several hundred pounds' worth, all gone.'

'Not necessarily,' Jessica said, more brutally yet. 'All that stuff is either in packets or well wrapped up. Providing we get her out of there in the next couple of days, it should be quite edible.'

'Oh ... you are unspeakable. I am going to bed. Kindly let me have a light.'

'Filly, would you light Mrs Lenghurst up to her room?' Jessica said. 'But I'm afraid we will need the light down here.'

Rowena flounced off, accompanied by Felicity.

'What's going to happen?' Theresa asked.

'That's up to your brother and his friends. With us all battened down, we're nearly impossible to get at. I imagine they're brooding on ways and means now. But while they outnumber us, and, I would say, have superior firepower, the ball has to be in their court. All we can do is wait. But just remember that every moment brings help closer.'

'Are you certain of that, Miss Jones?'

'Of course I am,' Jessica lied. 'Here's Filly. All peaceful up there?'

'That's not exactly how I would describe it. She's spitting blood.'

'At who, now?'

'At me. She wanted me to spend the night with her.'

'It might have been an experience. But we need you here. We have to feed Jerry.'

He was awake, and moving restlessly. 'God,' he muttered. 'Where am I?'

'In bed,' Jessica assured him.

'That woman ... she shot me.'

'You did rather bring it on yourself.'

'But...' His eyes rolled as he tried to take in his surroundings; although he could tell there were two other people in the room, in the light of the single torch he could not identify them.

'Don't worry,' Jessica assured him. 'She's not here now. Felicity and Theresa have brought you some food.'

'My leg ... God, I'm in agony. I should be in hospital.'

'We're working on it. You have to eat. Be a good boy, and we'll put you back to sleep afterwards. Theresa.'

She left her a torch, and she and Felicity returned to the games room.

'What's the drill?' Felicity asked.

'It'll have to be watch and watch.'

'OK. What about these?' The two retrievers were looking at them expectantly.

'If they're thinking about walkies, they'll have to grin and bear it.'

'I think we're the ones who will have to grin and bear it, by tomorrow morning. But right now, I'd say they're thinking about food.'

'Oh,' Jessica said. 'I'm afraid I don't know much about dogs.'

'We have four.'

'That figures. So...'

'I'll look after them.'

'Good girl. Then you'd better take first watch.' She looked at her Omega. The time was eight forty-five. 'Can you stand three hours?'

'Sure.'

'Right. I'll be up at half eleven. But call me if there is the slightest alarm, human or weather.'

'Will do. JJ ... thanks for everything.'

'You mean, for getting you into this mess?'

'I wouldn't have missed it for the world. But I meant – well, for being so understanding about what happened.'

'I've told you: forget it. You were saving the life of your client.'

She went to their bedroom, stripped off her sweat-wet clothes, stepped into the shower stall ... and nothing happened. She'd forgotten that without electricity there was no means of pumping the water from the reservoirs.

'Shit,' she muttered. But at least the bathtub was three-quarters full. She scooped some out to give herself a top and tail; then she scooped up some more to clean her teeth and have a drink.

The house was now absolutely, uncannily still; she supposed Theresa had given Jeremy another knock-out drop. Even the rain seemed to have slackened into a drizzle, and there was no sign of any wind, at the moment, although in the distance, now that the noise of both the air conditioning and the generator was stilled, she could just hear the rumble of the surf. She remembered this waiting period from the Pacific typhoon, when the yacht had rolled lazily in the huge swell, while the sky had slowly turned black. This time she couldn't see the sky, although from what she had seen earlier she didn't doubt it was black; but the swell was certainly huge, judging by the surf. The wind, she recalled, would sound like ... an express train going through a tunnel! She awoke with a start, realized it was her mobile. She fumbled in the dark, found it. 'Yes?'

'Would I be speaking with Detective-Sergeant Jones, Metropolitan Police Special Branch?'

'This is she,' Jessica acknowledged, muscles tensing; it was not a voice she recognized.

'This is Superintendent Hubert Stratton, Bahamas Police. Did I wake you up?'

She gathered the phone must have bleeped several times before it had penetrated her consciousness; the time was a quarter past eleven. 'I was asleep, yes, sir. But thank you for calling.'

'Does the fact that you were asleep mean that you have matters on Tiger Cay under control?'

'No, sir. My colleague and I are standing watch and watch. The situation here is still critical.'

'Confirm. You and your colleague are alone on the cay with two other women and a badly injured male, and you are being menaced by eight armed men.'

Hooray for old Adams, Jessica thought; he had said just enough, but not too much. 'That is correct, sir.'

'But you are also armed.'

'We are on protection duty, sir. I believe the matter has been cleared with your government. But the odds remain considerable. These people are equipped with automatic weapons.'

'I take you point, Sergeant, and I will have armed members of my force up there just as soon as is possible. Unfortunately, you must

306

understand that it is not possible at this moment, with a hurricane on our doorstep. Even if I could get them up to Cat Island, which would be a highly dangerous operation, I am not sure that I could get them across to the cay.'

'I understand this, sir.'

'Are you prepared for a blow?'

'We are shuttered, sir. I believe adequately.'

'And are you adequately provided with food and drinking water?'

'Yes, sir.'

'And cartridges, eh?'

Jessica sighed. 'Yes, sir.'

'Very good. Brigitte is presently forecast to strike Cat Island in a couple of hours' time. You should be having the rain there now.'

'It has been raining all afternoon, sir.'

'Then it's on schedule. Now listen: if she hits you before dawn, she should be through by lunch time. Unfortunately, by then she could be coming our way. No one can say which way she will actually go after hitting Cat Island, but if she continues on her present course, she could plough right into the central Bahamas. If she does that, we are not going to be able to move for another twenty-four hours or so, and even then it may depend upon how much damage she does. If she swings off, we should be with you by noon tomorrow. Can you hold for another twelve hours, at least?'

'It looks as if we will have to, sir.'

'I'm glad to hear you're so confident.'

'Well, sir, it occurs to me that we have an ace up our sleeve. If that hurricane really is going to hit us in an hour or two – well, we're snug in here behind our shutters and with ample supplies of food and water, but those baddies are outside with nothing save what they might be able to find in the village.'

'Good thinking, Sergeant. I look forward to meeting you, some time soon.'

Jessica switched off, listened to the dogs barking. She got out of bed, pulled on a pair of knickers and a bra, and saw the gleam of a torch in the corridor. 'JJ,' Felicity said, 'something's up.'

'So it seems.' She picked up her bag, went outside.

'There's someone at the back door,' Felicity said.

'One of them?'

'No. That's the strange thing. It sounds like a woman.'

'Right. Stay by me for a moment, then you can go to bed.'

She went into the games room, patted the excited dogs, and moved to the back door. Standing to one side, she asked, 'Who's there?'

'Sergeant Jones? I am Clarissa Pleass. Arnie's wife. Please let me in.'

'What are you doing there?'

'I have escaped from those thugs. Please let me in.'

'Are you alone?'

'Of course I'm alone.'

'Where is Arnie?'

'He's still with them. In the village. They have him tied up.'

'But you escaped.'

'Yes. Yes. Please let me in. It is so cold and wet out here. And there is a big storm coming.'

Jessica couldn't argue with that; the rain had now returned heavier than ever, pounding on the roof, and although there was no wind as yet, she again remembered from the past that it had to be close. But...

'I'm sorry,' she said. 'I can't open this door.'

'But you must.' Clarissa's voice ceased whispering and became loud. 'If I go back to them, they'll kill me. I know they will.'

'I don't think so,' Jessica said, 'seeing as how they sent you in the first place. Just tell them: no dice. You can tell them as well that I have just spoken to a Bahamian police superintendent – name of Stratton. You may know him. He reckons on being up here first thing tomorrow morning, so they had better make some alternative plans.'

'Let me in, you bitch!' Clarissa screamed, banging on the door. 'Let me in!'

'Suppose she's telling the truth,' Felicity asked.

'I hope she's not, for her sake. But that's the oldest ploy in the world. Now...'

'What's happening?' Rowena asked, emerging from the stairwell. 'All that screaming...'

'Just Arnie's wife, trying to get in.'

'Oh, the poor dear. We must—'

'Do nothing,' Jessica said. 'We are opening no doors. Now...'

From above them there came a resounding crash.

Rowena spun round. 'What in the name of God...'

Jessica listened to feet above them. 'Oh, Christ,' she said. 'They're in the house.'

A Fearful Thing

'Kill that torch,' Jessica told Felicity, and switched off her own, having spotted the shotgun leaning against the wall. She picked it up, levelled it as she heard feet on the stairs, squeezed the trigger. There was a shout, but more of alarm than of pain, she suspected. She pumped the gun and fired twice more, the buckshot splattering over the wall and through the open doorway. Then she handed the gun to Felicity. 'Get back,' she whispered. 'Take the lounge door, and reload, with solid shot. Rowena, in here.' She pushed her into the kitchen.

'What can we do?' Rowena asked.

'They have to come down the stairs.'

'We can't even see the stairs. And ... Oh, my God! Jerry.'

'And Theresa.'

'They're cut off!'

'Yes,' Jessica agreed, trying to think. 'What beats me is how they got in through those shutters.'

'Well...'

'Holy shit! You didn't.'

'It was so hot. I couldn't sleep.'

'And you described me as unspeakable.

311

And the bastards spotted the open window and sent Clarissa to distract us while they climbed up. Shit!'

'I didn't know they could do that – climb up, I mean.'

'They used the mango tree. Do you realize how lucky you are that you came downstairs when you did? Otherwise they'd have you. Quite literally.'

'Oh ... What about Jerry?'

Jessica felt like spitting. Because of this woman's crass inability to think of anything but her own comfort, JJ was being required to risk her life, quite unnecessarily. But Jerry had to be rescued, if it were possible.

'Filly,' she said, 'can you see the door?'

'Just about. What do you reckon they're doing?'

From upstairs there came a series of bangs and crashes, and the sound of splintering glass.

'Seems they're wrecking the place. Or looking for another way down. That suggests they don't have Arnie with them.'

'My beautiful house, being wrecked...'

'Oh, for God's sake, shut up. Filly, I have got to get through that door and into the bedrooms. You'll have to cover me.'

'But...'

'Just listen. You are now down to deershot in that shotgun. That is to say, if you don't aim at me you won't hit me, but you need to remember that anyone you do aim at, at a range which will only be a few feet, is going to

312

be cut right in two.'

'Jesus! Can't I use my pistol?'

'As a back-up. Those slugs will be more effective in keeping their heads down. You ready?'

Felicity drew a deep breath. 'Ready.'

'And you,' Jessica told Rowena, 'don't move, and don't utter a sound.'

She drew her Skorpion, stepped away from the kitchen doorway, and, back against the wall, edged her way towards the lobby. Only then did she remember she was wearing only bra and knickers. At least it made movement very easy.

She was only a few feet from the door when it suddenly swung wide. 'Say,' Theresa remarked. 'You guys around? There is one hell of a racket going on upstairs.'

'Don't shoot!' Jessica shouted, just in case Felicity was trigger-happy. 'Theresa...'

'Sergeant?' Theresa turned towards her, still holding the door open. Then there was a sudden ripple of fire from above her, and she gave a shriek and fell on to her face.

Jessica stepped away from the wall, into the doorway, and disobeyed her own orders, emptying her magazine up the stairs. There were screams and shouts and more crashes; Jessica thrust the gun back into the bag, and grasped Theresa's arms, dragging her clear of the door and against the wall.

Rowena was screaming, a prolonged high-pitched wail.

'JJ!' Felicity shouted. 'Are you all right?'

'Yes.' Jessica fumbled in the darkness, her hands becoming wet with blood, and at last located Theresa's throat. There was no pulse.

'Hey!' a voice called. 'You down there! Sergeant Jones! That was my sister, no?'

Jessica abandoned Theresa's body to crawl back to the kitchen doorway. 'That was your sister, yes,' she called over her shoulder.

'She is all right, yes?'

Jessica had gained the kitchen doorway, where she sat to change magazines. Rowena had subsided into a continuous low moan. 'Your sister is dead,' Jessica called.

There was a moment's silence. Then Arturo said, 'You have killed my sister?'

'Look, buster, I am being paid to keep your sister alive. If you'd like to come down here and look, you'll see she was struck by several bullets from an assault rifle, which is something I do not possess. Unfortunately,' she added in a lower tone.

There was a babble of voices from upstairs, all in Spanish and spoken too quickly from Jessica's limited knowledge of the language to interpret. Then one of the voices screamed something, to be cut short by a single shot.

'JJ,' Felicity said from the lounge doorway.

'I think we only have five against us now. Or less.' She had hit at least two of them, firstly with the buckshot and then with her Skorpion – though she did not know if either was dead.

'Jerry,' Rowena moaned. 'Oh, Jerry.'

What a fuck-up, Jessica thought. She had

314

had some hope of getting Jerry out with Theresa's help, covered by Felicity. But there was no way she alone could hope to move a heavy and inert man ... and if she had Felicity to help her, they would have no cover: Rowena was obviously useless.

'JJ,' Felicity said again.

'Ssssh. I'm thinking.'

'But, JJ, what's that noise? It sounds just like an express train entering a tunnel.'

'Shit!' Jessica muttered. 'Which window did you open, Rowena.'

Rowena moaned, and Jessica shook her shoulders. 'Which window, God damn it?!'

Rowena waved her hand. 'The north one.'

Of course; the one next to the mango tree! 'Oh, Jesus! Abriga,' she shouted. 'Listen to me.'

For reply, several shots rang out, smashing into the floor at the foot of the stairs.

'Listen to me,' she screamed. 'Shut the window! Close and bolt the shutters. You have only a few seconds.'

The reply was another shot, and it occurred to her that they didn't have hurricanes in Colombia, and unlike his sister he couldn't have been sent to school in Miami. But if he wasn't going to shut the window ... She had to make an instantaneous decision. The kitchen was the only room in the house without an exterior window, and the back door was firmly shuttered.

'Filly!' she shouted. 'Come in here!'

'I won't be able to cover the door,' Felicity

315

shouted back.

'Just do it,' Jessica screamed.

Felicity ran across the space and almost tumbled into the kitchen. As she did so the train seemed to arrive in the station, but without stopping. The roaring sound obliterated thought, and the house trembled as if shaken by a giant hand.

Rowena began to scream again, but could hardly be heard above the noise. Jessica slammed the inner kitchen door shut, and sat against it. Felicity collapsed behind her, but she had retained hold of both the shotgun and her shoulder bag. 'Those men will come down!' she shouted, her mouth against Jessica's ear.

'I think they have more to worry about than us.'

'Are we going to die, JJ?'

'No way,' Jessica promised.

She hoped she wasn't lying, as the house still shook, and now there came a series of strange noises from above them.

'What's that?' Felicity shouted. 'Sounds like...'

'A roof tearing off,' Jessica said. 'That's what's happening. The wind's got inside.'

Now they were surrounded by ripping, tearing sounds, while through even the whine they could hear a crackling sound.

'What's that?' Felicity asked again.

'Waves coming through the coconut trees.'

'Oh, Jesus! When they hit us...'

'They're not supposed to,' Jessica said.

'We're too high up.'

'Oh, JJ, I am so scared.' She put her arms round Jessica and hugged her. Jessica responded, holding her tightly. Now there was nothing they could do but wait, until ... movement, close at hand. Someone shouting in Spanish. Felicity raised her head, and Jessica shook hers. But she drew her pistol, and Felicity did likewise.

The shouted conversation continued for a few more seconds; then there was a thump on the door. The Colombians had worked out that there was nowhere else they could be. *How crazy*, Jessica thought, *that these people can still be trying to kill us, when we are all in danger from a force greater than anything mankind has ever been able to harness*; or, hopefully, ever would.

'The other side,' she shouted into Felicity's ear.

Felicity promptly rolled away from her to the far side of the door, while Jessica retreated from the panelling on her side. 'Lie down,' she shouted at Rowena.

Bullets slammed into the door. The wood was thin inside the house, and most of them got through. Rowena shrieked, but it was terror rather than pain. Sparks flew as the lead ricocheted from the stove and the freezer before slamming into the walls and ceiling. Then the shooting stopped as the men listened.

The temptation to return fire was enormous. But their pistols would not be very

317

effective fired through wood, and they needed to save the shotgun for a real emergency. 'Easy,' she called to Felicity.

She didn't suppose she could be heard above the howl of the wind, the crackle of the waves and the shattering of timbers, but the Colombians opened fire again. Jessica reckoned that Arturo Abriga had entirely lost his senses since the death of his sister. But the door was now shot to pieces, and she knew an assault was imminent.

'Ready!' she shouted.

'Ready!' Felicity shouted back.

Shoulders thudded against the door, and it crashed off its hinges, assisted by the wind, which was swirling around inside the house, carrying with it a concoction of flying sand and grit and vegetation and water which stung their faces and Jessica's exposed body. But both women had turned on their knees and emptied their magazines into the games room. Bodies tumbled to and fro, but Jessica reckoned only two had been hit; the other man had been out of the line of fire. In any event, there was no time for either side to continue hostilities. As Jessica dropped her now useless pistol and picked up the shotgun, she found herself being thrown backwards across the kitchen as the far wall of the games room collapsed. 'Filly!' she screamed, but she didn't know if anyone heard her.

Now the walls of the kitchen also began to shake. Jessica knew she had to get out in preference to being blown out. She grappled with the back door, flattened against it by the wind, and found Felicity beside her. Between them they slipped the bolts and fell out, down a short flight of steps into a shallow gully. This was filled with water, but it was fresh rather than sea water, as the rain continued to pound down on their heads.

'JJ,' Felicity shouted, 'I've lost my weapon.'

'Join the club,' Jessica shouted back. 'They'll have to wait.'

Above their heads the kitchen outer wall was falling, and with it came Rowena, still shrieking. She landed on the side of the hollow, while the wall fell right across it. But this actually provided some shelter from the rain, even if Jessica suspected that it might only be temporary.

She reached out from beneath the wood, found Rowena's ankle, and dragged her into the pit. 'Help!' Rowena shouted as she sank into the water. 'I'm drowning. You're drowning me.'

'Get your head up and take deep breaths,' Jessica recommended.

Rowena gasped for several seconds. Then she said, 'We're all going to die. I know we're going to die.'

'The good news,' Jessica pointed out, 'is that we're not dead yet. The bad news is that it is going to cost you a fortune to rebuild this place.'

'Rebuild it? My God! I never want to see it again as long as I live. Jerry!' she suddenly screamed. 'Oh, my God! Jerry! He's dead!'

'We don't know that,' Jessica said. 'He's in bed. Probably the best place for him.'

Rowena began to weep again, so Jessica let her get on with it, reached across the hollow to squeeze Felicity's hand. 'You OK?'

'As long as you are, ma'am. Is there anything we should be doing?'

'There is nothing we can do, until this passes through.'

'How long, do you reckon?'

'Another three or four hours, this way.'

'What do you mean, this way?'

'The storm will have a centre – what they call the eye. When that passes over, the wind will blow from the opposite direction.'

'Oh, my God! For how long?'

'Another four hours or so. But I believe it shouldn't be quite so strong.'

'Holy shit! By then we'll have frozen to death.'

'Not in this climate.'

'You reckon? You want to feel my tits?'

'Ice picks, again? Oh, come to mother.'

They huddled against each other. The house had just about collapsed, but the foundations and the few walls that remained standing protected them from the full force of the storm, although the noise – the howl of the wind, the booming of the thunder and the vivid flashes of lightning; the drumming of the rain and the roaring of the surf, seeming to be coming closer by the moment – continued to assail their senses so that they lost

320

all concept of time, nor did Jessica have the slightest desire to look at her watch. When, without warning, the wind suddenly dropped, the thunder ceased banging away above their heads, and the rain stopped, she was for a moment not certain where she was.

'Oh, Lord,' Felicity said. 'Oh, my! Oh, hallelujah!'

Jessica looked up at a brilliant moon, seeming to hang immediately above her head, and at the same time realized that it was not the moon alone that was brightening the sky: it was nearly dawn.

She was strangely reluctant to move. The long immersion in the water, even if that was not cold, had still chilled her. Her muscles felt flaccid, but not as flaccid as her brain. But she had to move. They all had to.

'How long have we got?' Felicity asked.

'Maybe half an hour. Maybe only fifteen minutes. Let's go.'

'Where?'

'Filly, we have to find shelter on the other side of the house, before the wind comes back from this direction. We have to find Jerry. And...'

'What about our friends?'

'I was going to say, we have to find our weapons. So let's hurry.' She stood up, uncertainly, water dripping from every part of her.

'And can we change our clothes?'

'If there's anything to change into.'

Felicity stood up, also dripping water..

'Well, you need something. You've lost you bra.'

Jessica looked down at herself. 'Oh, Lord!' She was so chilled she hadn't even noticed.

'Talk about ice picks,' Felicity commented.

'Oh, shut up.'

'Well, what about her? Do you think she's dead?'

Rowena was certainly very still, only her head showing above the water. But when Jessica touched her, she came to with a scream.

'Where am I? Oh, God! I'm so cold. Where am I?'

'Exactly where you were before you passed out.' Jessica pulled her to her feet. 'Let's get you a change of clothes.'

Rowena stared at her. 'Sergeant...'

'I know. I'm incorrectly dressed. But not around here, if I remember rightly. Let's hurry. We're running out of time.'

The steadily lightening sky began to reveal what had happened during the night. Swathes of coconut trees had been blown flat, as had the mango tree, which was uprooted. When they climbed up to the house they could look down on the rest of the island, which was still half-submerged, although the tidal wave that had swept across it was now receding.

The house itself was utterly destroyed, except, remarkably, for the section containing the spare rooms, although Jessica estimated that would also go when the wind returned from the south-west. For the rest ... the upper floor had disappeared, torn loose and deposited in scattered timbers down the slope to the beach, there to be pounded into splinters by the waves, which even on the sheltered, shallow side of the island were hurling themselves on to the sand.

The front of the house had also been torn apart, although the deep freeze remained in place. Cautiously picking their way into what had been the kitchen, Jessica and Felicity found their weapons easily enough, wedged under various pieces of wood. Jessica had no ammunition for her Skorpion, but she located the shotgun and Lucian's revolver, while Felicity had a spare box for her Ingram.

There was no sign of the Colombians, alive, but there was a dead body wedged in the remains of the doorway, and Theresa's body had been hurled – appropriately, Jessica thought – against the deep freeze.

'Jerry!' Rowena reminded them.

'Jerry.' Jessica led the way through the stairwell. As the upper floor had disappeared, so had the top of the stairs, but the lower rungs remained, mounting aimlessly.

'My clothes!' Rowena screamed. 'My jewellery! All gone!'

'Think of the insurance.' The door to the back corridor hung by a single hinge. Jessica pushed it open and it fell off. Compared with the rest of the house, which was covered in sand and debris, the back corridor was virtually clean.

'Hallelujah!' Felicity said, and opened their
323

bedroom door.

'Jerry first,' Jessica reminded her.

'Oh! Right. The sight of you ought to have him standing to attention.'

Jessica opened the door and gazed at the two empty beds. *Oh, Christ!* she thought, and then saw a leg sticking out from under the nearest bed. She knelt. 'Are you awake?'

He blinked at her. 'Sergeant? God, I've been scared. Boy, are you a sight for sore eyes.'

'Yes, well, don't press the point or I'll kick you in your bad leg. Come on out of there.'

He rolled out. 'My leg hurt like hell.'

'But it's better than it was. Can you stand on the other one? Filly.'

They each held an arm as he struggled up.

'Jeremy!' Rowena rushed forward.

'Hi, Mum. Boy, do you look a mess.'

'We all look a mess.'

'Well...' He looked at Jessica. 'There are messes and messes.'

'Mind where your hand goes,' she recommended, as she draped his arm round her shoulder. Felicity did the same with his other arm, and they got him out of the door. Rowena followed.

'Where are you taking me?' he asked.

'Somewhere safer than here.'

'Is there one? How's Terry?'

'Ah...' Jessica and Felicity looked at each other round Jeremy's chest.

'Theresa is dead,' Rowena said from behind them.

Jeremy stopped hopping.

'She was shot by her own brother,' Rowena said.

'I don't think that is quite accurate,' Jessica said, 'but it was one of his people.'

They reached what had been the games room.

'Holy Jesus Christ!' Jeremy commented. 'What a mess.'

'The wind got in,' Felicity explained.

'I can see that. So where is this brother now?'

He should have asked where Theresa is now, Jessica thought. *Or at least shown some grief.* Maybe that would come later. Or maybe he was thinking that he was well out of a liaison that had obviously turned sour. 'We have no idea where Arturo is,' she said. 'We will have to find him when the storm is over.'

'Isn't the storm over?'

'No,' she told him.

Although there was virtually no part of the north side of the house left upright, the foundations there were higher than those on the south side, and as there was nothing left to fall on them, Jessica and Felicity laid Jeremy on the ground against the sloping earth.

'Isn't this a bit exposed?' he asked.

'You'll get wet,' Jessica agreed, 'but at least you won't be blown away.'

'I wonder where the peacocks are?' Felicity asked.

'Now, they probably have been blown

away,' Jeremy said.

And those poor hens, Jessica thought.

'The dogs!' Rowena said. 'My dogs! Where are my dogs?'

'Shit!' Jessica muttered.

'They were in the house when it started to fall apart,' Felicity said.

'They were barking, up until the shooting started,' Jessica said.

'Shooting?' Jeremy asked. 'There's been shooting?'

'Of course there's been shooting,' his mother shouted. 'There are dead bodies all over the place. And now, my dogs...'

'I'm pretty sure they weren't shot,' Jessica said. 'We'll have to look for them later. Right now, I need some clothes, and Filly needs a change too.'

'I think you look great the way you are,' Jeremy said.

'Why don't you bugger off?'

'What about me?' Rowena asked.

'Sadly, I don't think either of us has anything that would fit you. Save ... we'll bring you Filly's dressing gown. Now listen, Filly, one of us has to stay here just in case someone turns up we don't like the look of. I'll be back in five minutes.'

Filly nodded.

'And bring some of those knock-out drops,' Jeremy said. 'My leg is giving me gyp.'

'Sorry,' Jessica said. 'We needs you to stay awake for a while. We may have to move you again.'

She hurried off before he could argue. The bedroom was actually dry. She left her still-soaking knickers on the floor, washed her face and cleaned her teeth with water taken from the tub, put on clean underwear, jeans and a shirt and sandals, brushed her hair, although it remained a bedraggled mess. Then she looked around her. She was pretty sure the room was going to disappear when the wind returned, but there was nothing she could do about it. She emptied the wet shoulder bag, made sure nothing was missing, including the tablets. But everything was soaking; the waterproofing had not stood up to the constant immersion. Most importantly, her mobile was dead; the water had got at the batteries, as it had also got at the spares.

She took Felicity's dressing gown from the hook behind the door and returned to the others. 'I don't suppose your mobile is operative?' she asked Felicity.

Filly tried it. 'Dead as a dodo.'

'Right. Hurry it up.'

Felicity climbed into the house.

Rowena removed her clothes and put on the dressing gown. 'Not that I feel any better,' she complained. 'And now you say we're cut off? What are we going to do?'

'I suggest we survive, until someone turns up from the mainland,' Jessica said.

Felicity returned in the nick of time, for the sky was darkening and it began to rain. Then the wind began to blow from the west, and the thunder and lightning returned. They huddled against each other, even Jessica's nerves close to breaking point, while time seemed to stand still in a constant crescendo of water and noise. When the wind finally abated, they were hardly aware of it for some minutes, for the rain continue to teem down.

Jessica was the first to realize what had happened. She disengaged herself from Rowena, who had been hugging her, and rose to her knees. 'Get down,' Rowena said. 'You'll be blown away.'

'I won't,' Jessica assured her. 'The wind has gone.'

Felicity also disengaged herself, in her case from Jeremy. 'Whee!' she said. 'Does that mean we're going to survive?'

'That means we have survived,' Jessica said. 'The storm, at any rate.'

She stood up. The wind still whipped at her hair, but it was merely fresh, not destructive. And the rain still stung her flesh, but it seemed to have been doing that for ever.

It was broad daylight now; a glance at her watch told her that it was just after ten. She thought that if she could find a warm bed, preferably her own, she would crawl into it and sleep for a fortnight. But there was so much still to be done before she could possibly get there.

She climbed up on to the ground floor of the house and looked around her. Never had she seen such devastation: it had previously been hidden by the darkness. Not a wall still stood in the house; the staircase had finally collapsed. The tennis court was still there although the net and its posts had disappeared, together with the high wire fencing, and the concrete surface was cracked where a huge jumble of twisted metal had been deposited in its very centre. The helicopter! It had to be at least a quarter of a mile from the pad.

All around the house palm trees lay uprooted and scattered, although oddly there were clumps which had survived. To the south the sheltered waters of the sound still tossed and heaved and surged at the beach; she thought they might be settling down, but it was obviously going to be a few hours yet before any boats would venture out from Cat Island, supposing there were any boats left afloat on Cat Island. And to the north and east the sea was still a raging maelstrom, thundering on to the beach, completely obliterating the cruiser's dock – but at least she thought that was still intact.

Felicity joined her. 'When, do you think?'

'Not for a couple of hours, at the earliest.'

'Shit! What do we do?'

'You hungry?'

'Not really. I could do with a drink. Do you think there'll be any water left in any of those tubs?'

'Let's first see if there are still any tubs.'

To her surprise, two had survived, and there was still some water in each. They scooped it up with their hands to drink, and found Rowena kneeling beside them, doing to same.

'What about Jerry?' she asked. 'He's dying of thirst. And he's in such pain.'

Jessica hunted round on her hands and knees and found a plastic tooth mug which had survived wedged between the shattered toilet and the remains of the wall. 'That doesn't look very clean,' Rowena objected.

'What makes you think the water you have just been drinking is very clean?' Jessica asked. 'Here.' She opened her bag and handed her a pill. 'Give him one of these.'

'You said he shouldn't have another right now.'

'That was four hours ago,' Jessica reminded her. 'I don't think we'll be moving him again in the near future, because there's nowhere to go. Give him the pill and do your mother act. Someone will get to us eventually.'

Rowena took the pill and the water and went off.

Felicity was rooting around in the remains of their bedroom. The beds had been overturned, as had the bureaux, with drawers and clothing scattered everywhere. 'They're all wet and covered in sand,' she said disconsolately. 'And I was hoping for another change.'

'Look on the bright side. The rain has stopped, and the sun looks like it might come out. You'll be dry in no time. Now, listen: as far as we know, there could be at least three, possibly four thugs still loose on this island.'

'You think they could have survived the storm? In the open?'

'We did.'

'I never thought of that. So...'

'We don't know the state of their morale, or their armaments, whether they're still on the job or whether they want to call it a day. But we have to assume they're still hostile.'

'And we're sitting ducks out there. What we have left isn't going to stop a man with an AK Seventy-Four.'

'Sure it will, if we use it right. Here's where your psychological-warfare training comes into play. These guys have two counts against them: one is that there is no way they can get off the island until help arrives, and they have to figure, correctly, that the help is going to be on our side, not theirs. Right?'

'Ye-es,' Felicity agreed, hesitantly.

'So the only way they are going to get off this island except in handcuffs is by the time-honoured way of taking hostages. Now they won't be thinking of you or me. They don't know whether we are important or not, and they do know that we are armed and prepared to fight. So their first aim will be to eliminate us.'

'Cheer me up.'

'I am doing that. Now, we know that they had a rifle, because that's what they fired at me. But they didn't use it to get at us through the kitchen door. So they either had only maybe one magazine for it, or they left it upstairs, in which case it could be in Cat Island by now. Equally, we have seen no evidence that they have pistols – just assault rifles. That means that they have to get fairly close to do any damage. That's to our advantage.'

'If you say so. And if you're right.'

'Now, they are not going to take Jeremy hostage, because they have come here to kill him, and equally they're not going to lumber themselves with a cripple who has to be carried. So, Rowena is the one they will want.'

'As far I am concerned, they can have her. If she hadn't opened that window...'

'She's a client, and clients are always doing stupid things. So the drill is this: we cover them both up with flora – there's enough of it lying about – and you take up your position in the house, suitably surrounded by debris. You have your Ingram, and you will also have the shotgun, which we will reload with scatter-shot. However, there is one small caveat. I think it would be to our advantage to take Arturo alive; he's our only hope of ending this feud. Wound him if you have to, but try not to kill him. That is, if he, and they, come at you at all.'

'Hold on,' Felicity said. 'You keep talking about me doing this, and me not doing that. What are you going to be doing while I am not doing things, if you follow me?'

'With difficulty. The plan is that, while you hold the fort, I am going to flush these buggers out.'

'Won't that be very dangerous?'

'It'll be less dangerous now than if we wait for the guys to get their nerves back and come at us. I'm pretty sure none of them have been in a hurricane before, or even have any idea what it's like. If they had, they wouldn't have risked coming up here last night with one pending. Now they've spent something like ten hours outside in one. If they've survived, they'll be totally shell-shocked. But that won't last for ever. I also need to find Arnie and Clarissa. Give me your handcuffs. Both pairs. There could be four of them.'

Felicity scratched her head. 'You intend to arrest four gunmen? Just like that?'

'It's my job, remember. Now get on with it.'

'Yes, ma'am. But, JJ ... please come back to me.'

Jessica kissed her. 'I'll come back to you the moment I hear a shot.' She put the extra handcuffs in her shoulder bag, and went first of all to what was left of the west verandah. The wind was dropping all the time, and the sea, although still big, was also beginning to ease. Above there was not a cloud in the sky and the sun was blazing down. And she didn't have a hat! However, sunstroke had to be at the bottom end of her list of concerns.

She stood on the steps, which were un-disturbed although half hidden beneath layers of sand, and looked left and right. Clarissa had still been on the verandah when the Colombians had broken in. What would she have done then? Tried to regain her husband, surely. And she had said that Arnie was tied up in the village. In which case ... but she had to check it out.

It was not practical to use the beach without running the risk of being knocked down by the still heavy surf. She retraced her steps to reach the path through the centre of the island, gave a wave in the general direction of the house, although Felicity was invisible, as instructed, behind a pile of rubble, and went down the path. The going was difficult, as coconut trees had fallen across it, which she had to climb over, and pools of water had been left by the storm. She tasted one of these and was relieved to discover that it was fresh rather than salt; she was still above the extent of the tidal surge.

She also paused every few minutes to listen, but although the generator was silent, and the wind no longer howled, the roar of the surf deadened all other sound. On the other hand, it obviously made it difficult for anyone to discover her unless he was actually watching the path ... or had a very keen sense of smell. She had not walked more than a hundred yards, though she was out of sight of the house, when she heard a low growl.

'Hi,' she said. 'Hero, Leander. You there, boys?'

The bushes beside the path rustled and the two dogs emerged. Both were bedraggled and obviously cowed by the experience they had undergone, but they wagged their tails as they recognized Jessica, and she stroked their heads and patted them. 'You can come along with me, if you like,' she said.

The idea seemed to please them, mainly, she supposed, because they thought she might be taking them to food. They followed her down the path and they arrived at the generator shed. Here the roof had disappeared, but the heavy machinery, bolted to the concrete floor, had withstood the wind, The storage tank had fallen from its supports, and lay on its side, but fortunately it had not burst, presumably because it was only a quarter full.

There were the usual puddles of water, and again Jessica tasted one. Still fresh. So the surge had not been as high as Lucian had suggested, although she reckoned she was still some forty feet above normal sea level. She was about to move on when the dogs began rooting through some bushes just beyond the shed. She drew the revolver and, going to them, found the body of a man. Although he had been mostly washed clean of blood by the rain, there remained traces of it, and his chest and face had been cut to pieces by the small shot.

So, he had been brought down here and abandoned by his probably terrified companions. Did that mean that they had sought shelter from the storm in the generator shed, which presumably would still have had its roof on when they got here? So, were they still around?

Although the surf still boomed, she was reluctant to reveal her presence by shouting, so she had to push and pull the dogs away from the corpse. Then she had to determine her best course of action, but much as she wanted to locate the gunmen, she felt she should find out what had happened to Arnie first. So she snapped her fingers, and the dogs followed her towards the village.

The reservoir came first. The sloping concrete catchment area seemed undamaged, but as with the generator shed, the roof over the tanks had blown away. The tanks themselves were overflowing, and the surround was several inches deep in water, into which the dogs splashed happily. But they did not drink it and, when Jessica tasted it, she found it was salt. So the tidal surged had got this far up, at least – and the reservoir was several feet above the village level.

She hurried now, through increasing numbers of puddles, some of them more than a foot deep, and in several of which there floated the corpse of a fowl, the dogs now barking excitedly, and came upon the village. The word which came to her mind was 'scattered'. Not one of the houses still stood, although there were various walls sticking up at odd angles. The dock had survived, even if waves were still breaking over it, and the sea between the cay and the mainland was seething as if it were boiling.

No one who had been in the village when it had been struck by the storm surge could possible have survived, so she supposed she would never know whether Arnie had been a willing assistant to Abriga or whether he had been coerced, probably by threats against Clarissa. She preferred to think the latter, and it made her very angry, especially as it seemed unlikely that Clarissa had survived, either.

'Come along, guys,' she told the dogs, and set off back up the path. But she had not gone more than a couple of hundred yards when she heard the sound of a shot.

Instinctively Jessica dropped to her knees, while the dogs barked more excitedly than ever. But the bullet had not been fired at her. Yet it had not been a shotgun, and she was too far away for the report of the Ingram to have carried. Thus it had been a single shot from either a high-calibre pistol or one of the assault rifles. But as there had been no response from Felicity ... 'Go get 'em,' she told the dogs. They were, after all, retrievers, even if she did not suppose they had ever picked up a bird in their lives.

They certainly set off with enthusiasm, and she had to trot to keep up with them, but lost them as they left the path and went into the bushes, and she tripped and landed on her hands and knees. She looked down and discovered that she had fallen across another body. The man was dead, but he was actually still bleeding from the wound in his chest. *When thieves fall out*, she thought.

She regained her feet and set off again, making for the house now, regardless of any noise her progress might create. If she couldn't hear them, they couldn't hear her above the roar of the surf. Then she did hear a noise: shouts from surprisingly close at hand. The man was speaking Spanish, and she could understand very little of what he was saying, but she did catch the word 'perros'. It was no part of her plan to have the dogs hurt, so she drew the revolver and sent a shot in the general direction of the voice, at the same time dropping to her stomach – which saved her life, for in reply there came a burst of automatic fire. This passed over her head, but she realized she had overestimated the effect the storm had had on their morale, even if Abriga might have had to shoot one of his people to get the other one to follow him; and she had at least diverted them from their obviously proposed assault on the survivors at the house, even if she might have landed herself in a spot of bother.

She rolled to one side, but remained prone, the revolver held in both hands, trying to peer through the bushes – and heard more shouts, from even closer at hand. Again the man was speaking Spanish, but one of his words was unmistakable: *helicoptero*. She lay on her back and looked up, trying to find the sky through the trees, and spotted a Chinook, swooping low over the cay. *Holy hallelujah*, she thought, all the tension and exhaustion of the past twenty-four hours dissipating in a feeling of utter relief. Too soon. There was a crackling sound from close at hand, and although she rolled back on to her stomach again, revolver thrust forward, she was too late. A booted foot flew through the air to kick the revolver from her grasp and leave her feeling her hand was broken.

She sat up, and the muzzle of the assault rifle was thrust into her chest. 'You must be the policewoman,' the man said, in heavily accented English. 'Jones, eh? Bridge told me about you over the phone. Classy looker, he said. Well, for once he was telling the truth.'

Jessica pushed hair from her eyes. She had never seen this man before, but from his resemblance to Theresa she knew he was Arturo.

The other man spoke, his expression twisted.

Arturo grinned. 'He wants me to shoot you in the belly. And listen to you scream as you die. He does not like women, you see. But he is also a fool. According to Bridge, you are very well known. You are famous. Is this true?'

Jessica had got her breath back. 'That depends on which press you read.'

'Ha ha. You have courage. But I think it is true. I do not think the Bahamas Police will wish you to be killed. So you will be our ticket out of here. Get up.'

Slowly Jessica got to her feet. She wondered where the dogs were. But they could not possibly be any help to her, when faced with two assault rifles and the pistol.

Arturo spoke to the other man, who went into the bushes in the direction that the revolver had flown, obviously to find it. 'You walk in front of me, eh?' Arturo told Jessica. 'But first...' As she turned, he pushed the muzzle of the rifle into the middle of her back and stepped against her, running his hand over her shirt front and down the sides of her jeans. 'You have a lot in there,' he said. 'But no other weapon, eh? Now walk. Go to the house. We have time to finish the job my father gave me. That helicopter is still circling, making sure it can come down safely. It is large for that pad, eh? Oh, it will come down eventually. But by then, as I say, we will have completed the job, and we will have three female hostages. They will not wish to let you die.'

Jessica was getting her thoughts under control. 'What are you going to tell your father?' she asked.

'He sent me to do a job, and I am doing that.'

'He didn't send you to kill your sister.'

'Do you not think I grieve for that? But I did not kill her. It was that fool Ramon. And he has paid the price.'

'You were in command. Whatever happened was your responsibility. That is how your father will see it.'

'Listen, woman, you talk too much.'

'It would be better for everyone if you persuaded your father to call off this feud. There is no point to it, now that Theresa is dead. She loved Jeremy Lenghurst. He did not abduct her. She eloped with him because she loved him. They were going to be married. If you were to do this, I would intercede for you.'

'You? Intercede for me? How do you think

340

you will do that?'

'By explaining the circumstances. You are guilty of a lot of crimes, but so far you have not yet actually committed the murder of anyone except your own people. If you kill Jeremy Lenghurst, you will be hunted down and locked up for life, if you are not executed.'

'Who will do this hunting down? You?'

'If need be.'

'You?' He gave a shout of laughter. 'You are a little woman. So you are a good shot, maybe. But you know nothing of killing. How can a little woman know anything of killing? When I leave here, I will return to Colombia. No one can touch me in Colombia. No one would dare.'

'I wouldn't count on that, if I were you. Do you recall an incident a couple of years ago, when a helicopter filled with armed men was shot down from the ground?'

'That was a freak accident. The person who fired the shot was executed. Or died in the jungle.'

'She wasn't, you know.'

'You are saying ... You? *You?* You are lying.'

'The helicopter was a Chinook, just like the one about to land here, and it was operating on behalf of Señor Ramon Cuesta, a Bolivian gentleman who is currently serving a life sentence for murder and various assorted crimes. I put him there – in prison, I mean.'

'You,' he said again. 'I should shoot you

now. Some of my friends were in that chopper.'

'You win some, you lose some. But I have never lost yet.' She pushed aside the last piece of broken foliage, and gazed at the wrecked house. To their left, the helicopter was just settling, and Rowena was standing up and waving her arms, while the dogs were beside her, barking. But there was no sign of Felicity.

'You will lose this one,' Arturo said. 'She will do as a hostage. Turn round.'

Jessica drew a deep breath, and turned. She had no intention of tamely accepting being shot, but he was too far away for her to reach him.

He grinned at her as he slowly levelled the pistol. 'It is a pity. I would rather fuck you than shoot you. But you are too dangerous to live. So, how do you say – This will hurt you more than it will hurt me.'

Then this is it, Jessica thought. *What a miserable way to go.* She drew another deep breath as she saw his finger tighten on the trigger ... and a shot rang out. Hit in the shoulder, Arturo half-turned as he dropped the gun, and fell to his knees.

Felicity stepped out of the bushes. 'You told me not to kill him.'

'The other one,' Jessica shouted, throwing herself down beside the moaning Arturo.

'Eh?' Felicity turned as the gunman, walking some distance behind his boss, fired the revolver he had retrieved from the bushes. Felicity uttered a little shriek and fell back

342

into the bushes. The gunman then fired at Jessica, but the shot went wide, and Jessica had already picked up the pistol Arturo had dropped. This she levelled and fired in the same instant, and the man went down, shot through the heart.

Felicity was sitting up. 'He wasn't a very good shot. But thank God you are.'

'You disobeyed my orders,' Jessica pointed out.

'I'm sorry. When I heard that shot, and the dogs turned up, all excited, I knew you were in trouble. And by then the helicopter was on its way down, so I figured you needed me more than the Lenghursts. Have I blotted my copybook?'

Jessica kissed her. 'Admirably. You saved my life.'

'Help me,' Arturo groaned. 'I am in such pain. And I am bleeding to death.'

Jessica knelt beside him, presented the revolver to his head.

'Please,' he begged. 'Please don't kill me.'

'Well,' she said. 'I might reconsider the situation, providing that from here on you do, and say, exactly what I tell you.'

'And he seems to have done just that,' the commander said. 'Will Abriga really call the whole thing off, do you reckon?'

'I believe he will, sir.' Jessica wore uniform and was again her immaculate self. 'He came to Cat Island to collect the body of his daughter, and especially asked to see me. We had

343

quite a long chat, and I was able to put him entirely in the picture. What I told him was corroborated by the statement Arturo had already made to the Bahamian Police.'

'As dictated by you, I gather.'

'I may have jogged his memory a bit.'

'And what did his father have to say to him?'

'I don't really know, sir. It'll be a little while before they can have a heart-to-heart chat. Not until he comes out of Nassau gaol. But as I was able to convince Abriga that Jeremy Lenghurst is going to be a cripple for life ... I'm afraid I rather let the departmnt down there, sir.'

'Not at all, as he has admitted that he brought it on himself by attempting to, ah, molest the Garcia woman. And Lord Blandin merely seems happy that, in all the circumstances, the Florida Police have agreed not to proceed against the boy. As I said at the beginning, Blandin was far more interested in the health of his daughter than his grandson, and now that she has finally decided to ditch this fellow Lenghurst ... I don't suppose you had anything to do with that?'

'Nothing at all, sir. The fact is, Lenghurst let her – let us all – down, by not returning to the cay. He claimed it was because he couldn't find anyone willing to crew him, but we all knew it was because he was scared. I don't suppose he would have been much help, but he should have tried.'

'Absolutely. What do you think will happen

to him?'

'Mrs Lenghurst has settled a small income on him, and I believe he means to remain in the Bahamas.'

'Doing what?'

'Probably what he's been doing all his life. So he's very likely to wind up in a Bahamian gaol. With Arturo. That should be fun.'

'One almost feels sorry for the fellow. Tell me something: what was Abriga like? I mean, face to face.'

'He was charming. He offered me a job, as his personal bodyguard. A hundred thousand a year.'

'My word. But...'

'Oh, I didn't accept. So he asked me to become his mistress. At two hundred thousand a year. I am speaking in dollars, of course.'

'Good heavens! But...'

'I declined, of course. So he asked me to marry him. His wife died some years ago. Half his fortune.'

'Good God! But...'

'It was tempting, but it would have meant I'd have become Arturo's stepmother, and a lot of other thugs' as well. So I declined.'

The commander gazed at her for several seconds, uncertain whether or not she was pulling his leg. Then he said, 'Well, JJ, as usual I have to congratulate you. I cannot always approve of your methods, but they do get results. You could try looking a little happier. You appear to be unscathed ... I take it Hewitt is all right?'

'Yes, sir, she is.'

'She didn't let you down, I hope?'

'She was magnificent, sir. She saved my life. I hope she will be commended.'

'You will both be commended. So, what's on your mind?'

'I suppose, just a lot of innocent lives, all the result of that bastard's lust. Garcia, and then his wife. Theresa. Arnie Pleass and his wife...'

'What happened to them?'

'Arnie's body was washed up on Cat Island. They never did find his wife.'

'They were friends of yours?'

'They were innocent bystanders. And then, those people from Tiger Cay...'

'None of them were killed, were they?'

'No, sir. But they lost everything: their homes, their possessions, the better part of their livelihoods...'

'I'd hate to think you were going soft on me, JJ. Now I want you to take some leave. And Hewitt, of course. And first I order you to go out and get drunk. Without, if possible, being arrested.'

'Yes, sir.' Jessica stood up.

'And I'll be in touch.'

'I'm sure you will, sir.' She went outside.

'How were the Bahamas?' Mrs Norton inquired.

'Absolutely stunning. Sun, sea, sex, hurricanes, gunmen...'

Mrs Norton assumed her lemon-sucking expression. 'Let's see: the place you were at is called Tiger Cay, isn't it?'

346

'It is, and I couldn't recommend a better place for a holiday. Nothing but beach. No people, not a house left standing ... If you're lucky, you could even stumble across a dead body. Send me a postcard.'

She closed the door behind her, joined Felicity, who, also in uniform, was waiting, anxiously, in the lobby.

'How'd it go?'

'You're to get a commendation.'

'Am I? Oh, tremendous. The folks will be so pleased. But what about you?'

'Oh, I'm to get one too.'

'So what happens now?'

'We each have a week's leave. But first, we are required to obey a very specific command from the boss. I know just the place to do that.'